WHISPERS ON THE WIND

DANA WAYNE

Book Liftoff
1209 South Main Street
PMB 126
Lindale, Texas 75771

This book is a work of fiction. Therefore, all names, places, characters, and situations are a product of the author's imagination and used fictitiously. Any resemblance to actual persons, living or dead, places, or events is entirely coincidental.
Copyright © 2018 Dana Wayne

Book design by Champagne Book Designs
Cover design by Just Write.Creations

Library of Congress Control Number Data
Wayne, Dana
Whispers On The Wind / Dana Wayne.
Ghosts—Paranormal—Romance—Fiction.2.
Supense—Romance—Fiction.
BISAC: FICTION / Romance / Fantasy. | Fiction / Ghost.
2018935060

ISBN: 978-1-947946-31-6

www.danawayne.com
www.bookliftoff.com

BOOKS BY DANA WAYNE

Secrets Of The Heart

Mail Order Groom

Whispers On The Wind

CHAPTER ONE

You let him kill her.
     The angry female voice in the pre-dawn hour jolted Cooper Delaney from a restless sleep.

Adrenalin pumping, he rolled to the right and automatically grabbed his pistol from the nightstand, fully expecting to see a stranger beside the bed.

Nothing but moonlit shadows. He swiveled his head to the left.

The room was empty.

He blinked and drew in a deep breath, trying to dispel remnants of the dream making sleep all but impossible for over a month. Always the same dream; a shadowy figure begging Coop to find her. That was it…*find me, please.* Two weeks ago, the voice changed and insisted Coop had to stop him.

Stop who? From what?

Tonight, the dream exploded into a full-blown nightmare.

He put the gun back on the table and lay down, right arm over his eyes. "Shit," he whispered as the vision replayed through his mind. *Powerful hands gripped her throat, the eerie silence punctuated by ragged gasps as she struggled for air. Blood trickled from her nose and the corner of her mouth. Dark hair wedged into a jagged cut across her forehead. Terror-filled eyes stared at the figure bent over her.*

All the while, the voice reproached…you didn't stop him.

At forty-three, Coop considered himself a straight-forward, no nonsense lawman, well known and respected as the Sheriff of Baker County, Texas. He looked at the facts, the evidence, and made logical, rational decisions. And yet, the dream was so real, he smelled the metallic odor of blood, felt the dampness of the earth around her.

"Dammit." He lowered his arm and punched the bed. *I'm losing my fricking mind.*

It was bad enough when the voice invaded his sleep, but two days ago, he heard it at the kitchen table where he sat eating breakfast. Wide awake. This time, she warned he—whoever *he* was—would kill again.

He tossed the sheet aside and sat on the edge of the bed. Heart pounding, his breath hissed as he gulped in air. Elbows on his knees, he cradled his head in his hands. "Just a dream," he murmured, "a bad dream."

He stumbled to the window and shoved it open with an angry thrust, gasping when the rush of cool night air caused gooseflesh to prickle his sweat-coated body. "A dream," he whispered, willing himself to believe. "Nobody died." He pulled down the sash and pressed his forehead against the glass pane. "Nobody died."

When his racing heart finally slowed, he pushed away and headed for the bathroom, stopping at the foot of the bed as he tried to remember if Miss Eva had guests tonight. A curse escaped parched lips as he grabbed his jeans from a chair. *Why in the world did she want to go into the B&B business anyway?*

Even as the thought flitted through his mind, he knew the answer. She decided he needed a wife and used the lovely

Antebellum home to lure prospects. Hence, the majority of her guests were single women looking for a good time, or to change their marital status. He lost track of the propositions, both subtle and otherwise, thrown his way in the last six months. *When had women become so forward?*

He opened the door and padded on bare feet to the bathroom he shared with his son, Jason, when he was home from college. Guests used the one across the hall.

Since sleep was out of the question at this point, he threw on a shirt and headed downstairs for coffee.

Light showing under the kitchen door stopped him cold. "Crap. Company."

Today is the first step of starting over.

Samantha Fowler gazed out the kitchen window, transfixed by the beauty of daybreak, convinced the magnificent sunrise was a good omen. The sky, once dark and gloomy, now showcased varying degrees of orange, blue and purple. Giant oaks, pecans and pine trees, previously hidden by darkness, sprang to life, as did the beautifully landscaped yard of the bed and breakfast she would call home for the next two weeks.

Her best friend, Barbara Walker, who grew up in Bakersville, suggested Pecan Grove B&B for her much-needed sabbatical to contemplate what to do with her life. A quick perusal of their website convinced her to give it a try. Located two hours from Dallas in rural Baker County, it was a beautiful antebellum-style home re-constructed after a fire in 1920.

Everything from the graceful columns on the front, to the upper-level porch running across the back, conveyed old-world-south. The interior was painstakingly decorated and furnished like its predecessor built in 1880. Modern upgrades included air conditioning and wi-fi, but the majority of the house retained the serene elegance and charm of the time.

"Oh, Jack, you should see this." A soft sigh of wonder arose as she took in the panoramic view. "No way could I capture this with a camera."

Her companion, a huge crossbreed dog of indeterminate lineage laying at her feet, merely grunted.

She sipped her coffee, still rooted by the window. "Don't be such a grouch. We've been up a lot earlier than this."

The mutt didn't bother to grunt this time.

"Ms. Benton said breakfast will be ready by the time we get back."

A soft groan followed by the swish of his tail on the worn linoleum floor acknowledged he heard what she said.

"No exercise, no food. Time to rock and roll, old man."

Suddenly, Jack growled low in his throat and stood in front of her, attention fixed on the kitchen door as it slowly opened.

A man, barefoot, shirt half-buttoned, sporting a severe case of bed head, strolled into the kitchen.

Every cell in Sam's body began a happy dance.

As a doctor, she was trained to quickly assess every situation and did so now. He towered over her, at least six-three or four, dark, curly hair in need of a trim touched the collar of a half-buttoned chambray shirt, while streaks of gray edged around the temples. Ruggedly handsome, his dark beard stubble projected an explicit manly aura.

Storm-cloud eyes, sharp and focused, assessed her as well.

Feminine radar pinged. Hard.

He liked what he saw.

Her fingers tightened around the cup. She attempted to speak but nothing came out. She settled for what she hoped was a smile of welcome but feared it may look more like a grimace.

Her protector didn't appear happy at the intrusion and bared his teeth in a menacing snarl.

She fumbled for the dog's collar. "Down, Jack."

Man and woman stared at each other in silence as seconds ticked by.

She reminded herself to breathe.

He cleared his throat as he ambled over to the pot on the counter. "I didn't expect company." He glanced her way, then focused on pouring his coffee. "Guests usually aren't up this early."

His voice, deep and sensual, coupled with that just-out-of-bed look sent ripples of awareness through her.

Oh my God. Looks like sin and sounds like Sam Elliott. "Oh, yes, well, we arrived late last night."

He looked around the kitchen. "We?"

His mouth moved so she knew he must have spoken, but it took a moment for her brain to stop fixating on the mat of chest hair peeking out the top of his shirt. She blinked and gestured toward the dog. "Me. And Jack. My dog. We arrived last night."

"Don't think I've ever seen a dog like him. What is he?"

An irresistibly devastating grin accompanied the question, and her stomach lurched.

She gulped in air. "Vet said maybe a cross between Mastiff and Rottweiler but even he was stumped."

The man cleared his throat—again—and looked

everywhere but at her.

Warning bells sounded.

Holy crap. He feels it, too.

"Unusual coloring," the man offered at last. "Like someone splattered black and brown paint all over him."

She patted Jack's head. "Yeah. He's so ugly he's cute." *Really? That's the best you can do?*

Jack, apparently satisfied the visitor was not a danger to his mistress, lay back down with a heavy sigh.

Silence filled the room.

She set her cup on the counter. "Um, I'm Samantha Fowler. Are you a guest here, too?"

When his laser-sharp gaze fixed on her mouth, a swarm of butterflies invaded her stomach.

A muscle flexed in his jaw. "Cooper—Coop—Delaney. Guess you can say I'm a permanent guest."

Awareness bounced off the walls like a rubber ball, charging the room with explosive energy.

She let out an audible lungful of air and moved away from the counter. "Well, I think it's light enough to explore."

Jack snorted.

The edges of Coop's lips turned up. "He doesn't seem interested."

"Yeah, but he needs the exercise."

"Got a route in mind?"

Every word he spoke rolled over her in a tidal wave of heat. A quick shake of her head sent her ponytail sliding to the side. "Just riding around, checking out the area. Got in too late last night to see much of anything."

"Well," he pushed away from the counter, "enjoy your ride" He headed for the door, stopping to speak to the dog.

"Nice to meet you, Jack."

A soft rumble and a couple of weak tail thumps indicated acceptance.

Cooper grinned and walked out.

Sam closed her eyes and took a deep breath. "No. No. No," she commanded, "Hormones fooled me once. I won't let it happen again."

She nudged Jack with her toe and headed out the back door, her unhappy companion lagging behind.

What the devil is wrong with me? Sam sped down the road, tires kicking up rocks and dust. She looked straight ahead, but her mind's eye recalled the chance meeting in sharp detail. Her body still hummed with the force of his effect on it. Lust at first sight? Is that a real thing?

"Oh my God, Jack. What must he be thinking?"

Her silent companion watched intently, head cocked to one side as though listening while she ranted.

"I ogled like a fricking school girl." She shook her head, cheeks burning as she relived the encounter. "But at least, thank you God, I stopped short of drooling, though I'm sure I would have if he hadn't left when he did."

Jack's head cocked the other way, as though silently urging her to continue.

"Okay, okay, I looked. I admit it. I couldn't help it." She licked her lips. "Oh my. That chest," she murmured. "So much hair." Her fingers arched as she imagined running them through the thick mass of dark curls. "And didn't he sound a little like Sam Elliott to you? Kinda gravelly and raspy, and when he smiled—" She slapped her palm against her temple. "What the blue blazes is wrong with me? Did Paul not teach me anything?" She shook her head, sending her lopsided ponytail lower. "But his eyes, they were so, so, intense. Such an unusual color, too. Not grey, not blue; more, I don't know, like the ashes of a cold campfire or the color of storm clouds rolling in. The minute I looked at them," she paused as a light shiver rolled over her. "I swear it jolted me down to my toes." She wagged a finger at her companion. "And I'm not some sex-starved divorcee who can't control herself, either, though I'm sure he thought so. I stared. Fine. Not a crime. God took a lot of extra pains with him, and it would be extremely rude of me not to notice." She focused on the road. "My *goodness* did I notice. If ever a man was built for seven kinds of sin…"

Sam gave little thought to conversing with Jack as though he understood. In fact, sincerely believed he did. She found him beside a dumpster near the hospital two years ago more dead than alive from two bullet wounds. After he healed, they were constant companions. Paul, her now ex-husband, complained constantly about him being in the house, going everywhere with her, but she ignored his rants. Their marriage was already rocky by then, and she needed the mutt as much as he needed her.

Which no doubt explained why Paul and Jack never liked each other. Or maybe Jack was a better judge of character than her.

She sped down the road, wheel gripped in her left hand, her right waving around as she poured out her thoughts. "What did he expect anyway waltzing in there half-dressed?" She inhaled deeply and rested both hands on the wheel. "I shouldn't be surprised, though. Males in general are self-centered jerks who should be lined up and shot at sunrise." She reached over and patted Jack's head. "Well, except you, of course."

A soft whine and a thump of his tail drew her gaze.

"Again? You just went."

Another whine.

"Okay, okay." She searched ahead for an appropriate exit. Seeing what appeared to be a lane off to the right, she slowed and signaled a turn. It was little more than a well-traveled dirt lane leading to a briskly moving stream surrounded by willows, pines and an assortment of East Texas foliage. The nearest bank held a collage of mementos from past visitors, classifying the area as a primo make-out spot. Her mind's eye marked the location of beer cans, towels and discarded condoms even as she pulled under a towering pine. She rummaged in the glove box for tissues and finding them, opened the door and stepped out.

"Come on you big whiney-butt."

Jack jumped out and headed for the pine tree.

Sam headed in the opposite direction and gave a sharp, "Stay," when he turned to follow. Rounding the lone holly bush, thumbs tugging on the waistband of her pants, she saw the body.

CHAPTER TWO

Coop shaved with a shaky hand, mulling over what happened in the kitchen and the newcomer's perplexing effect on him. *At least I maintained some control over myself and didn't let her see what she did to me.*

He couldn't remember the last time he felt such an immediate attraction to a woman. Granted, she was stunningly beautiful, even in baggy sweats and a tee shirt, but it went beyond the physical. Eyes blue as a summer sky, ringed by ebony lashes, pulled at him like a powerful magnet. High, exotic cheekbones, inky black hair pulled into a lop-sided ponytail, and a perfect bow-shaped mouth that begged to be kissed. By him. Desire rushed through him in waves unlike anything he had ever experienced.

He was in for an agonizing two weeks.

Short term flings and one-night-stands were not his style. But, given his body's reaction to their brief encounter, he knew it imperative to stay far away from her.

In the space of the next few seconds, his over-charged, sleep deprived mind conjured countless ways this newest guest could make his life miserable for the duration of her stay.

I'm not myself today, that's all. Probably just my lack of sleep and crazy dreams. Even as the thought popped in, he dismissed it. This was real. Too real, and not something he wanted to study too closely.

Fifteen minutes later, he entered the kitchen where Miss Eva prepared breakfast. At sixty-five, Eva Benton was still an attractive woman with an infectious smile, and an endless capacity for caring. Her short gray hair rested in soft curls around her head, and the ever-present apron circled a slim waist.

"Morning, Coop," she said over her shoulder, "almost ready."

He shuffled to where she stood scrambling eggs and gave her a quick kiss on the cheek. "Morning, Beautiful. I'm starved."

He re-filled his mug, and reached for the paper lying beside his place at the table. He watched as she moved about the kitchen, humming softly to herself. His mother's best friend, she'd always been a part of his life. After his parents were killed by a drunk driver when he was twenty, she took him in without a second thought, sharing every triumph and failure in his life.

Her most recent, self-appointed role, was matchmaker. For him.

"You'll be happy to know, Coop," she said as she worked, "I've one guest for the next couple of weeks and she's not the least bit interested in finding a husband."

Coop sucked in a breath as the memory of captivating azure eyes and lush lips swamped him.

"I misjudged the last one so badly, I thought I'd give you a break."

He tipped his head back and glared at the ceiling. "For the last time…I am perfectly happy with my life. I don't need, or want, a wife."

If she heard him, she simply ignored it and continued. "Dr. Fowler—Samantha, but she goes by Sam—will be here a couple of weeks. She's a friend of Doc Harper's niece, Barbara Jean Reynolds. Well, she's Barbara Jean Walker now. You remember her, don't you? I think she was a year or two behind you in school. She's a social worker in Dallas at the same hospital with Sam." She paused, shaking her head. "Bless her heart, just went through a pretty nasty divorce. Sam, not Barbara Jean. I got the impression men were on the top of her things-to-avoid-at-all-costs list."

Coop groaned, caught between wishing it was true, and hoping it wasn't.

"Oh, stop groaning. You're safe." She set a plate of scrambled eggs and bacon in front of him. "For now. Sam is just the sweetest thing, too. The prettiest eyes you ever saw. BJ told Doc Harper it was such a shame someone as wonderful as her got taken in by that scoundrel. Why he just sucked the very life right out of her."

"And you believe all that?" Coop didn't bother to hide the sarcasm in his voice, "Without even knowing her?"

"I believe in first impressions," she replied neatly, "As do you. She has a kind and caring heart. I'm certain of it. You can judge for yourself when you meet at dinner tonight."

The sharp ring of the phone saved him from further discussion of Sam's attributes.

"Delaney. What? Calm down, Alice, calm down. Now, start over. Where? Get JD and Johnson and tell them to meet me there. Call the judge, too. Tell her to stay put till I get there. And Alice…don't you dare say anything to anyone else. Understand?" He hung up and hurried back to the table, knowing full well the gossipy secretary, who happened to be the mayor's pampered daughter, would likely not heed his instructions.

"What's wrong, Coop?"

He consumed his coffee in one scalding gulp and headed for the back door, grabbing his hat from the rack as he passed. "Someone found a body down by Simmons Creek."

"Oh, Lord, no!"

Coop rushed out the back door, the condemning voice trailing after him.

You should have stopped him.

CHAPTER THREE

Sam slid the phone in her pocket and mentally prepared for the ordeal to come. The 911 call took longer than normal because Baker County used a central call center, which then routed the call to the appropriate person. In this case, the sheriff's dispatcher who couldn't believe Sam actually found a dead body. When finally convinced otherwise, she brought up another series of anxious questions about the woman's identity. It took time for Sam to calm her down enough to provide the information needed. Afterward, the dispatcher put her on hold for almost ten minutes, and came back only long enough to say she was not to move under direct orders from the sheriff.

Sam smirked at the command. Clearly, when the sheriff gave an order, he expected it to be followed to the letter.

Sensitive to her every mood, Jack whined and pushed his nose against her arm.

"Don't worry, baby," she said rubbing his ears, "everything will be okay. Just stay put like I told you."

The sun sat well above the horizon now, and September's Indian summer heat began to climb. Resigned to being stuck here a while, she put the top down, and debated taking pictures. While not a professional per se, she did have a knack for it. An old high school hobby, photography provided a much-needed creative outlet. The stress of being a doctor evaporated with each click of the lens. Over the years, her skills improved to the point she equipped her home with a state-of-the-art dark room, and every wall showcased her favorite pieces.

Being from a family of cops, she briefly considered forensic photography. But, she wanted people to see the joy and beauty in life, not the pain and suffering, so she kept to her still life and landscape photos.

She understood the routine involved in a crime scene, and the importance of not disturbing anything. But, if Bakersville was anything like the multitude of small towns in Texas, half the population owned a police scanner. Company could already be on the way.

"Easier to beg forgiveness than ask permission," she mumbled as she retrieved her camera from the back seat. She took a series of shots of the road behind her, the area around her car, and what she could see of the clutter along the riverbank up to where the body lay. She used both a wide-angle and zoom lens to get as much detail as possible without moving from her spot by the car. At one point, she stood in the seat to get a different angle. The proximity of the holly bush prevented any shots of the body itself, but she managed to get the area leading to it. Satisfied at last, she placed the camera in the front seat, and leaned against the door.

Jack nuzzled her arm, trying in his own way to comfort.

"Well, my friend, looks like we've found ourselves in the middle of a crime scene."

She absently scratched his ears and wondered about the dead woman. Who was she? How did she end up here? Did she have a family?

Sam sighed and considered her own complicated life. She loved being a doctor despite the long hours, and even managed to donate time to a local free clinic. Paul begrudged any time she allocated to something with no monetary return, but she refused to give it up. Her work meant everything to her. Maybe too much.

Paul, the jackass, told her so more than once, adding it was why he cheated, which of course was crap, but, still the allegation hurt.

A toss of her head banished the depressing image of them fighting over every stipulation in the divorce settlement. It crushed her to realize he wanted more from ending the marriage than he ever put into saving it.

When it was all said and done, she resigned her positions at the hospital and clinic. The house and most of the contents were sold. A few keepsakes, as well as her favorite photographs and lab equipment, ended up in storage.

Now, two weeks later, her future remained unclear. *Guess that's what happens when you're thirty-three years old and your husband of five years decides he wants his freedom and as much of your money as he can legally steal.*

In hindsight, she pegged herself as lonely and vulnerable, and perhaps even a little naïve. She devoted her life to fulfilling the dream of being a doctor, leaving little time for anything else. Consequently, she easily fell for the smooth-talking pharmaceutical salesman. It took time to admit her mistake, and still more to gather the courage to end the charade.

She took a deep breath and refocused her thoughts, thinking instead of the woman behind the bush. Sam worked enough assault cases through the ER to know she died a painful, prolonged death, and hadn't given up without a fight.

"I need to be a fighter, too."

Ever the optimist, Sam believed she still had a chance for some kind of happiness, and she'd fight tooth and nail for it.

The distant wail of a siren said things were about to turn serious. She snickered at the mental picture she developed of the approaching sheriff; overweight, balding, a wad of chewing tobacco in his mouth the size of a tennis ball, belt buckle hidden by a massive beer belly, and an attitude to try the patience of Job.

Her day got off to a wobbly start and was about to take a significant downward turn.

Coop raced down the highway, cell phone pressed to his ear. "Affirmative. Just off forty-eight, half mile east of county road four-sixty-three. There's a dirt road on the east side leading to Simmons Creek. No specifics yet, other than one female body. Caller indicated she was nude with some obvious physical injuries. Can you roll now? Good. Thanks."

Coop wanted the Texas Rangers Mobile Crime Unit on site ASAP. There hadn't been a homicide in Baker County in over forty years, and his office wasn't equipped to handle one. Another call had State Troopers on the way to help with crowd control. Bakersville was a small town with an active rumor mill. Something like this would spread like wildfire. He wouldn't be surprised if a few locals even beat him there.

He slowed as he approached the one lane road but still took the corner too fast, dirt flying as the late model Ford Bronco skidded down the lane. Fifty yards farther, he spotted a vintage fifty-six Chevy convertible parked under a pine tree.

The Fowler woman stood beside the car, one hand shading her eyes.

"Crap," he muttered, "It had to be her."

He slid to a stop and marched past her without a glance, ignoring the dust cloud he generated. "Where's the body?"

"Over there," she pointed off to the right with one hand, waving the other in front of her face to ward off the powdery onslaught, "behind the holly bush."

He moved in the direction indicated, scanning the area carefully for anything out of the ordinary. A favorite make out spot for local teens, he steeled himself against what he might find on the other side of that holly bush. Bare feet extended beyond the edge, toe nails painted a bright red that somehow seemed indecent under the circumstances. He held his breath when he rounded the bush to get his first look at the body, hoping against hope he didn't know her.

He froze mid-step.

It was her. The woman from the dream last night.

What the hell?

No mistake about it. Every detail was present. The gash on her forehead, the dried blood in the corner of her mouth, and crusted in her nose. He stared for several heartbeats, unable to process the fact she was the woman in the dream. He clamped his jaw tight, and focused on the job.

She lay on her back, unseeing eyes focused upward, legs straight, arms flat against her body like a soldier at attention. He stepped closer, careful not to disturb anything, looking for something to help identify her, and maybe the killer.

Nothing. No shoes, no clothes, nothing. He squatted down beside her, gritting his teeth as he surveyed the brutal scene. He was no stranger to death, but that didn't make it any easier. And this one had been painful and prolonged. He saw it in the bruises, cuts and scrapes covering her body.

Could I have stopped this? Was the voice right?

He shook his head. No. He could not have prevented this horrific crime. He forced his mind back to the moment, and continued his perusal of the area.

The killer was good. He left zilch behind except a once beautiful woman used and discarded like yesterday's news. With one last look around, he stood and strode back to where Sam waited.

"*You're* the sheriff?"

Under different circumstances, her shocked exclamation would have been funny, but not today.

Coop looked past her to the cars streaming down the one-lane road, led by Billy Ray Thomas, one of his jailers, who brought his car to stop behind Coop's, jumped out, and walked toward him.

"Keep those people behind my truck, Billy Ray." He glared at the growing crowd. "If anyone gives you any shit, I'll throw 'em in jail."

Coop bowed his head slightly toward Sam. "Sheriff Cooper Delaney, Dr. Fowler."

At her surprised look, he offered, "Miss Eva told me." He removed his aviator glasses. "I hope I didn't disturb you this morning. I wouldn't have barged in so disheveled had I known she had guests. Frankly, can't recall the last time one of them got up before ten."

A couple of blinks preceded her reply. "Oh, okay, um, okay."

He replaced his shades and started Cop 101. "What do you know about this?"

She jerked her gaze to him, brow creasing. "She's dead."

"How did you find the body?"

"Beginners luck."

He jerked his head around and pinned her with his best don't-jack-with-me-I'm-a-cop look.

She stared right back.

"Nature called," she said at last, "This looked like a good place to answer. Went over there, found her, called you, end of story."

Coop barely managed to hide his surprise as he took her right arm, leading her toward the Bronco.

"Where are you taking me?"

He stopped when he reached the vehicle and opened the door. "Get in. Don't talk to anyone until I get back."

"Why?"

"Because I said so. Dammit, Billy Ray," shouted Coop, "Keep these people behind my truck."

"Come on, folks, you heard the sheriff, move back."

"Aw, come on, Coop," came a voice in the crowd, "we just wanna see what's happening."

"Yeah," whined another, "I ain't never seen a dead body. Not like this."

"Shorty, if your fat ass isn't behind my truck in ten seconds," roared Coop, "you'll spend the rest of the weekend in jail. That goes for the rest of you, too. Now move it!" Turning back to Sam, he lowered his voice. "Get in. Please."

She pulled her arm free and stepped toward the door, tripping over a root in the process. Her head just missed the corner as Coop caught her against him, causing her to mutter a startled squeal.

Immediately, Jack jumped from the car and raced for the

sheriff, teeth bared, his growl deep and menacing. "No, Jack! Stay," shouted Sam, still encased in his arms as she turned toward the dog.

Jack slowed, but inched toward them, his size alone enough to intimidate, but coupled with that low rumble, it was terrifying.

Her voice calm and soft, she told Coop, "No sudden moves. Let me go."

He slowly released her and waited.

"I'm sorry," she whispered, "he's very protective."

Turning to the dog now a mere two feet away from his leg, she reached down. "Good boy, Jack, good boy." She rubbed his ears and stroked his head. "I appreciate your concern, sweetie, but, really it isn't necessary."

Jack didn't appear to agree, and crept forward.

She rose and stood beside Coop, slipping her arm through his.

"What the hell are you doing?"

She glanced at him from the corner of her eye. "Say something to him and be nice. He's not as dumb as some dogs…and most men."

CHAPTER FOUR

"Better do as she says, Coop," came a voice from the crowd, "I think 'at sucker means business."

Snickers could be heard above the roar in his ears as he waited while her bad-ass guardian angel debated his next move.

Who says God doesn't have a sense of humor, thought Coop as he endured being laughed at by half the town.

"What the devil am I supposed to say to him?"

"What would you want to hear from the person who hurt someone you loved?"

"This is ridiculous," he snapped and started to pull away.

Jack snarled and Coop froze, belatedly realizing the seriousness of the situation. And to add insult to injury, by tomorrow, the whole county would be buzzing about Sheriff Cooper Delaney, ex-Army Ranger and lawman extraordinaire, being held hostage by a mutt of indeterminate heritage.

Shit. Shit. Shit.

He took a deep breath and looked at the creature glaring back. The mottled black and brown fur covering his body stood on end as he watched Coop with deadly eyes. With an inward groan, he knew if he didn't convince him he truly meant no harm, things would go to hell in hurry. He slowly pushed his sun glasses up until they perched on top of his head. "See here, uh, Jack, I didn't hurt her." He kept his voice light, ignoring the ever-growing laughter from the crowd. "I know it probably looked like I did somehow, but I didn't. I swear."

The mutt glared, his expressive eyes accusing.

Without forethought, Coop argued—with a dog. "I didn't push her, she tripped and I grabbed her so she wouldn't fall."

Jack's defensive stance weakened, and his growl grew less menacing. He looked from one to the other, but didn't appear totally convinced.

The snickers spiraled into belly laughs. Coop ignored them. "I didn't hurt her. I swear. I couldn't."

Jack eyeballed Coop, and sniffed once.

"I promise."

The dog studied the crowd, now laughing hysterically, then Coop, and finally, Sam. Satisfied at last, he wagged his tail, and ambled back to the car, jumping over the door in one smooth move to settle in the front seat.

Coop immediately stepped back and put on his sunglasses.

"Hey, Coop," came a voice from the crowd, "you think she done it or the dog?"

"She don't look like no killer to me," came another, "but that dog, now, he's another story."

At his thunderous glare, the crowd shuffled back, still laughing at the incident, no doubt altering the details to suit themselves.

"You're hurting me."

He looked at her, then stared at his fingers, surprised to see how tight he held her. He didn't even remember reaching for her. A quick look at Jack told him the dog saw no reason to get hostile again, though he continued to watch. He loosened his grip.

Lips forming a tight line, she glanced at his hand, then shot ice-blue daggers at him until his hand dropped away.

The imprint of his fingers was clearly visible, and he mentally kicked himself for such a deplorable lack of control. He didn't hurt women. But he'd hurt her.

"On second thought, maybe you should wait in the car with the dog. I don't want him getting excited and hurting someone."

"Fine."

He gritted his teeth at the sharpness in one four letter word. He probably had it coming. And then some.

Jack stood in the seat as they approached. A snap of her fingers, and he hopped into the back seat.

"I have a g-u-n. I'm licensed to carry and sorely tempted to use it."

He ignored the jibe. "Where?"

"Glove compartment, a thirty-eight revolver, loaded, not chambered."

"I'm going to look at the gun," he said firmly. "Keep him off me."

"Just tell him what you're doing. The g-u-n will upset him."

Surprised when she spelled the word again, he asked "Why spell it out?"

"When I found him, he had two bullet holes in him."

Coop shook his head in disgust, and shifted to the dog. "Look, Jack, I'm going to come around and get the...," he stopped and looked at Sam. "The gun, okay? I'll unload it, and lay it on the seat. No need to go all nasty on me."

Coop slowly opened the passenger door, one eye on the

dog. "I'm just gonna reach in, and get the gun, okay? No need for us to get sideways again."

Jack whined every time he said the word *gun*.

Slow and precise, he reached toward the glove box, released the catch, and let it drop. "I'm gonna take the gun out and unload it, okay?"

When he reached for the weapon, Jack tensed and growled.

Sam reached over and patted his hindquarters. "Shhhhh, baby. It's okay."

"Look, boy, one hand," said Coop. "See? One hand." He grasped the butt of the gun, and pulled it toward him.

Jack whined.

"It's okay," Sam murmured as she stroked his arched back, "it's okay."

A quick glance at the dog ensured he wasn't ready to attack, so Coop unloaded the gun and dropped the shells in his pocket. He placed the gun on the seat next to the camera, then turned to end the one-sided conversation. "See, Big Fella, just like –"

Jack's nose was three inches away.

He froze, afraid he'd scare the dog as bad as the dog scared him.

Neither moved for several heartbeats. Then, to Coop's utter astonishment, Jack's tongue snaked out of that massive jaw and licked him from chin to eyebrow. Twice.

Then, with a swish of his tail, the dog moved to the opposite corner of the back seat and sat down, head hanging out the back window.

"Well, I'll be damned," said Sam, "first time for everything."

Coop shut the door with more composure than he actually

possessed as he walked back to where Sam stood, wiping dog slobber off his face with a bandana. On impulse, he reached over and patted the head hanging over the side of the car.

The dog's tail wagged so hard his butt rocked back and forth on the seat.

"We understand each other, don't we?" *Because dead people and dogs talk to me.*

Jack's chocolate-colored eyes scrutinized him, and the tail-wagging kicked up a notch.

"Traitor," huffed Sam.

Coop leaned against the car and crossed his arms. "So, Dr. Samantha Fowler, what are you doing in Make-Out Cove with a dead body?"

CHAPTER FIVE

Before Sam could answer, another patrol car sped down the lane, tires kicking up rocks and dirt as it slid to a stop beside Coop's SUV. Fascinated on-lookers scattered like frightened birds to escape the flying debris.

A deputy stepped out, cocked his grey Stetson to one side, and looked around. While the sheriff exuded a quiet, but potent sex appeal, this newcomer flaunted his. All muscle and sinew, his uniform stretched tight across a broad chest and muscular arms. A square jaw, offset by matching dimples in each cheek, drew the eye to a sensuous mouth wearing a come-hither smile. Pearl white teeth sparkled against golden brown skin. He glanced at a woman on his left and the smirk widened. His index finger touched the brim of his hat, and one eye closed in a suggestive wink.

The lady licked her lips and winked back.

The man did not lack self-confidence. In fact, he reminded her of a strutting peacock looking for another notch on his bedpost.

The newcomer sauntered toward Coop, shoulders swaying side-to-side, his stride practiced and proud, the muscles in his legs flexing as he strutted forward.

"What've we got, Coop?"

"Help Billy Ray string tape. And keep those people behind it."

The stranger turned the charm meter up a notch and faced Sam. "Jimmy Don Cannon, ma'am. JD to my friends. I'm sure we'll be seeing each other again."

"Cut the crap, JD," snapped Coop, "I want this area cordoned off. Stuff's in the back. Start over there behind my truck and bring it around to the pine tree."

"Sure thing, Sheriff." He tipped his hat and winked at Sam before heading off to complete his assigned task.

Coop reached over and plucked the camera from the front seat. "What were you taking pictures of?"

The curt question put her teeth on edge, like fingernails on a chalk board. "The Taj Mahal."

A muscle flexed in his jaw and his eyes narrowed.

She huffed out an exasperated snort. "I took some pictures before you got here because I thought you could use them later on. I'm a photographer—"

"I thought you were a doctor."

"I'm both. You can have the film, just don't screw around with my camera."

He pushed it toward her, mouth drawn into a tight line.

She snatched it from his outstretched hand, ignoring the quiver when her fingers brushed his. She pressed the rewind button, and quickly handed him the roll. "I could print it for you if I had access to a dark room. It's black and white film, but might be helpful. It's time and date stamped, too. I know everything today is digital but I prefer the old-fashioned way."

Coop's brow furrowed, but he remained silent. He dropped the spool in his pocket, glanced over to where the other deputies worked, then back to Sam. "Start at the beginning." He leaned against the door again, arms again crossed over his chest, "and don't leave anything out."

The intensity of his gaze drilled through mirrored sunglasses and sent her pulse through the roof. Everything about him disturbed her on some primal, unexplored, and intense level.

The man was sexy as seven kinds of hell, and it was difficult not to react, which ticked her off, so her voice took on the clipped, no-nonsense tone she used with unruly patients.

"I told you. I was driving around when Mother Nature called. This looked like a good place to answer. Saw this road and took it. I walked over there," she indicated the area just to the right of the body, "found her, called you. End of story."

"Did you see anyone else?"

"No."

"No one came out as you drove in?"

"No."

"But you took pictures?"

"Yes."

"Why? Plan to sell them to a tabloid?"

Sam bristled, but held her temper. Barely. "I grew up around cops. I know the drill. I knew you would do your own photos, but decided more wouldn't hurt. Even if they were old-fashioned black and white prints."

He pursed his lips while he mulled over her statement. "Tell me exactly what you did, where you stood, where you, you know."

Sam flushed and nodded toward the body. "I went over there," she pointed to a pine tree on the right. "I didn't—not after I saw her."

"Go on."

"I followed the same path back here, and called it in."

"Tell me about the pictures."

"I stood here and shot the area with a wide-angle lens in sections. I tried to capture the area from over there by the holly bush, to the spot where those people are standing. I used a zoom for some close ups of the garbage along the bank, and what I could see of the area where I found her." She waited for the next question.

"What about Jack?"

"He went to the big pine by the passenger side door. When I came back, he was in the front seat."

"Did he go near the body?" Clipped, rigid, his voice radiated tension.

I bet he gives lessons on how to be brusque. "I told you. He was in the car."

Jimmy Don returned from his assigned task. "What's next, Sheriff?"

Coop pushed away from the car, and looked back toward the body. "Judge on his way?"

"Yeah. Alice got him out of bed. He'll be here in a bit."

Coop nodded and looked back to his deputy. "Start a log, then work on diagrams. Stuff's in the back of the Bronco. I'll do the pictures."

"You got it."

"So," Coop turned back to Sam, "what kind of doctor are you?"

His tone tweaked her patience, and put an edge to her voice. "A good one."

"Where?"

"Dallas."

"How long?"

"Too long."

"*How long?*"

Sam glared, trying to discern what had his shorts in a wad. Other than a dead body, of course. "Ten years, give or take."

"Where in Dallas?"

Arms crossed over her chest, her tone exuded defiance. "What difference does it make?"

A muscle flicked in his jaw, but he remained silent.

His implacable expression unnerved her. "Central Valley Hospital, their community clinic, and a contributing partner in The Wellington." *Until I had to sell it to pay off Paul.*

"Wellington, huh?" An edge of derision filled his voice. "Home of mega-dollar nose jobs."

Sam couldn't decide if it was his sarcastic attitude or her ambivalent feelings about him making her testy, but testy she was. "I didn't work there. I worked at Central Valley Hospital, and volunteered at the Community Clinic. I'm a damn good doctor."

He turned and spoke to Billy Ray who stood a few feet away. "Dammit, Billy Ray, keep those people behind my truck." He shook his head in disgust and directed his attention back to her. "I can have someone drive you back to town or you can wait here." He nodded toward her car. "I can't let you drive out until I'm done."

Anticipating an extended wait, she'd resigned herself to a long day. "If it's all the same to you, I'll just wait. This car is… special. I won't leave it unattended."

Mouth tight, he shook his head slightly as though dealing with a temperamental child. "Have it your way," he said at last, "liable to be a while."

She got behind the wheel but remained silent when he shut the door with more force than she thought necessary. The man was stubborn, snappish and tried her patience to the max.

So why did her body tingle and her mouth go dry watching him walk away?

CHAPTER SIX

Sam parked in the driveway, but lacked the energy to get out. A glance at her watch showed two in the afternoon, and she hadn't eaten all day. At least Jack had dog food in the car. Around noon, Delaney let her take him to the creek on the other side of the road for a drink, and he dozed in the back seat the rest of the time.

Her discomfort extended well beyond the gruesome circumstances, though. Cooper Delaney played a huge role in her distress. He intrigued her, and ticked her off; and those conflicting sentiments wreaked havoc with her already twisted emotions.

His image danced around the edges of her mind, and she easily recalled the last sight of him. His back to her, he stood alone in the middle of chaos, focused and determined as he processed the scene.

The broad outline of his shoulders strained the seams of a soft cotton shirt and faded jeans hugged his body like second skin. One pant leg balanced on the top of worn boots, while the other rested in folds around an ankle.

When he shifted, her eyes riveted on his well-formed derriere, highlighted by the washed-out denim covering it. The immediate reaction of her body caused heat to flood her face, and she quickly looked away.

This up close and personal experience with a murder investigation left her drained and ill-tempered. The Texas Ranger who quizzed her was patient and kind, but relentless. She repeated her story so many times, she was sick of hearing it. About one-thirty, he handed her a bottle of water from his car and let her leave the scene.

She stopped in town for fuel and a snack at a convenience store and discovered she had suddenly acquired celebrity status. Half a dozen people wanted to know all the gory details, and she told them, as politely as she could, nothing. When the cashier discovered she was a guest at Miss Eva's, the grilling began again, but this time, about the sheriff. In the end, she just paid for her gas and left, her stomach protesting in earnest.

She heaved a weary sigh and pulled herself from the car as the back door of the house opened.

Ms. Benton came down the steps drying her hands on a towel. "My goodness, child, I was worried sick. How are you? Alice told me you found the body. Have you eaten anything? You look exhausted."

Sam struggled with the sudden urge to cry. Taken aback, she tried to gather herself together. She faced traumatic situations almost daily, and learned to compartmentalize, but for some reason, this situation was different. "This has been a trying day for sure."

"You come inside this minute." She put her arms around Sam's waist, and led her toward the back door. "I've got fresh coffee on and lunch is waiting."

"Thank you, ma'am, but really, you needn't trouble yourself on my account."

"Nonsense," she said as they entered, and urged Sam into

the nearest chair, Jack on their heels. "You are a guest in my home. And frankly, you deserve a little fussing over." She nodded toward Jack. "Has he eaten?"

Again, Sam fought back tears. What was wrong with her? It wasn't as though she knew the woman, had no involvement other than finding the body, yet she felt such sorrow and loss, hot tears hung a heartbeat away. She hadn't had such a strong emotional response to anything in years.

She pushed the disturbing thoughts aside. "I keep dry food in the car, and fed him around one." She swallowed hard past the lump in her throat. "Thank you…Ms. Benton. You're very kind."

"Everyone calls me Miss Eva, and I love having people to fuss over. Makes me feel needed." The warmth of her smile echoed in her voice. "I put a bowl of water there by the door, and saved a plate of scraps for him. If you don't mind, of course. Some folks are picky about such things."

"I don't mind. And my friends call me Sam. Or did I tell you that already?"

"You did," she replied brightly. "I believe its short for Samantha, right?"

"Yes ma'am. My brothers thought Samantha was a silly name, and called me Sam from day one."

"How many brothers do you have?"

"Two. Frank is the oldest, Thomas two years younger." She grinned. "I'm the baby of the family, and the only granddaughter. Between my parents and my grandmother who lived with us, I was pretty spoiled."

"Where do they live?"

"Frank lives in Dallas and Thomas is a cop in Houston."

"And your folks?

"Both retired. He was a cop, she's a nurse." As the words flowed, she relaxed, and some of the tension leached from her body. "Last time I talked with them, they were somewhere near Williamsburg, Virginia." She beamed at the memory. "They bought this used motor home, and planned to travel the country for a solid year, then they'd vegetate back in Houston." She shook her head. "That was six months ago. I bet another six won't be enough."

The older woman deposited a bowl on the floor for Jack who promptly scarfed up the treat. She returned to the stove and filled another plate with roast beef, mashed potatoes, and green beans for Sam. "I traveled some in my younger days," said Miss Eva as she placed the food in front of her. "Until one day, I realized everything I needed was right here in Bakersville."

"I wish I knew what I wanted." Heat rushed to her cheeks when she realized she spoke out loud. She barely acknowledged the thought to herself much less someone else.

Eva reached over and patted her hand. "When the time is right, dear, you'll know." She turned toward the stove. "What would you like to drink? Coffee, tea or something else?"

"Coffee please. I haven't had my ration of caffeine today."

She pulled a mug from the cabinet and filled it. "I think Coop needs about a gallon a day."

At the mention of his name, her heart jumped. "Coop?"

"Uh-huh. Cooper Delaney. The sheriff. You must have met him, well, out there."

"Of course. The sheriff."

"Uh-oh. I recognize that tone. Don't let his blustery I'm-the-sheriff attitude fool you. He's a sweetheart."

Her voice rose in surprise. "A sweetheart?"

"Oh, my, yes. Why I don't know what I would do if it weren't for him and Jason."

"Jason?"

"His son. He's twenty-two and a student at SMU. Handsome as his father and twice as charming."

Unable to picture the man she met today as charming, Sam shook her head. Efficient, yes; focused on his job and authoritative, certainly, but charming? No way. *Let's not forget sex appeal oozing out every pore.*

"Um…what about Mrs. Delaney?" Immediately, she regretted the query. It was none of her business, and she didn't care in the least. *Liar, liar, pants on fire.* She ducked her head to hide the flush creeping up her neck.

"Oh, there isn't one. Not anymore."

"I'm sorry, I shouldn't have asked. It's none of my business."

Miss Eva wiped at a non-existent spill on the countertop. "Judy just up and left them both when Jason was almost seven. Sent divorce papers in the mail and never looked back. Can you imagine leaving your child like that?" She queried softly, then shook her head before deftly changing the subject. "Can I get you anything else, dear?"

"Oh, no, thank you, I'm fine. And thank you for lunch. I didn't realize how hungry I was until I started eating. Everything was delicious."

"You're welcome, dear. Dessert? Fresh apple pie."

"Oh, goodness no. I'm stuffed."

"Well it's here if you decide you need something later. And there's always coffee on the stove." Her voice glowed with pleasure as she continued. "I never know when Coop will be in, so I make sure there's always a fresh pot on."

Sam wanted to ask about her relationship to the sheriff, but decided it crossed the line of casual conversation, and switched to neutral topics. "Do you happen to know Dr. Harper? I understand he's a local physician."

"Oh yes, he's been a fixture in this town for over forty years. Do you know him?"

"Not really. His niece, Barbara Walker, is my best friend. In fact, she's the one who suggested your lovely home for my vacation."

"How sweet of her. Poor dear doesn't make it back home very often anymore." She tilted her head to one side as though in thought. "I believe she works at a big hospital in Dallas."

Sam nodded. "We met at Central Valley Hospital and became best buds right away. I promised to check in with her uncle while I'm here. Now, what is there to do in Bakersville? I understand it's a fairly small town."

There was something warm and enchanting in the older woman's laughter. "Well, we're a little behind the times here, Sam. No malls or fancy stores. But, we do have a drive-in theater."

"Really? I had no idea those things still existed."

"I am proud to say The Sundown Drive-In Theater is one of the few still operating in Texas. It's only open on weekends. And they use the old speakers you hang on your car window. You can also tune in on your radio, but it takes the fun out of going to the drive-in."

"I'll make sure to give it try while I'm here."

"They do double features on Friday and Saturday nights. The late shows are always old movies. I just love those, though I can't stay up as late as I once did. And then a single feature on Sundays. There's a playground area for the kids and the best hot dogs you ever tasted."

"Really?"

"Absolutely. They're open year-round, though the weather can be unpredictable sometimes and affects the schedule."

The next hour passed in pleasant conversation as she gave Sam tips on scenic places she could photograph, the history of Baker County, and some of its more interesting people.

Sam headed up to her room filled with peace and contentment for the first time in over a year. Paul's cheating, the quarrels, and finally, the drawn-out divorce process, robbed her of all spirit and drive. But, here, in this place, strength returned and despair lessened.

I was right to come here. Now I can figure out what to do with my life.

CHAPTER SEVEN

Monday, 5:30 a.m.

Coop parked and killed the engine, hands resting in his lap as he leaned back and closed his eyes. The two-hour drive from the morgue in Dallas took his last reserve of energy. No time to rest. A quick shower, hopefully decent coffee, then off to the office to continue the process of finding out who the victim was, and who killed her. And, just as important, why.

He sighed and recalled the coroner's observations.

"This little lady definitely didn't give up without a fight. Preliminary COD (cause of death) is strangulation, with time of death sometime between midnight and 4 a.m. She took one hell of a beating, too. All the bruises are pre-mortem, a couple of broken ribs, haven't gotten the full tox screen yet, blood alcohol was point-0-two, so she wasn't drunk, still could've been drugged, though. No tattoos or scars. Doubt I'll find anything under her fingernails"

"Why?"

"Looks like they were scraped clean, but we'll see if he left anything. And he used a condom." He pointed to the woman's right hand. "Her right index finger is broken"

Coop was bone tired and not sure he heard right. "What?"

"Broken. In two places, like maybe he pulled it, then snapped it like a twig."

"Why on earth would he do that?" An instinctive and rhetorical query, he didn't expect an answer.

"They pay you to figure out the whys. Me, I just tell you what I find."

He opened his eyes and stared at the trucks' roof. *Why the finger? What the hell does it mean? Is it significant or not?*

A former combat soldier, with two tours in Afghanistan, Coop was no stranger to death. Murder was a totally different matter; depravity personified; everything vile and heinous one human could do to another, with no regard for the victim or those who must deal with the carnage left behind.

After his stint in the military, he joined Dallas PD and worked his way up the ladder to homicide detective. Faced with violence every day took a toll on you, destroyed your ability to feel normal. Which was why he returned home and took a deputy job in Bakersville after Judy left. He wanted a normal life for him and Jason, not one filled with images like he faced today.

No wait, that was yesterday. A full twenty-four hours had passed since he last closed his eyes. He rolled his shoulders to loosen the tightness. He had to get moving or fall asleep where he sat. A light in the kitchen window lifted his spirits. Miss Eva no doubt waited for him with food and hot coffee in hand.

Except wasn't Miss Eva.

Sam yelped and jumped at his entrance, dousing her hand with hot coffee.

"Crap." He rushed over, grabbed paper towels from the roll under the cabinet and formed a dam to keep the liquid from rolling to the floor. "I'm sorry I startled you. Can I help?"

She ran cool water over the scalded patch on her hand. "I'm fine."

When she turned off the water, Coop pulled more towels off the roll, and handed them to her. "I'm so sorry. Does it hurt much?"

She dabbed at her hand with the towel. "I'm fine, really."

"I expected to see Eva."

She shrugged. "I'm an early riser. Thought I'd go for a run."

When she looked at him, once again he felt the tug of those fascinating eyes. Bone tired, his groin tightened in response, and his heart rate kicked up a notch. *Down boy. Down.*

She nodded toward the pot. "It's fresh but may not be to your liking. I'm afraid I like it stronger than most folks. Since you weren't back yet, and I didn't know when you'd return, I made it to suit my taste."

At the end of her rambling dissertation, she took a breath and reached for her mug, the tinge of a blush racing up her cheeks like a fever, eyes darting around the kitchen.

"I'm sure it's fine. Besides, I'll need the extra kick today." He grabbed his favorite cup and took his time filling it before taking a cautious sip. His eyes widened in surprise. Perfection. He took another sip and savored the rich flavor as it passed over his tongue. "Umm…thought Eva was the only woman around who knew how to make good coffee." His body vibrated with new life. "I was wrong."

She glanced up, surprise and pleasure etched on her face. "Thank you. I, um, grew up drinking my dad's cop-coffee as he called it. It's what got me through med school, my residency and stuff. Can't drink anything else now."

He nodded, reluctant to leave, though he knew he needed to get a move on.

She sipped her coffee. "I guess –"

"Where's Jack?"

"What? Oh, um, hiding under the table. I don't think he wants to run today."

Coop stooped over to check out the dog.

Jack lay sprawled out, head on his paws, eyes closed.

"Hey Big Fella, how's it going?"

A light swish of his tail on the floor was the only indication he wasn't dead. Coop chuckled. "Some bodyguard you got there."

Sam set her cup on the counter, looking everywhere but at him. "Yeah, well, he has his moments. Besides, if he didn't trust you, it would be a different story all together."

Coop could certainly vouch for the protectiveness piece. Propped against the counter, he blew across his coffee before taking another drink, idly wondering if the warm feeling pulsing though his veins was the caffeine or the company. "I'll need you to come down to the office later and give a formal statement."

She nodded. "Any particular time?"

"Whatever works for you, but the sooner the better."

"No problem." She eased one hip against the counter beside him, compelling eyes now studying his face. "You're exhausted. How long since you slept?"

For whatever reason, the hint of concern in her voice lifted his spirits. "I don't even remember." He drained his cup and set it on the counter. "Thanks for the coffee." He turned toward the door to the dining room.

"Have you eaten?"

No mistaking it; concern. For reasons he chose not to examine, he liked it. "Junk food from the vending machine and piss-poor, uh, sorry, bad coffee at the morgue."

"Eva left a sandwich in the fridge. I'm guessing sleep isn't an option, but you really should eat it before you go out again. Trust me. I know what sleep deprivation and lack of decent food will do. You can't be productive running on adrenalin and bad coffee."

"I'll get it on the way out."

"Make sure you do." She pushed away from the counter. "Doctor's orders."

His disposition took another upward climb. "Thanks, Doc."

She nodded and walked out the back door, presumably for her morning run.

He paused, and snapped his fingers. Immediately, Jack opened his eyes and looked at him. "Go with her," he said tightly, pointing to the back door. "There's a murderer on the loose."

Jack jumped up and waited for him to open the door before trotting out to catch up to Sam.

CHAPTER EIGHT

"No missing persons matching her description."

While not surprising, JD's report wasn't what Coop wanted to hear. "Get out a teletype to Region 1. Prints will be in the system this morning. Maybe we'll get lucky." The dream's warning popped into his head. "Look for anything similar."

"Similar? You think there might be more?"

"Just covering all the bases. Cause of death is strangulation."

Jimmy cleared his throat. "Was she raped?"

"Yeah. She fought back, so hopefully they have enough for a DNA match when we catch him." Coop pushed back in his chair. "Put in the details her right index finger is broken in two places."

Jimmy hesitated, brow crinkled. "Is that important?"

"Maybe, maybe not. We check every detail so we can rule out what doesn't apply. And the tidbit about the finger is need-to-know only for now. Got it?"

"Yes sir."

"Get the teletype out before you do anything else."

"Will do." The deputy's familiar affability disappeared and his voice resonated determination. "I've never been involved in a murder investigation. I wanna make sure I do stuff right."

"By the book all the way, JD," said Coop firmly, "by the book."

Face tight, he nodded agreement and left the room.

Alone, Coop stared at the ancient computer screen. Modern technology had yet to make it to the Baker County Sheriff's Office, but at least they had high speed internet. He spent the next hour surfing various law enforcement sites for anything useful, and got zero for his effort.

He still had a contact in the Dallas FBI office, so he left a message for him to return the call, hoping he could offer insight.

The ancient leather creaked as he leaned back in his chair and rubbed his eyes. *God, I'm tired. And hungry.* He rubbed his face and thought about the sandwich still sitting in the refrigerator. He left in such a hurry he forgot it.

"May I come in?"

At the sound of Sam's sexy voice, desire flickered to life. Something about her struck every male molecule in his body, and apparently, he was powerless to do anything about it. Would he survive for two long weeks?

"Of course." He stood and eyed the cloth-wrapped object in one hand, a thermos in the other. "If that's food and decent coffee, I may have to kiss you." The words were out before he could stop them, and heat flooded his cheeks.

She hesitated at the door, eyes widened slightly, then she stepped into the room, holding the plate out to him. "You left without eating the sandwich she left. I figured you'd be busy and not eat for a while, so I brought lunch."

He looked at the clock on the wall, surprised to see it neared the noon hour. "Didn't realize the time." He took the plate, and flushed again when his stomach growled loudly in anticipation. "I'm starved."

He moved back to his chair and sat down, the plate of chicken fried steak and mashed potatoes slathered in cream gravy, a side of fresh peas and a biscuit getting all his attention.

Sam passed him napkin-wrapped utensils, along with the thermos, then sat down in the chair in front of his desk. "When did you eat last?" A light laugh punctuated the question.

"Candy bar at the morgue," he mumbled around a mouthful of potatoes, "about midnight." He sighed with contentment as he wolfed down the plate's contents.

He finished the meal and poured himself a cup of real coffee from the thermos. This time, he couldn't stifle the contented exhale as he took his first drink.

He's not done.

He jumped at The Voice's unexpected intrusion, barely able to remain in the chair, choking on the coffee he inhaled. He covered his mouth with the napkin as he sputtered and glanced at Sam.

She shuddered and shifted in her chair, arms folded across her chest as she glanced around the room.

For a moment, he questioned her response. *Did she hear it, too? Not possible. I'm the one who hears voices in my head.*

"Are you cold?" He was surprised his voice sounded so calm considering his racing heart.

She rubbed her forearms. "Had a sudden chill." Her gaze focused on the overhead air vent. "I should have brought a jacket. You could hang meat in here."

Thankful for the diversion, he swiped his mouth with the napkin and stood. "I'm hot-natured." Heat rushed to his face again, and this time, it was he who avoided eye contact. "We'll get your statement, and you can be on your way."

"I'm good. Unless you want to do it right now."

She gasped and those baby blue's locked on his, the easily inferred double-meaning loud and clear.

Frozen in time, neither moved.

He heard each hasty breath she took, saw the rapid pulse at the base of her graceful neck. Unable to stop, his gaze dropped to slightly-parted full lips, and fixed on the tongue lightly tracing the lower one. He just managed to stifle a groan as forbidden images sent blood rushing south.

He gave himself a mental kick, and stomped to the coat rack in front of the window. He grabbed his jacket and handed it to her. "JD will take you next." He stumbled as he returned to his chair and picked up his cup. "Your statement. He'll be back shortly and get your statement."

Well, hell. Just pull the pin on the damn grenade and be done with it.

Sam draped the leather jacket around her shoulders and flinched as the stimulating scent of leather and man assailed her nostrils. Self-control vanished around him; like a marionette whose strings are pulled by unseen hands. The harder she tried to deny the attraction, the stronger it persisted.

It's pointless to get involved with him. I'm only here for two weeks. There's no room in my life for romance. Not now, maybe never.

Her brain might know it, but her body had other notions. She doggedly pulled her wandering thoughts together and looked at him.

Bad idea.

The intensity radiating from those storm-cloud eyes drew her like a magnet. She tried to throttle back the dizzying current racing through her, to no avail.

The fact that he felt it too showed in his own labored breathing, the flared nostrils, and the hand clutching his coffee cup so tight, the knuckles turned white.

Holy mother of pearl.

"Sheriff, I got –" JD stopped in the doorway. "Sorry. Didn't know you had company."

Sam seized the opportunity to end the unnerving encounter and sprang from the chair, shrugging out of the thought-altering jacket. "I came to give my statement." She hung it on the rack without looking at Delaney, who remained seated. "Dee said you'd take care of it."

The deputy frowned. "Who's Dee?"

It took a moment for the question to penetrate the desire-clogged recesses of her brain. "Oh, sorry. I have a habit of assigning nicknames to people without even realizing I do it."

JD grinned. "Ahh, so, the sheriff here is Dee, for Delaney, huh?"

No. For danger, delectable. "Uh, yes, right. Delaney."

The smile widened, emphasizing dimples in each cheek. "So, what's mine?"

For some reason, repartee with the cocky deputy wasn't the least bit unnerving. Some of the tension dissipated, and she chuckled. "I haven't decided yet."

"Room Two is set up to get her statement." Coop's rough command abruptly ended the friendly banter.

The deputy stepped around Sam and handed a folder to the sheriff. "My report on things you wanted me to do."

He turned back to Sam and the grin reappeared. "This way, ma'am."

"My friends call me Sam."

"A beautiful woman shouldn't be called Sam." The charm meter pegged out. "I'll call you Sunshine. Because you brighten up the room just by being in it."

"Your charm is wasted on me."

He winked. "Issuing me a challenge, Sunshine?"

The exaggerated eye roll didn't appear to faze him.

He cupped her elbow and headed toward the door. "I like a challenge."

CHAPTER NINE

The surge of jealousy blindsided him. Coop watched JD put a hand on Sam's elbow to lead her down the hall, and wanted to punch him. He scrubbed his face—hard—with both hands and picked up Jane Doe's folder. He thumbed through the contents but couldn't concentrate. *I'm just tired. I need some sleep.*

He tossed the folder onto his desk and swiveled his chair to look out the window, gaze pausing on the framed accolades hanging on the wall. *What would the townspeople think if they knew I heard voices in my head?* He snorted. *I'd be out of a job so fast I wouldn't know what hit me.*

The law was his life, and he prided himself on being good at it. For whatever reason, that no longer appeared to be enough. Something was missing though he could not precisely define what.

You have to stop him.

This time, the directive didn't surprise him. In fact, he almost welcomed it. He closed his eyes and leaned back in his chair. "What do you want from me?" he whispered. "What do you want?"

Two hours later, Sam left the station, stopping on the way out to retrieve the plate and thermos from Coop's office, refusing to be disappointed when he wasn't there.

She deposited the items in the front seat, and looked around. The old courthouse sat in the middle of the town square, its beautifully landscaped front anchored by giant pecan trees, a small military memorial and several benches. The streets were cobblestone and well maintained. The buildings facing the front of the courthouse, some dating back to the mid-1800's included a small drug store, Arnolds's General Store, and Ruby's Diner. Other businesses graced the remaining three sides, with a couple of empty buildings on one corner.

Light posts around the square appeared to be old, and, upon inspection, were indeed gas powered. She moved to an unoccupied bench under the nearest pecan tree and sat down, watching the ebb and flow of people as they went about their lives. A mild late-September breeze brought with it the faint aroma of flowers, no doubt from the delivery truck parked in front of the florist shop on the corner. She closed her eyes and leaned her head back, savoring the gentle brush of air on her skin. Murder notwithstanding, Bakersville was a nice place to be.

"Mind if I join you?"

Coop's unexpected question elicited a slight jump.

"Sorry." He sat beside her, their hips a hair apart. "I didn't thank you for bringing me food and coffee."

She shrugged. "Eva worried about you not eating, so I told her I'd bring it with me."

"I appreciate it just the same."

"You're welcome."

The ensuing silence wasn't unpleasant. In fact, for the

first time since they met, she was actually comfortable in his presence.

"I grew up in a busy suburb of Houston. Moved to Dallas for work. I've always been surrounded by noise, lights, and people." Sam looked around. "I never thought I'd be happy anyplace else. But here…"

Coop nodded. "I left Dallas PD when Jason was seven so he could grow up in my hometown. Best move I ever made."

The groan of a loud motor had them both looking south. A dark blue, late model Cadillac rolled slowly up the street.

Sam squinted. "Is she the lady they call Big Mama Eva told me about?"

Coop sat up a little straighter. "Uh-huh."

"I understand she only comes to town on Fridays, parks out front of the store, and waits for someone to bring her groceries. Wonder why she's coming in today?"

The car neared the store in question, and stopped in the middle of the street, horn blaring.

"John Austin's in her spot." As Coop stood, a man exited the store and hurried to the car occupying the space Big Mama wanted.

"Sorry, Big Mama," he shouted, "didn't expect you in town today."

As soon as he moved his truck, the old caddy rolled into it, and the horn blared again.

A young man rushed to the driver's side window, then gestured wildly for Coop to come.

"Now what," he muttered as he crossed the street. A quick look inside and he yelled at Sam. "Doc. Get over here."

When Sam saw the blood on the old woman's face, she morphed into doctor mode, gently tilting the woman's chin so she could get a better view of the cut above her left eye. "What happened?"

"Who the devil are you?" snapped the woman, "I want Doc Harper."

"I'm Dr. Fowler. Did you fall?"

"Well as sure as heck didn't hit myself in the head with a hammer."

Sam bit back a grin. The crusty matriarch reminded her of her late grandmother. "Are you hurt anywhere else?"

She squinted at Sam, mouth tight, and didn't answer.

Undeterred, Sam continued to probe her arms and hands. When she touched the left shoulder, the old woman winced. "Coop, she needs to get to the hospital. At the very least, she's going to need a couple of stitches on her forehead. Her shoulder needs to be x-rayed to make sure it's not broken. She doesn't appear to have a concussion, but it can't be ruled out without some tests."

"I'm not going to no dang hospital. I want Doc Harper." She glared at Sam. "And nobody else."

An hour and a half later, Sam stood beside Doc Harper as he filed away the x-rays. He not only invited her to hang around during the exam, he asked her opinion on the film prior to talking with the patient. In the end, he had his receptionist take the older woman home after Coop arranged to have her car returned there.

"Mable's a tough old bird," he said without rancor, "but her bark is much worse than her bite."

"She's lucky she ended up with a bruised shoulder and couple of stiches instead of broken bones."

He closed the file and placed it in the holder outside the exam room, limping a little as he moved about. "Let's talk in my office."

Seated across from him, she eyed the clutter on his desk. She'd anticipated this conversation later rather than sooner.

He got right to the point. "I guess you know Barbara Jean is my niece?"

"Yes. We've been friends since I moved to Dallas ten years ago."

"She thinks you're the person to take over here for me."

Nervous, she shifted in her seat. "I told her I'd discuss the prospect with you."

"She said you already quit your job in Dallas."

"True. But I haven't decided what I want to do yet."

"How do you like our little town?"

"It's only been a few days, but I like it. Nice people, slow pace."

"She tells me you're a good doctor."

"Well, we're best friends, so I think her opinion may be a little biased, but I appreciate her saying so."

"Not just her." He cleaned his glasses with the tail of his crumpled tie and slid them in his pocket. "I did some checking after she suggested you. Lot of folks think the same thing." He folded his hands on top of a pile of papers. "Let's cut to the chase, Dr. Fowler. I'm sixty-five. I'm tired. I wanna go fishing with my grandsons, go on a cruise with my wife. Won't happen if I'm tied to this office."

Sam's heart jumped, anticipating his next statement.

"I want someone I can trust to take care of my town, my people. I think you're that someone."

CHAPTER TEN

Tension seeped away as Sam enjoyed the gentle sway of the rope swing hanging from an ancient pecan tree. The wooden seat, worn smooth from years of use, and the creak and rasp of the thick, braided line as she swung was more therapeutic than any drug. Her gaze drifted to the glitter of sunlight off a pond in the distance, then to the giant pine trees waving in the afternoon breeze. A blue jay chased a robin from a bird feeder at the end of the veranda with a loud squawk, as an orange tabby watched from the corner.

This moment in time, she conceded staying here, taking over Doc's practice as a workable solution to the dilemma of what to do with her life. But what about later? Would she miss the benefits of city-living? As much as she loved being a doctor, was she really ready to jump back into the grind of hospital rounds and patient appointments?

She pushed the doubts away, refused to let anything negative impose on the tranquility she enjoyed right now. She'd earned the peace and quiet.

A little push with her foot put the ancient swing in motion. She gripped the rope, leaned back and pushed again, sending it higher and higher. She couldn't stop the laughter bubbling up when Jack played chase with her feet as she flew along the ground. This is how life is supposed to be lived. In the moment. To the fullest.

What about Delaney?

The peacefulness ended with a jolt as she drug her feet on the ground to stop the swings motion. She couldn't deny her attraction to him, but she wasn't ready for another relationship, and a one-night-stand was out of the question.

Which meant she would have to find her own place. She looked around the beautiful back yard, thought of her well-appointed room, and the companionship of Miss Eva. Did she really want to give it up?

If she stayed, would her body betray her determination to avoid the weakness of desire and be made a fool of again? "I have to nip this in the bud right now."

At her terse comment, Jack's ears perked up, and he sat down in front as though waiting for her to continue.

"I won't be duped again. I was naïve and lonely when Paul came along. I'm neither of those things now."

Jack cocked his head to the side and gave a delicate "*woof*".

"How do you know we can trust him? We just met him. Anyone can be nice when they have to."

A second "*woof*" sounded like a rebuke.

"I heard today Miss Eva wants him to get married and he wants none of it." She wrapped her arms around the rough rope, swaying a little. "Okay, he's nice to you which means a lot, but it doesn't alter the fact he's not marriage material and I'm not fling material, so I just need to set him straight, and we can move on."

Her four-legged friend glared a moment, shook his head, and took off after the tabby, leaving her to resolve the situation on her own.

Coop stood at the kitchen window and watched Sam swing. Even at this distance, he saw the happiness in her face as the wind whipped her hair around, while Jack chased her feet. He couldn't hold back a lop-sided grin as her joyful laughter penetrated the glass pane. Sunshine suited her for a nickname because she *did* brighten up a room.

As usual in a small town, everyone knew everyone else's business, and word leaked out about Doc's wish to retire. His nurse, Jan, happened to be best friends with Coop's secretary, Alice, whose love of gossip was surpassed only by her love of anything George Strait. Her parting words today still had him astonished.

Yesterday, Doc Harper asked Sam to take over his practice. Which begged the question, *Is that why she came to Bakersville in the first place?*

He admitted to being undecided about the possibility. On the one hand, she would be here indefinitely. Given their attraction, it could be a double-edged sword. He was not in the market for a wife. Period. And she didn't strike him as a casual-sex kind of woman. But, at the same time, his male ego sensed a mutual pull. *And this leaves me where?* "Between a rock and a hard place," he muttered, then snorted at the unintended pun.

When Jack took off after the cat, he poured himself a cup of coffee and mentally prepared to tell her, in no uncertain terms, how a relationship between them would be impossible. His resolve wavered when she turned toward the house, and that radiant smile faded the moment their eyes met.

She stopped, squared her shoulders, and strode forward.

Inside the kitchen door, she hesitated. Then, appearing to reach a decision, she barked, "We need to talk."

Surprised by her sense of urgency, he rested his cup on the counter, hands braced on either side of his hips. "About what?"

"Us. This –" She waved one hand back and forth between them. "Whatever it is between us. It ain't happening."

He opened his mouth to respond, but she continued with renewed vigor.

"I don't do flings. You're not into marriage, so whatever you have mind, you can just forget it."

Wait…what?

Ego dented, he moved toward her. "Forget it?" he asked quietly, "So, you're not attracted to me at all?"

Those baby-blues widened and she sucked in a breath. "Don't be silly. Of course I'm attracted to you."

Ahh, that's more like it.

"I'm just not going to act on it."

"Why not?"

She took a step back, eyes darting around. "I was fooled once. I won't be fooled again."

"And you think…." He paused for her to fill in the blank.

"I know. You don't want a permanent relationship. If you did, we wouldn't be having this conversation."

"Because…?"

"Because some woman would have snared you by now."

"Snared me?"

She waved a hand in front of her. "Okay, okay…bad choice of words, but you know what I mean."

"Maybe I've been waiting for the right woman to snare me."

His comment made her eyes squint as her forehead creased in confusion. "I'm not her."

"How can you be so sure?"

"You're a cop. Don't you believe in gut instinct?"

"I do." He took another step toward her, enjoying the play of emotions across her face as she struggled for control. "What's your gut telling you? Avoid me? Take a chance?"

Her jaw clenched and those amazing blue eyes speared him. "Not to trust you."

Four little words cut him to the bone. He had trust issues out the wazoo, but he'd never had anyone not trust *him*.

He was close enough to smell the floral fragrance of her perfume mixed with the light perspiration on her blouse, to see the varying shades of blue around the iris of her eyes glittering with a hurt so raw, it made him step back.

"I see." The sharp ring of the telephone saved him from having to rebut her censure. When he turned to answer it, she darted through the door. He heard the hard slap of her shoes on the floor as she raced up the stairs.

He grabbed the phone only to be greeted by a cheerful telemarketer advising him of a free trip to somewhere. With a grunt of frustration he slammed the phone back in the cradle.

She doesn't trust me. The words echoed through his brain, and suddenly, he knew: no matter what, he could not let her maintain such a low opinion of him.

CHAPTER ELEVEN

Wednesday, 4 p.m.

Five hours sleep in the last forty-eight made concentration difficult as Coop listened to JD's report.

"Got nothing off the prints in AFIS," the deputy said. "And no similar cases, either. Anything from your FBI friend?"

"No. He left a message late yesterday. He's out all week and will call back on Monday. Spoke to the ME in Dallas a few minutes ago. Said he found some blue thread in one of the gashes on her back, silk, possibly from her blouse."

"I showed her picture at the gas stations and cafés like you suggested. Ruthie down at the Shell station said she might have seen her Sunday night, but couldn't be sure. Said a woman in a fancy red car drove up to the pumps. Couldn't get a good look at her since she was on the opposite side. Most people use the pay-at-the-pump feature now. No need to come inside."

Coop tossed his pen on the desk and leaned back. "Fancy red car?"

"Her words. Said she's never seen one like it."

"Did you get a copy of the credit card receipt?"

"I asked about it, but she didn't know how to get one. Not very tech savvy. Said she'd have the owner get it to you."

"What about surveillance tapes?"

He shook his head, voice laced with frustration. "They have some, but the system is down more than up because he's always messing with it. Seems he's some kind of techno geek and has all this equipment in his office he plays with. She'll have him get a copy as soon as he gets back in."

"Okay. Check the motels and B&B's next. If she was passing through she might have stopped somewhere in town. I'll go talk to Ruthie and see if I can get a better description of the car."

"She got off at two today. Said she was going shopping with her sister in Texarkana. Won't be home till after supper."

"What about the owner?"

"He comes and goes a lot."

Coop rubbed his temples to ease the growing headache. He hated hurry up and wait. "Leave word to have him call me as soon as he gets in."

"Already did." Jimmy paused and shuffled his feet. "Sheriff, I know it's not my place to say so, but you look like hell. Why don't you go home, get some rest. I'll call you if anything turns up."

"Sheriff Delaney?"

Both men turned to see a young man standing outside the door, worn baseball cap in his hands. "The lady out front said I should come on back."

Coop swallowed a groan. Alice didn't care who came in or how busy he was, she sent them back without bothering to let him know. He made a mental note to talk with her about it. Again. "What can I do for you?"

"Well, um, I'm Arlis Barton. I work at Teddy's Place."

"You're Frank Barton's boy, aren't you? He let you work there?"

"Yes sir, but I don't work in the bar part. I work in the back doing the dishes and stuff."

"What can I do for you, Arlis?"

"Well, it's about the dead woman. I might've seen her Sunday. Teddy said I needed to come tell you."

Coop sat forward in his chair. "When? Was she with anyone?"

"Not when I saw her. I went out back to the dumpster and seen this red Corvette off to the side by the metal building we use for supplies." He made a tsk-tsk sound. "Man, what a car. A 2005, candy apple red, shined like new money, and not a scratch on it. I bet that sucker runs like a scalded dog."

Trust the boy to notice the car and not the woman. "You said you saw the woman?" prompted Coop.

"Yes sir. She was leaning on the front fender, talking to someone on her phone. She sounded mad. I couldn't make out what she said exactly, cause her back was to me, but I did hear her say she'd kick someone's ass if she got stood up."

"Anything else?"

"No sir. She hung up and saw me standing there." He ducked his head as his cheeks flamed. "She told me to stop eavesdropping and get the hell away from her." He looked up, face stricken. "I wasn't trying to eavesdrop, Sheriff, I promise. I was taking out the trash."

Adrenalin spiked and chased away the fatigue. He had a lead.

"What about the woman? What can you tell me about her?"

"Well, kinda pretty, long hair, like down past her shoulders, dark brown, a lot of makeup like those city girls wear. She had on this bluish colored, slinky tank top. I couldn't see her legs so I don't know if she had on jeans or whatever."

Coop and Jimmy exchanged looks. It was her. It had to be. "What time was this, Arlis?"

"I get off at ten and was finishing up, so a little before ten. That's all I know, Sheriff. I'm sorry."

Coop extended his hand. "You've been a big help, Arlis. Thanks for coming in."

After promising to call if he remembered anything else, the kid left.

"Get out another teletype." Coop's voice rang with command. "There can't be that many red Corvettes in this area. Add the part about the blue tank top." He grabbed his hat from the wall. "I'm going out to Teddy's and see if I can get anything else."

An hour later, his euphoria faded. No one remembered seeing a woman matching her description on Sunday night. Ladies Night, and the place was packed with folks from every surrounding county, as well as truckers and interstate traffic. Just one more face in a sea of strangers. They did have security cameras on the parking lot but not the area where she parked. He secured the stuff from Sunday anyway, hoping they would produce something.

He stood beside his SUV and debated what to do next. Getting some much-needed sleep topped the list. He strolled around behind the tavern to the spot Arlis indicated he last saw her. Eyes on the ground, he cautiously scanned the area. A mixture of asphalt, gravel and concrete made up the parking lot which offered nil in the way of evidence. He widened the search, but after nearly an hour of looking, admitted there was nothing to be found.

Hands on his hips, he took one last look around, then

headed back to his car. The sharp blare of his cell phone stopped him at the door.

"Delaney."

"DPS may have found her car," Jimmy's voice vibrated with excitement.

"Where?"

"Oil road out past two-o-six, the one leading to the old abandoned oil well near the county line."

"On my way. Tell Josh I want him on Day Dispatch for a while." Night calls would go through central before routing to the deputy assigned after hours. Alice was the last person he wanted on those lines right now. "Either of 'em don't like it, they can see me."

"Yes sir."

Twenty minutes later, he stood talking with the highway patrolman who found the car. "It's registered to a Lana Watkins from Dallas. Crime scene van on the way."

"Anything inside?"

"No purse or anything personal. Not locked. No keys inside. There's a lady's jacket in the passenger seat. I looked around some, but didn't find anything. Looks like she just parked here and left."

By the time the crime scene guys hauled the car away, Coop had trouble keeping his eyes open. After a quick call to bring JD up to speed, he headed home.

Light thunder rumbled in the distance as he parked in the drive.

Jack ran from the corner of house and bounced around his feet, tail wagging so hard his whole body shook.

"Well, Big Fella," he said as he rubbed the head thrust his way. "Glad to know I'm on your nice guy list."

Man and dog made their way into the kitchen.

After a quick lap from his water bowl, Jack plopped down under the table, then flinched and whined when thunder rolled again.

The dog evidently didn't care for storms.

Sam sat at the table, laptop open in front of her. "Hey." Her tentative greeting was accompanied by a nervous shifting in her seat.

Their last meeting fresh on his mind, he tried to keep the mood light. "Please tell me there's coffee."

She nodded toward the pot on the counter. "No offense, but you look like death eating a cracker."

He barked out a laugh. "Yeah, well, I feel worse." He took a cautious sip of the caffeine rich drink and sighed. Unlike some people, coffee didn't keep him awake. And given his current state of fatigue, he'd be lucky if he didn't fall asleep standing up.

"Sit down before you fall," she directed. "I'll get your dinner."

He considered arguing, but only a moment. He was so damn tired. Every movement took more effort than the previous one. As he passed her open laptop, he nearly dropped his cup.

The headline at the top of the page jumped out at him: *Ghosts Are Real.*

CHAPTER TWELVE

Sam moved about the kitchen, pulling the meal together, trying not to focus on the intimacy of the act. *I'm a doctor. I'm concerned for his health. Nothing more.*

The denial worked its way through her brain, but she was honest enough to admit she enjoyed it. Even if she didn't trust him. Or herself around him. Or something.

"Where's Eva?" Exhaustion made its way into his voice, dropping it an octave.

"Ladies Guild meeting."

"Um."

She turned to bring his plate to the table and stopped. His shoulders sagged and his head drooped forward, then jerked back up, the coffee in his cup sloshing out.

The man was falling asleep in the chair.

She put the plate in front of him. "You need to eat and go to bed. You're dead on your feet."

He jerked upright and shook his head. "Sorry. Guess I'm more tired than I thought."

She went to the sink and wet the end of a towel. "At least wipe your hands first. No telling what's on them."

The dark beard stubble emphasized a weak smile. "Yes, Mother." He dutifully wiped his face and hands, then proceeded to scarf down the roast beef and vegetables with renewed vigor.

She refilled their cups and sat down across from him.

A strange expression crossed his face as he nodded toward her laptop. "You believe in ghosts?"

The question sounded more curious than critical, but she stiffened anticipating ridicule. "I...believe there are things in this world we can't explain."

"Like ghosts?"

"You don't believe they exist?"

He ducked his head and forked another bite into his mouth. "Never thought much about it."

"I think this place has one." *Crap. He'll think I'm nuts.*

A coughing spell followed the remark, and she waited for him to regain his composure.

At last, he sat up straight, the light in his eyes electric. "You think we have a ghost? Here?"

Nervous now, she fidgeted in her seat. Why did she speak out loud? Paul mocked her mercilessly when she told him of her belief in ghosts. Would Coop do the same thing?

"Well, I haven't actually *seen* one, it's more of a feeling. Cold spots, the sense of not being alone, strange sounds. That sort of thing."

"And it doesn't frighten you?"

"No."

"Why not?"

"It doesn't...feel evil." She closed the top on her computer. "You must think I'm crazy."

"Why would I think that?"

A long exhale preceded her reply. "Some folks think it's a silly notion." *Paul said I was crazy to believe my grandmother sometimes visited me when I was scared or troubled.*

He watched closely. Too closely. "What makes you so sure they exist?"

She met his steady gaze, trying to determine how to answer. *What the hell. Cat's already out of the bag.* "Sometimes I hear her voice. My grandmother. And I smell gardenias where none exist. She loved gardenias. That's how I know she's close." She held her breath and waited for him to tell her how ridiculous that sounded.

Instead, he nodded and sipped his coffee. "Your research tell you why ghosts hang around after they're dead?"

She sensed an underlying intensity he tried to mask. This wasn't a conversational question. He really wanted to know. Why?

"Well, there are different schools of thought. Personally, I think they either have some unfinished business or they're keeping an eye on a loved one."

His head came up and those mesmerizing grey orbs locked on hers. "So you think she's keeping an eye on you?"

She squared her shoulders, daring him to make fun of her. "Yes. We were very close."

He maintained eye contact, face giving away none of his thoughts. "Is the car hers? You said it was special."

"Yes. She taught me to drive in it. My grandfather died when I was five, and she came to live with us. Mother worked odd hours at the hospital, so Granny looked after me."

He offered no comment as he finished his meal, wiped his hands with the towel, and reached for his plate. "I hate to leave good company, but I'm beat. Thanks for doing this."

"Leave it. I promised Eva I would take care of you. I mean, see to it you ate when you got home." She stood and took the plate from his hand. "Go to bed, Dee. Now. Doctor's orders."

He stopped at the door to the dining room, glancing over his shoulder, features softened by tired grin.

Her stomach fluttered like it did the first time she rode the roller coaster at Six Flags, only more extreme. He was so damned good looking. And sexier than any man had a right to be.

"A friendly ghost, huh?"

His gravelly voice, deepened by fatigue, and a spark of amusement in those stormy eyes, sent the sensuality level off the charts.

It was impossible not to return his disarming smile. "Yep."

His light chuckle as he turned and walked out sent shivers through her.

Holy mother of pearl.

Convinced she was the biggest fool to ever strap on a bra, she cleared the table. Thunder rolled outside as she put the kitchen to rights and prepped the coffee pot for the next day.

She wanted to watch the storm roll in from the porch off her bedroom. A quick glance at Jack said he wasn't stressed, at least for the moment. For whatever reason, he sometimes became antsy during storms, and wouldn't leave her side. Tonight, however, he didn't appear upset. Yet.

She refilled her mug and headed upstairs, stopping dead in her tracks as Coop exited the bathroom across the hall, shirtless, his baggy sweatpants resting low on his hips. A rush of awareness so intense her breath caught, crashed through her. Of their own volition, her eyes dropped to the broad expanse of his chest, the dark mat of curls tapering down to a thin line that disappeared below his waistband. She fought for air, fingers curling tightly into her left palm, then snapped her eyes back to meet his intense gaze.

In a flash, a slender, delicate thread formed between them; a mutual understanding.

She wanted him.

He wanted her.

They may not be happy about it, but neither could they deny it. The only question being, who caved first?

The spell broke when Jack padded up to Coop, tail wagging, and pushed his nose into the hand hanging at his side.

"Get a grip," she whispered as she fled to the relative safety of her room, leaving the door ajar for Jack in case he wanted company.

Wrapped in a light blanket and ensconced in a comfy rocker on the porch, she pushed the disturbing encounter to a darkened corner of her mind as she watched the late season tempest approach. The lightning flashes, the deep rumble of thunder, and the sound of rain on the roof were hypnotic. Memories of other storms, enjoyed from the safety of Granny's lap, filled her with a quiet peace. "I miss you," she whispered. "I miss your sage advice." A hard swallow kept the tears at bay. "Jack's a good listener, but he isn't much for talking."

Coffee forgotten, she pulled the blanket tighter around her.

It's going to be all right, child.

Surrounded by fond memories and the faint smell of gardenias, sleep claimed her.

CHAPTER THIRTEEN

A scratching sound, like nails on wood, penetrated the veil of exhausted slumber. Coop concentrated to pinpoint the origin. There it was again, followed by a low whine. *Jack?*

He stumbled to the door and pulled it open. The dog padded into the room and made himself a spot on the foot of the bed.

Coop glanced across the hall and saw her door open. He looked at Jack, curled up on the bed, seemingly content. If something were wrong, he would indicate it. Wouldn't he?

He gave a disgusted grunt, and stepped across the hall to peek inside Sam's room. A soft night light showed the covers turned back on an empty bed. He looked back toward his new roommate who now occupied one whole side of the bed. Shaking his head in disgust, stepped into the room. "Doc?" When he got no answer, he turned to leave and saw the open French doors to the balcony. He crept forward, not wanting to startle her, but concerned because Jack came to his room, maybe because hers was empty. Who knew how a dog's mind worked?

She sat wrapped in a quilt in one the rockers, sound asleep. The storm had passed and the waning moon bathed her face in a soft glow, her enticing mouth slightly open.

He needed to wake her so she could get in bed. Her bed. Not his. Unless she wanted to, of course. He shook his head, silently muttering a curse. "Doc," he crooned, "come on, wake up. You'll catch your death out here."

A soft snore greeted his entreaty.

The sudden cool breeze reminded him he stood there wearing only his boxers. "Sam," he touched her lightly on the shoulder. "Wake up." When he got no response, he muttered another heartfelt curse, then slid one arm under her knees, the other behind her shoulders and pulled her toward him. Her head nestled against his chest as he stood. One hand poked out of the blanket to skim across his chest accompanied by a soft sigh.

Desire, hot and potent, seized him. He struggled for control as slender fingers worked their way through the dark whorls on his chest. Ebony tendrils tickled his chin and an enticing floral scent tested his control. Eyes closed, he tried not to think about her in his arms as a more powerful surge of need engulfed him. His groin tightened, anticipating what his mind conjured, and a frustrated groan rumbled in his throat.

Shit. Leaden feet moved forward. Arms trembling as he struggled for control, he eased her down.

Her hand slid down his chest, brushing a taunt nipple, and he gasped. *You're killing me, Doc.*

She lay on her back, Coop's arm trapped under her neck, face turned toward him, as she blew out a heavy sigh.

His store of self-discipline vanished in a heartbeat. He lowered his head and kissed her softly, a light brushing of the lips because he couldn't bear not to.

A sound from the doorway made him jerk back.

Jack's gaze appeared more curious than distressed. Thank God.

As gently as he could, he extricated his arm and stood on shaky legs before pulling the covers up to her chin.

No wonder she doesn't trust me. Hell, I don't trust me.

He stepped away from the bed, and Jack led the way back to his room.

Once inside, the dog reclaimed his spot, chocolate colored eyes spearing a hole in him as he left the door ajar.

"What the hell did you expect me to do you crazy-assed mutt?" He gestured with his hands as he stomped into the room. "I'm not made of stone. And what are you doing in here, anyway?"

Head cocked to one side, Jack's ears twitched.

"I kissed her. I couldn't help myself." He plopped down on the bed, one arm over his eyes. "I couldn't."

Jack rested his massive head on Coop's shoulder as though he understood the torment his new friend endured.

Sleep, when it finally came, provided little respite, and he woke with dog breath in his face, a dreamed-induced erection, and a headache.

But, at least he wasn't crazy.

The matter-of-fact way Sam discussed hearing her grandmother speak, convinced him of it. However, the questions remained: Who the hell kept talking to him? And why?

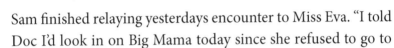

Sam finished relaying yesterdays encounter to Miss Eva. "I told Doc I'd look in on Big Mama today since she refused to go to the hospital."

"She's a hoot for sure," said Miss Eva, "but has a heart of gold. It's such a shame she has no family around."

Jack nosed the door open and entered, Coop right behind him.

It took a great deal of effort not to react, though she couldn't stop the flood of heat to her cheeks as questions and images from her dreams last night swirled around in her head. *How did I get to bed? Did I dream that kiss?*

"Sam was just telling me what happened with Big Mama yesterday," said Miss Eva.

His reply could best be described as a grunt as he reached for his cup.

Jack went to the back door, barked once, and looked at Coop, who opened the door for the dog to go outside.

"Sam is going over there today to check on her," said Eva, "Can you draw her a map? You know I'm terrible with directions."

"Sure." He leaned against the counter and faced her. "It's not too far from town. I'll drive you."

"Aren't you working today?"

He nodded. "It won't take long."

"I'll be fine driving myself. You have more important things to tend to."

"I'd feel better if I took you."

She stiffened. "I can take care of myself."

"She lives down a dirt road. After the rain last night, it's gonna be a mess." A trace of envy in his voice, he added, "Take my bronco. Your car is too nice to drive down a muddy road."

"How will you get to work?"

"You can drop me off at the office."

Suddenly nervous, she argued. "I can't leave you without wheels."

"I'll take a squad car if I need to go anywhere." His brow

furrowed, and he looked at her. "Can you drive a standard shift?"

Affronted, she glared at him. "Of course."

His smile sent the butterflies in her stomach on a rampage.

Jack reappeared at the back door and Coop let him in before he sat down across from Sam, the dog at his feet.

Irritated, her voice rose slightly. "He has never, ever taken to anyone the way he has to you." She moved her coffee cup aside as Eva positioned a plate of sausage, eggs and biscuits in front of her. "He even slept with you."

Amusement flickered in the eyes meeting hers. "Jealous?"

Cheeks so hot, she thought surely they would blister, she snapped, "In your dreams."

The rich timbre of his laugh filled the room. "How did you know?"

"Coop," admonished Eva, "stop teasing and eat your breakfast."

He sipped his coffee, gaze fixed on Sam. "She's so cute when she blushes."

Unable to come up with a suitable retort, she stabbed her eggs.

"Doc asked Sam to take over his practice," said Eva. "Isn't that wonderful?"

Sam didn't bother to hide her surprise. "How on earth did you know? I haven't said anything to anyone."

"Small town," said Coop, as if two short words explained everything.

"Edith Watkins mentioned it last night at the Guild meeting," said Eva. "She heard it from Janet at the bank."

Silent, Sam looked to Coop for more information.

"Doc's nurse is best friends with Alice who works for me,"

he offered. "She also happens to be the Mayor's daughter, and the biggest gossip in Baker County." The butter he slathered on a warm biscuit melted and dribbled down his hand as he added a dollop of grape jelly. "If you want something to spread like wildfire…telephone, telegraph or tell Alice."

Sam watched with fascination as he licked the gooey mess from his fingers, then pushed half the bread in his mouth.

He had such a nice mouth.

She jerked her eyes up, but not before he caught her ogling.

The toad had the audacity to wink.

Miss Eva set a carafe of coffee in the center of the table, ending the silent exchange. "I'd offer my old clunker, but today is my day to deliver meals."

Sam tackled her food, trying to corral her roller coaster emotions. "I won't need it long; couple of hour's maybe."

"No problem. Lot of paperwork to do. Should be in the office all day."

"Do you know who she is yet?"

Eva voiced the question Sam wanted to.

"Not yet." The teasing note in his voice vanished. "Some leads, though." He ducked his head and continued eating.

For reasons she refused to examine, Sam wanted the teasing Coop back. "I just hope Alice doesn't see me drop you off at work."

When he looked up, she managed a tentative smile. "Who knows what the rumor mill might generate then."

CHAPTER FOURTEEN

"I really think I should drive you." Coop snapped his seat belt as Sam got behind the wheel. "The killer is still out there."

"We've been through this already. I'll be fine. I have Jack with me." She slid her hands along the rim of the steering wheel, and glanced around the interior. "This is an eighty-nine, right?"

"I'm impressed. Most women wouldn't know that."

"My brother has one. His is two-tone brown. I love this baby-blue and white, though."

"Flattering my ride won't change the subject."

She backed out of the drive. "We'll be fine."

He didn't miss the note of exasperation in her voice. "Call me as soon as you get there and when you leave."

"I will."

He saw the tightness in her jaw, reasoning her patience ran low. Too bad. She'd just have to get over it. "Sure you can find the place?"

She glanced his way, spacing her words evenly. "I am sure. Your directions are very explicit."

"You have my number programmed into your phone?"

A perturbed smile showed the slightest dimple in her

right cheek. *How did I miss that?*

"Yes. I will call if I get lost, have a problem, to say I'm there, and I'm headed home."

"Good. And –" He paused his instructions to answer the phone. "Delaney."

"Detective Rollins, Dallas PD. Lana Watkins isn't your vic."

"Are you sure?"

"Yeah. Spoke to her myself. Most likely her roommate, Joyce Ayers, though. Seems she borrowed the 'vette for the weekend. Emailing you a picture and pertinent info now."

"Thanks."

"We did secure some DNA stuff just in case. Wanted to let you know."

"Thanks." Coop ended the call and dropped the phone on the seat beside him.

"Bad news?" Sam kept her eyes on the road as she eased her way through a school zone.

He leaned back in the seat. "Wasn't who we thought, but we may have an ID today."

At a four-way stop sign, she glanced his way, head shaking side to side. "I just don't understand this kind of violence."

"Me neither."

"You'll get who did this," she said firmly.

"That's a lot of confidence in someone you don't trust."

The tightness in her jaw was the only indication he struck a nerve.

"I'm sorry…I didn't mean that the way it sounded."

She hesitated. "It's not that I don't trust you, exactly. It's…"

"What?"

She sighed and glanced his way, doubt and anxiety

flashing in those baby-blues. "I let my emotions, hormones, whatever, guide my decisions once. Then spent five years regretting it." She looked forward, face tense, hands gripping the wheel tightly. "I won't make the same mistake again."

He'd let emotions control his decisions a time or two himself so didn't argue the point. Could be they were more alike than different after all. "Maybe we could start over?"

She missed a gear as she drove through the intersection and had to try again. "What?"

He rubbed his hands on his thighs so he wouldn't reach for hers. "I think it's safe to say we're attracted to each other, and both have…issues to deal with which will no doubt require some time to work through."

"…Um…agreed."

"And, unless you take over Doc's practice, which I hope you'll consider doing, you're only here for a couple of weeks."

She nodded without replying or looking his way.

"How about we see if we can be friends? For Now." The question surprised the hell out of him. Friendship was the last thing on his mind.

Unless it turned into friends with benefits.

Widened eyes flickered his way. "Friends? You want us to be friends?"

"What? You don't think we can?"

She waited so long to reply, he wondered if she would.

"I'd really like us to be friends," she said at last.

Silence surrounded them for the remainder of the short drive to his office. The very normalcy of the action soothed his soul, lightened the burden he carried.

She pulled into his designated spot and killed the engine. "Did you put me to bed last night?"

Her whispered question stopped him in the act of reaching for the door handle. It was rhetorical at best because who else would have? "Jack woke me. I thought something might be wrong. I found you on the porch."

"Why didn't you wake me?"

He turned toward her slightly, arm resting on the console. Cheeks flushed with color, she nonetheless met his steady gaze.

A man could get lost in those azure depths. "I tried. You were dead to the world. Never even flinched when I picked you up." *You fingered the hair on my chest and nearly sent me over the edge.*

She chewed on her lower lip, eyes dipping down. "Is that all?"

Oh shit. The kiss. "I covered you up." As an afterthought, he nodded toward the dog who dozed in the back. "Jack can vouch for me. He was there."

One perfectly arched brow lifted, and she shook her head. "My dad is the only other man Jack has anything to do with."

"Animals, especially dogs, are great at reading people." He flashed her his best smile. He hoped. "So…friends?"

She hesitated. "Yeah. Friends."

"So, friends can have dinner together, right?"

Blinking quickly, she stared at him. "You want to have dinner?"

"And a movie. If we can take your car. Can I drive?"

After a slight hesitation, she giggled, and his spirits lifted.

"I'll have to think about letting you drive Ethel."

"Ethel? You call your car Ethel?"

She shrugged. "My grandmother's name."

"Well, I let you drive mine, so turnabout is fair play."

"I'll think about it."

"How about tomorrow night? It's Friday and the football game is in McKinney so the town will, hopefully, be quiet. We can have an early dinner, maybe catch a movie at the drive-in."

"What's playing?"

"*Jaws*, I think. Last Friday late show is always old scary movies."

"The shark movie? You've gotta be kidding. It's over thirty years old."

"I know. Ever seen it?"

"No."

"I can't believe you've never seen *Jaws*. I've seen it umpteen times on TV but never on the big screen." He reached for the door handle again, then winked at her. "You can hang on to me if you get scared."

She regarded him with gentle amusement. "What am I going to do with you?"

He raised his brows a couple of times in rapid succession, his voice seductive. "I have a list."

She snorted, then inclined her head toward the front of the courthouse where Alice stood watching them. "Uh-oh. Busted."

"Aw, hell." Eyes closed, he shook his head in defeat. "You may as well know what everyone else does. Eva's been matchmaking for months." He turned back toward his secretary who watched them intently. "Alice will have a field day with this."

She turned in the seat, her knee brushing his. "How could she make something out of us just sitting here?"

He laughed. Really laughed for the first time in a long time and it felt wonderful. "You do realize that by the time you get back, it will be all over town we were necking in the courthouse parking lot."

"What?"

"Darlin', this is small town East Texas where, murder notwithstanding, nothing interesting ever happens. And when something does, everyone puts their own spin on it before they pass it on to someone else. I know you've heard some of the altered versions going around about what happened between me and Jack at the creek."

"Surely it won't be so bad."

He settled his hat on his head, mouth tight. "Just wait." He got out and started up the sidewalk.

"Dee!"

He turned back to the driver's side window.

"You forgot your phone."

He took it from her, allowing his fingers to lightly brush hers, enjoying how her cheeks turned a lovely shade of pink. "Call me."

He dropped the phone in his pocket and strolled away whistling. Alice could make what she wanted to of it.

CHAPTER FIFTEEN

"Got the pictures back from Harvey over at the Gazette." Jimmy handed Coop the envelope. "Did you know he was a forensic photographer back east before he came here?"

"News to me." Coop took the envelope and quickly sifted through the shots, using the dates stamped on them to separate the crime scene photos from Sam's personal ones.

"Yeah. Got tired of it and ended up here ten years ago. He said Sunshine did a good job on the photos."

Coop's jaw clenched at Jimmy using the nickname he gave Sam, but he kept any comments to himself.

The deputy didn't appear to notice his boss's displeasure as he left the room.

Coop pulled the papers from his inbox as his phone rang. A quick glance at caller ID and he smiled. "Hiya, Doc."

"Checking in as ordered, sir."

He liked that sassiness in her voice. "Any problems finding the place?"

"Nope. As I said, your directions were very explicit."

"How's she doing?"

"Haven't seen her yet. Thought I'd better call you first so you wouldn't get your shorts in a knot."

He leaned back in his chair, mood suddenly cheerful. "I appreciate your concern for the state of my shorts."

Her heavy sigh made him laugh out loud. "Can't help it, Doc. You give me too much ammunition."

"Yeah, well, it's obvious I'm off my game, but I will do better."

He enjoyed the gentle sparring and decided she did as well. "I'll play any game you want to play."

She tried to sound peeved, but he heard the smile in her voice. "I'll call you when I'm headed back to town."

"Have fun with Big Mama."

"Yeah, right. Later."

He ended the call and turned his attention back to comparing the photos Sam took to the digital ones taken by him. His admiration grew as he noted the details she captured.

After an hour of sifting through the images, with nothing new discovered, his cheerfulness vanished.

"Sheriff?"

Jimmy Don's enthusiastic voice cut through Coop's concentration. "Yeah?"

"We have an ID."

"Is it the roommate?"

"Yeah. Joyce Ayers."

Brow crinkled in thought, he leaned back in his chair. "Okay." He pointed to a DVD on the corner of his desk. "Teddy sent the parking lot surveillance from Sunday. I went through it, saw a few folks didn't expect to see but nothing that ties to our vic." He didn't mention the banker he saw getting it on with one of the waitresses or the preacher's son leaving with a trucker. "At 9:45, her car pulls around back where Arlis saw her. Didn't see anyone else back there, but they could have come from the other side, and there are no cameras back there. She was alone, and didn't stop to talk to anyone." He rubbed his face with both hands. "I left a message for Teddy to send the videos from inside. He only has a couple of cameras there, and one of those covers mostly the bar and register. Maybe we'll get lucky."

Jimmy held up another DVD. "Just got this from the gas station manager along with a copy of the sales receipt. Confirms it was Ms. Ayers. I haven't looked at this yet."

Coop took it and together they ran through the rough footage which provided no additional information other than the time she filled up.

"Okay. She got gas at 9:30, hit Teddy's at 9:45." Coop folded his arms across his chest, frowning as he constructed the timeline. "ME puts time of death between midnight and four a.m."

"So, where was she between 9:45 and midnight?" asked Jimmy. "And with who?"

"That's the sixty-four-thousand-dollar question."

"I'm waiting for data from her cell phone. Maybe we can piece something together."

"Let me know as soon as it comes in."

"Sure wish Teddy had more cameras out front."

Coop heaved a disgusted sigh. "You and Johnson rotate going back there over the weekend. See if anyone recognizes her picture. She had to have met someone there, either inside or in the parking lot before she ended up at the oil well."

"Why on earth would she meet someone way out there? It's in the middle of nowhere. Granted, it's close to the interstate, but a good six miles from town."

"People do crazy things for even crazier reasons."

"Yep." Further discussion ended when Coop's phone rang. "Delaney."

"Well, judging by your less than cheerful greeting, your day hasn't been any better than mine."

Just hearing Sam's voice improved his disposition. "I take it Big Mama wasn't happy to see you."

"She's a pistol, for sure. Um, I was wondering if have time to cruise around Baker Lake? But if you need the Bronco, I'll come straight in."

"I'm good. Still doing paperwork." He glanced at his watch. "It's eleven now. How about you pick me up around noon, and I'll treat you to the best burger ever for lunch?"

"Works for me. But if you need me sooner, just say the word." Cutting off his snappy comeback, she added, "Not in this life."

Mouth twisted in amusement, he replied, "See you at noon."

He ended the call, and caught Jimmy's observant glance. "I guess it's true then?"

"What's true?"

"You and Sunshine."

"What about us?"

He lifted one shoulder. "You're an item."

He almost denied it, but thinking JD would immediately pick up the hunt, he changed his mind. Besides, he *wanted* to be an item. "You got a problem with that?"

"Not me. Ruby might, though."

Coop stared at the back of the deputy as he left. *Damn.*

He'd forgotten all about the owner of Ruby's Diner. Friends for years, she made no secret of the fact she wanted more from him, but the sentiments weren't shared. In fact, he always felt rather sorry for her because of the string of temporary relationships she went through. In a moment of weakness a few months ago, he accepted her offer of a no-strings-attached night out after her last break up. Too late, he realized his mistake, for she immediately took it to mean more than it did, despite anything he said to the contrary.

Ever since, she'd repeatedly insinuated they take things a step further, and he'd grown weary of trying to find nice ways to say no, and finally resorted to avoiding her and the diner.

Look close.

The Voice's plea interrupted his trudge down a slippery slope. "Dammit woman," he muttered, "you're gonna have to give me something more." He shuffled through the photos on his desk, then pulled up the crime scene shots on the computer. "Is something here?" he muttered, "What am I not seeing?"

Sam stopped in the parking lot near the boat ramp on Baker Lake, got out and moved the seat so Jack could join her. She stood for a moment enjoying the balmy breeze off the water, eyes taking in the tall moss-draped cypress trees on the near bank, water hyacinth along the edge and the small island in the middle covered with white birds. To the right of the ramp, maybe fifty yards away, two people cast lines from what appeared to be a fishing pier.

"We may have to invest in some new gear, Jack." Leash in hand, camera around her neck, she headed toward a trail on the back side of the lot.

A weathered sign stapled to a tree identified it as walking trail on the west side of the eight-hundred acre lake. She didn't have time to explore much, but decided to look around a little, anticipation of her lunch date with Coop uppermost in her mind.

His suggestion they become friends filled her with both trepidation and joy; as did the dream last night.

Did she dream the kiss? Even now, her lips tingled at the thought, and her fingers relished the coarse texture of chest hair as they pushed through it.

She gritted her teeth and concentrated on the narrow, rock-filled trail.

About a hundred yards in, gooseflesh pebbled her arms when a sudden chill enveloped her. Sounds of the forest ceased immediately, and the sudden silence became unnerving.

Jack growled low in his throat, ears thrust forward, listening.

The hairs on the back of her neck tingled, and she whirled around. Nobody there.

Despite temperatures near eighty, another cold breeze swept her face, followed by feelings of loss and sadness so acute, her knees buckled, and she grabbed the nearest tree for support. She flinched when something brushed against her ear, soft as a butterfly's kiss. Not a voice, no words, but the sense of someone needing help overcame her.

Find me.

CHAPTER SIXTEEN

By the time she pulled into the gas station on the edge of town, the shaking ceased and Jack no longer whined. The whole experience left her unsettled and the sensation that something horrible had happened there still lingered.

Maybe I can ask Coop at lunch.

Even as the thought formed, she dismissed it. He would think she was crazy. She made a vow to return as soon as possible and…do what?

She inserted the nozzle in the tank, and looked up when a maroon pickup swerved into the spot behind her.

A young man in worn jeans and dark Stetson hat slid out. His smile faded to a scowl as he approached the Bronco.

No one had to tell her he belonged to Coop. The resemblance was uncanny.

"You must be Jason," she said as the pumped kicked off.

He scowled and took another step. "And you are…?"

She waited for her receipt to print, then walked toward him, right hand extended. "Samantha Fowler. I'm a guest at The Grove."

His grip was firm, his gaze steady. "That's my dad's Bronco."

"He let me use it today."

He blinked, eyebrows shooting upward. "What do you have on him?"

"Excuse me?"

"I can count on one hand the number of times he's let me drive it. And he was usually in the seat beside me."

"Really?"

"Really."

His Coop-like grin made her stomach clinch.

"What do you have on him?"

"He said my car was too nice for a house call today down a dirt road. He insisted I use this."

"Must be some car."

"I guess you could say a fifty-six Chevy convertible qualifies."

He stood up straighter. "You have a fifty-six? A convertible?"

"I do."

"V6 or V8?"

"V8, three speed manual, dual exhaust, four barrel carburetor, blue and white."

"Can I drive it?" A dimple appeared in his left cheek, and the corners of his eyes crinkled.

She laughed. "Like father like son."

His face settled into an unreadable mask. "I didn't know he was seeing anyone."

She stuffed the receipt in her back pocket. "We're not… seeing each other. I'm a guest at The Grove."

"Uh-huh. He let you drive it." He nodded toward the Bronco.

Completely at a loss as to what it had to do with anything, she changed the subject. "I'm supposed to pick him up for lunch. I'm sure he'd love for you to join us."

"Three's a crowd, Miss Fowler. I'll just see what Miss Eva has, and talk to him when he gets home."

"My friends call me Sam. Today is her day to deliver meals so she isn't home. Dee said something about treating me to a fantastic hamburger."

"Has to be Bub's Place. Best greasy spoon burger you'll ever put in your mouth. I've missed them."

"All the more reason to join us."

"Sure you won't mind me horning in on your date?"

"It's not a date. And you're more than welcome to join us."

He looked at the Bronco, left brow arched upward. "I'll give dad a call. If he doesn't mind, I'll meet you there."

A few minutes later, she pulled into Coop's designated parking spot as he strolled down the sidewalk, cell phone pressed to his ear. His long-legged swagger sent shivers down her spine and heat coiled low in her belly. "Holy mother pearl, woman, get a hold of yourself."

At her terse comment, Jack poked his head over the top of the seat and looked at her. When he spied Coop, the tail wagging started.

He stuffed the phone in his shirt pocket and got in the passenger seat, his happiness almost tangible. "I like a woman who's punctual." He fastened his seat belt and glanced her way. "I'm glad you invited Jason for lunch. He'll meet us there."

"You're letting me drive?"

"Everything's set for you."

"Most men I know wouldn't be happy doing so."

"I'm not most men."

Holy cow. That smile should be outlawed as a lethal weapon. After she remembered to breathe, she said, "No.

You're not. Where to?"

Ten minutes later, she parked in front of a rather drab looking building with two small, grease-stained windows on the front.

"Don't worry, Doc," said Coop, "you're not going to get sick eating here."

"If you say so."

He was out and beside her door when she opened it. After rolling down both windows, she got out and stood beside Coop.

The dog lumbered over the center console, and sat in the driver's seat, head out the window for Coop to pet.

"I'll bring you back a treat if you behave," he said, then led the way inside.

The pungent aroma of onions, hot grease and burgers cooking filled the air, and made her mouth water. She refused to think what a steady diet of this would do to her arteries. And her waistline.

"Hey, Dad…over here."

Coop laid his hand in the small of her back, and guided her toward the table where his son waited. Surprised to hear someone calling her name, she looked toward them, stumbling slightly on the uneven floor. Immediately, his arm slid around her waist and pulled her against him.

Jason stood and shook hands with his father, eyes flicking to the arm around her waist. "Bout time you got a girl. And a danged pretty one, too."

Unsettled from the effect of being pinned to his side, Sam couldn't come up with a coherent reply and merely smiled as Coop pulled out a chair for her.

"Great to see you, Son. Didn't expect you until next weekend."

"Nothing going on, so decided to come home for a few days."

A look passed between father and son, and she intuitively knew the real reason for the unexpected visit. The murder, the investigation, and concern for his father. It was obvious they shared a special bond, and for a moment, her biological clock ticked a little too loud.

Restrained at first, Sam soon joined in the conversation, answering questions about her life and listening as Coop and Jason caught up on each other. Locals stopped at the table to say hello or inquire about the progress of the investigation.

The number of people who singled her out to greet, as though she were an established part of the community amazed her. Some even asked about Jack.

Everyone appeared to know about Big Mama, and expressed their appreciation to her for acting so quickly to help someone they obviously cared deeply for.

Such acceptance would never happen in the big city, and a warm, fuzzy feeling bloomed inside her.

Toward the end of lunch, the waitress handed Coop the ticket, and set a small carry-out tray on the table beside Sam. "Bub said give this to Jack."

Surprised by the gesture, it took a moment to process. "How thoughtful of him. Please tell him I said thank you."

"Bub has a real soft spot for dogs," she said, "has a whole slew of them."

As she looked around the crowded eatery, she had a sudden epiphany. Was it possible to fall in love with a whole town in a few days?

It was. She did.

And she would accept Doc's offer.

The thought hadn't fully formed when Coop's phone rang. "Delaney. Yeah. Okay. I'll let her know." He slipped the phone back in his pocket. "Doc wants you to stop by his office when we're done."

"Why didn't he call me?" Mouth open, she stared, unable to say more.

He laughed and patted the hand resting near his. "Told you, Doc. Small town."

"I'm going to check in with the guys," said Jason as the waitress cleared the table. "I'll see y'all at home."

"Would it be too much trouble for you to drop me off at home first so I can get my car?" asked Sam. "I need to see what Doc wants."

"No need," said Coop as he tossed bills on the table. "Keep mine. You can pick me up at five."

Jason looked at her and winked. "I gotta know what you have on him."

Two hours later, Sam floated on cloud nine as she and Jack left Doc's office. It was official. They would begin working together next week. He'd get a letter out to his patients today letting them know of the impending change. He would stay through a transitional period while all the formalities were dealt with, then clinic would be hers. Hers.

Excited, but nervous, she glanced at her watch. Almost four. Coop would be off soon, so she decided to stroll around town. She parked in his spot at the courthouse, and crossed the street to the diner, a cup of coffee and a slice of pie on her mind.

Inside, the place could be a showroom for fifties-style diners. Black and white tiles covered the floor, and booths clad in red vinyl lined the left side. A few patrons occupied red Formica-topped tables scattered around the deep, narrow room, which also boasted barstool seating at a long counter. A juke box on the back wall cranked out an old Elvis tune, and she smiled. *Gotta love a small town that didn't change with the times.*

"Just sit anywhere you like," chirped the young waitress passing by with someone's order, "I'll be with you in a sec."

Sam chose a booth where she could look outside and checked out the tunes on the table-top juke box as she waited.

"What can I get for you?"

Taken aback by the chilly tone in her voice, Sam studied the woman standing beside the booth. "Coffee, please. Black. And do you have any pies or sweet rolls?"

"Apple, Coconut and Pecan Pie."

She glanced at the name tag on the white uniform shirt, "Ruby". *Well, if that's the Ruby in Ruby's Diner, she needs to work on her tableside manners.* "Apple please. And could I get it warmed with a slice of cheese?"

The woman's stare wasn't malicious or even curious; it struck Sam as more sad in nature, and she couldn't help but wonder about it as Ruby turned toward the back without a word.

A few minutes later, the young waitress, her tag read "Bethany", brought her pie and coffee. "So, you're gonna be the new doctor in town?"

Sam didn't bother to correct her, having already decided it would do no good. "I'm going to be working with Dr. Harper."

Bethany's eyes darted toward the register where Ruby

talked with a departing customer. "I saw you driving Coop's Bronco."

Sam couldn't believe people made such a big deal about her driving his car, and once again, chose not to address it. "This pie is delicious. My compliments to the cook."

She nodded toward the register. "Ruby's the owner and does all the baking. I'll tell her you said so."

By the time she paid out, Ruby was nowhere around and Bethany manned the register. "Is Jason coming home this weekend?" she asked a little too casually.

"Actually, he came in today."

Her pixie face brightened. "Great. Um, tell him Bethany at the diner said hello."

"I will."

Back at the SUV, she grabbed Jack's leash. His tail wagged furiously as he waited for her to attach it before jumping to the ground.

No particular destination in mind, she started walking around the square, scoping out the store fronts and window shopping. Halfway around, Coop came walking down the sidewalk.

Jack pulled on the leash, dragging her forward in his haste to greet him.

"Hey, Jack," he said as he squatted down to rub the hound's head. "Good to see you, too."

She glanced at the huge clock adorning the entrance to the courthouse. "It's not five yet. You done for the day?"

"Yeah." Jack licked at his face and Coop barely ducked out of the way in time. "No face-licking, dude."

His gravelly voice made her girl parts quiver.

"I still don't understand why he's so taken with you." She

couldn't decide if she were annoyed or pleased. "He's never taken up with anyone other than my dad. Not even my brothers."

"Jack knows I'm one of the good guys." He patted the dog's head, "Ain't that right?"

Jack responded by laying down on the ground, belly up for a rub.

Thoughts of those big hands on her sent tingles to the pit of her stomach. Acutely conscience of his virile appeal, she admitted to herself alone, a friends-only arrangement would never work. Yet, the thought of not being around him was too unsettling to entertain. She gave herself a mental shake and moved to safer ground. "Thanks for the use of the Bronco today."

"You're welcome." He stood and reached for Jack's leash. "Are we engaged yet?" The laughter in his voice said he knew the talk around town.

"What on earth is the big deal about me driving your stupid Bronco?"

"Would you let just anyone drive Ethel?"

Good point. "No."

He shrugged as though she answered her own question. "Guess what else I heard today?"

"I'm afraid to ask."

The look he gave her, slow and appraising, coupled with a deep, totally male laugh, added to her discomfort.

"You're ready to sign the papers and take over Doc's practice in two weeks."

She stamped a foot. "Dang it! I wanted to be the one to tell you."

"Sweetheart, if you want to beat the rumor mill, you have to act fast."

"I'm not sure I like all this, this openness about my business."

He turned and they started walking again. "Well, folks may talk out of turn, and discuss your business like it was their own, but I guarantee you one thing." He stopped and faced her, gaze intent. "If you ever needed anything, anything at all, you'd have it in a heartbeat."

They stared at each other in silence as the truth behind his statement settled in. "You love it here."

"I do. Wouldn't trade it for anything."

She thought about the people who had welcomed her so warmly, the honesty in their friendship, the simplicity of life here, and nodded. "Me, too."

He watched from the corner of the courthouse lawn, not surprised to see the woman and the sheriff together because it confirmed what he already thought—she was special. How else to explain it?

He had watched in amused silence for years as others tried, without success, to be in Sam's place. Like Ruby. Poor thing. Didn't realize she was way too weak. But, Sam, now there was a formidable woman. Even the dog exuded authority and strength. He would be a bonus.

The silent observer followed their progress around the square, noted the smiles of contentment each wore as they chatted, looked in windows, and spoke to folks passing by, tamping down the spurt of jealousy it triggered. *Soon, my pretty. Soon. I have plans for you.*

A couple stopped to chat, and as usual, the conversation

quickly turned to the dead woman. When they speculated on who could do such a thing here in their little town, he really wanted to tell them, but not today. The time would come, of course, but not today.

For now, he was content to watch the sheriff wander around in a fog trying to find him.

I am the master. No one is my equal.

He inhaled deeply as the certainty of his superiority hummed through his veins.

He joined in when his companions made fun of the sheriff and the dog at the crime scene, and voiced hollow words of sorrow when they talked about the dead woman.

Mostly, though, he watched the woman with the dog as he mentally planned the next step.

CHAPTER SEVENTEEN

Dinner was a jovial affair with Jason, Coop and Miss Eva sharing stories about life in a small town. Obviously, they were very close, and, not for the first time, she wondered why.

When the meal ended, she rose and reached for her plate.

Jason tapped her on the arm. "I got it, Sam. Miss Eva cooked and you're a guest. You and Dad take your coffee to the porch." He grinned and winked at Coop. "There's a full moon tonight."

Sam shook her head. "Your son is about as subtle as you are."

Coop grinned. "More coffee, Doc?"

She shook her head. "I think I'm coffeed out for a change."

"Me, too," said Coop as he guided her to the porch.

A few minutes later, they were seated in the oversized swing suspended from the ceiling. Suddenly, nervous, Sam wished for more space between them.

"I'm not going to bite, Doc," said Coop, his arm resting on the back as his foot set the swing in motion. "Nibble a little, maybe, but not bite."

Thoughts of him nibbling anywhere jacked up her heart rate. In an effort to get on safer ground, she nodded toward the full moon just over the tree tops. "Beautiful night."

"Uh-huh."

Okaaaay. Let's try something else. "This is a great swing."

"Thanks. I made it."

"You made this?" She ran a hand over the smooth slatted design, then took in the big chain hooked to the ceiling. "I'm impressed."

He nodded without comment.

Since he didn't appear in the mood for conversation, she listened as they were serenaded by the occasional croak of a frog, mingled with a band of crickets. In the distance, two owls joined in the chorus. Above the tree line, stars blinked on one-by-one. When was the last time she actually watched the stars come out?

A passing breeze elicited a light shiver and she rubbed her arms. "Should have brought my sweater."

Quick as a flash, she found herself tucked against his side. "Better?"

Better? It was heaven. His warmth seeped into her, filled all the places left hollow as she sighed and melted against him, curling her feet up beside her on the colorful cushion. "I thought we were going to be friends."

"We are."

"I'm not sure friends…cuddle like this."

"Of course they do. What kind of friend would I be if I let you sit there and shiver?"

She folded her arms across her chest, confident her tremors had nothing to do with the cool night air.

He ran his hand slowly up and down her arm as he held her against him. That's all. Just held her close as the swing slid gently back and forth, the light creak of the metal links adding to the therapeutic sounds of the night. Like a drug, his closeness, this moment in time, lulled her into euphoria, and a sense of rightness filled her.

Slowly, by degrees, she relaxed and rested her head on his shoulder. She closed her eyes when he placed a soft kiss to the top of her head. So soft, she almost missed it.

Time passed, how much, she couldn't say. Lights blinked off inside the house. She pressed her cheek against the corded muscle of his chest, inhaling the intoxicating scent unique to him.

Engulfed by a desperate need to feel the touch of his lips, she pulled back and met his open, intense scrutiny.

"I don't want to make another mistake," she whispered.

"I know."

"This is…this is nice."

"It is for a fact."

"…I want us to be friends."

"Me, too."

"But…I want to kiss you." Those whispered words hung between them.

His gaze dropped to her lips, voice deepened by desire. "Me, too."

Gradually, she eased herself upward, never taking her eyes off the prize—his mouth. He didn't move as she brushed his lips lightly with her own, her tongue tracing the soft fullness before pressing her open mouth to his.

"Dad, there's an –" Jason stopped in mid-sentence, quickly turning his back. "Sorry."

Sam jerked away so fast she would have toppled from the swing if Coop hadn't grabbed her.

"Dispatch is on the phone." Jason said. "There's some kind

of fight out at Teddy's and they need you there."

Coop grabbed her hand as she scrambled off the seat. "Doc…"

"I'll see you later." She couldn't look at him as she pulled her hand free and darted through the door and up the stairs.

Oh my God! What am I doing?

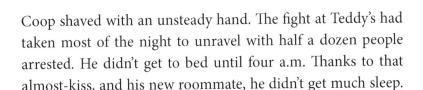

Coop shaved with an unsteady hand. The fight at Teddy's had taken most of the night to unravel with half a dozen people arrested. He didn't get to bed until four a.m. Thanks to that almost-kiss, and his new roommate, he didn't get much sleep. Again. Who knew dogs snored?

A soft knock on the bathroom door roused him from his fuzzy musings. "Come in, Son."

Jason stepped inside and closed the door. He lowered the commode lid and sat down.

Coop smiled. How many father-son conversations took place in this room? He sobered when he realized how few of these moments remained for them.

His son was a grown man now. When had that happened?

Coop watched Jason's reflection in the mirror as he continued to shave. "What's up?"

Jason clasped his hands in front, then unfolded them and straightened.

"Just spit it out, Jay. Putting if off won't change it."

"I'm sorry about last night."

Coop rinsed soap from his razor. "No apologies needed, but, thank you."

"It's obvious the timing sucked."

"Yeah, well, it did, but such is life. Stuff doesn't always work out the way you want."

"…I heard about the investigation. I was worried about you."

Coop assumed as much. "So you ditched classes to come home a week early?"

"Only one class, and yeah, that's why."

"I appreciate your concern, Jay, but I'm fine. This ain't my first rodeo."

"I know." Jason looked up and met his father's gaze. "She seems really nice." He rubbed his palms on his thighs. "Sam, I mean. She seems nice."

"She is."

"I saw y'all walking around the square yesterday. You looked happy." He paused. "I've never seen you like that…I'm really glad you found someone."

"Well, I wouldn't go sending out invitations yet. We barely know each other."

"But you do like her, right?"

Coop wiped his face with a towel and turned to face his son. "Yeah. I like her."

"And she's going to be around for a while, right?"

"Looks like it." Coop leaned against the sink, arms folded over his chest. "Out with it, Jason."

The young man stood and paced around the small room. "I promised I'd finish school before I made any major decisions about my life."

"And?"

"I graduate in December."

"I know."

"I have a job offer in Houston with a big graphics design company."

Coop's heart skipped a beat. He knew this day would come, but wasn't ready for it. Not yet. "Is that what you want?"

"Yes. And no." Jason sat down, clasped and unclasped his hands.

"What's holding you back?"

He blew out a long breath, then looked at his father. "I want to get married."

Of all the things Coop thought he might say, marriage was the one thing he never considered, though he should have. Laurie Hammonds and Jason were childhood sweethearts. They graduated high school together and attended the same college. "Laurie?"

"I love her, Dad. Have since the sixth grade. She wanted to get married last summer, but I couldn't do it."

"Why not?"

His voice dropped. "I couldn't leave you alone."

CHAPTER EIGHTEEN

How many ways can one person screw up their life? Sam sat on the edge of the bed, her knee bouncing up and down as she anticipated seeing Coop and his son at breakfast. *Oh God. I crawled up his body like a cat! And Jason saw it. How can I face them?*

She huffed and stood, rubbing sweaty palms on jean-clad thighs. "Suck it up, Buttercup. Putting it off won't make it easier." It took two attempts to get her feet moving forward, resigned to whatever catastrophe awaited.

The sudden jingle of her phone provided a welcomed distraction as she entered the kitchen. She pulled it from her hip pocket, and cradled it against her shoulder as she filled a cup with coffee. "Hello."

Barbara's cheerful voice always put Sam in a cheerful mood. "Hey there. Got your message. Congratulations! Told you it was perfect for you."

"I'm thrilled about the prospect."

"Still want your truck this weekend?"

"If you're sure I'm not imposing. I know it's asking a lot."

"It's no bother at all."

"Thanks, BJ. You're the bestest best friend ever, you know that, right?" She paused to sip her coffee as her friend laid out plans for the weekend. "Thanks, BJ. I owe you big time. I'll see you tomorrow."

"BJ?" Coop's words were muffled by the huge bite of buttered biscuit he popped in his mouth.

"Barbara Jean. Doc Harper's niece. And my best friend. She and her husband are visiting family this weekend. He's going to drive my truck here."

She sat across from Jason and his mischievous grin sent heat rushing to her cheeks.

He snickered when she ducked her head and fumbled with her napkin which added more heat.

"I didn't expect to make a decision about Doc's practice so soon, or I would have driven it down here instead of Ethel."

"You know you can use the Bronco whenever you want. I can sign out a squad car today, so you won't have to worry about picking me up."

She hesitated, scrolling through her phone to avoid looking at Coop. "Maybe just today. I'll have my truck tomorrow. I'd like to look around and see what kind of housing is available."

"You know you can stay right here for as long you want." Eva placed a plate of pancakes and bacon in front of Sam. "You don't have to leave at all."

"I'll stay the two weeks I booked while I look around." She bit into her meal. "But if I move, I might starve to death, because I can't cook like this."

"Sam needs to take that beautiful Chevy to the car show at the Dairy Barn tonight," said Jason, "it'll be over in plenty of time for your date."

She opened her mouth to argue the point. It wasn't a date. *Okay, maybe it's a date; just not that kind of date.*

"A date?" asked Miss Eva, "How wonderful. Where are you going?"

"He's taking her to see *Jaws* so she'll get scared, and he can protect her." Jason grinned at his father. "Right, Dad?"

Coop ignored the comment as he addressed Sam. "Last Friday of the month is Classic Car Night at the Barn. Ethel would be a big hit."

"I'll think about it. I rarely had time for car shows in Dallas, though I did go to this thing called Coffee and Cars a time or two."

"So, Dad, she gonna let you drive Ethel on your date so you can sit side-by-side like in the old days?"

Coop glared at his son.

"Jason Robert Delaney," chided Eva, "behave and eat your breakfast."

The culprit turned to Sam with a conspiratorial wink. "Maybe y'all can finish what I interrupted last night."

She sputtered and coffee dribbled down her chin. "You're incorrigible."

One dark brow arched and his lips curled up in an irresistible grin. "Part of my charm."

Try as she might, it was impossible not to smile. "You do understand paybacks can be…heck?"

He toasted her with his orange juice. "Wouldn't have it any other way."

The rest of the meal passed in pleasant conversation and occasional teasing as her companions tried to convince Sam to stay at The Grove for the foreseeable future.

"I need to get going," said Coop as he deposited his dishes in the sink, "you ready?"

"Yeah." Sam got up and added hers to the pile. "Is Jack

still outside?"

"Chasing the cat a few minutes ago."

When they reached the Bronco, she stood aside for him to unlock the door.

Instead, Coop laid his hat on the hood, and gently turned her toward him. "I've been thinking about that damn almost-kiss all night."

He cupped her face with his hands, thumbs caressing her cheek. His lips brushed hers, then gently covered her mouth, demanding a response. Mouth parting, she raised herself to meet his kiss. Like the soldering heat capable of joining metals together, it sang through her veins, his tongue sending shock waves through her body as it stroked and explored her mouth.

Heart hammering, she shuddered when his hands dropped to her hips and pulled her against him.

Too soon, he pulled back, eyes gazing deeply into hers. "Damn, Doc," he whispered. "Damn."

Surprised and embarrassed by her own eager response to his kiss, she stepped back, cheeks scorching hot. "We should get going."

"Please don't do that. Don't push away from me. From us."

She focused on a shirt button, unable to meet his intense scrutiny.

He took a step back. "I'm sorry if I crossed the line. After last night…" He raked his fingers through his hair, huffing out a long breath. "Okay. Let's go." He reached for the door handle.

"You didn't cross a line, Dee. I…I wasn't prepared…to like it so much."

He cupped her chin, tilting her face up to meet his gaze. "We might be on to something here, Doc. Just give us a chance."

To her dismay, her voice trembled when she spoke. "Okay." She paused. "You can drive Ethel tonight if you want to."

His brows shot upwards. "Will you sit beside me like the good old days?"

"...Yeah."

"Now you're talking."

After dropping Coop off at the courthouse, Sam spent the morning getting acquainted with the town. By mid-afternoon, she found herself back at Baker Lake.

Jack sat in the front seat, muscles taunt, and ears pointed forward as he looked out the window, and whined.

"I know, baby. I'm scared, too. But, I have to know if those sensations yesterday meant anything or not." She pulled a large, gold hair clip from her purse, twisted her hair into a long strip and secured it with the clip. She paused for a moment beside the truck and listened.

From an early age, she sensed emotions in others more acutely than most. As she grew up, the ability ebbed and flowed. More than once, she would be alone somewhere and be engulfed with unexplained sadness or fear or even happiness, though such times were rare.

In her mind, this deep empathy helped her be a better doctor, enabling her to reach even the most reluctant patient. During those tension-filled years with Paul, however, it all but vanished.

Apparently, since coming here, it returned.

Just last night as she got to her room, a prickling on the back of her neck made her stop and look around. The feeling of being watched caused gooseflesh on her arms. A whisper of sound made her glance behind. Nothing there.

A flicker of unease coursed through her, and disappeared as a smile found its way through the veil of apprehension. *Maybe there's a friendly ghost here.*

"Or maybe I'm imaging things." She shook her head. "Come on, Jack. Let's see what's out there."

They walked slowly toward the trail, stopping just inside the entrance.

Jack glanced up, sniffed once, and stepped forward.

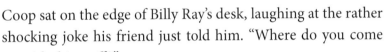

Coop sat on the edge of Billy Ray's desk, laughing at the rather shocking joke his friend just told him. "Where do you come up with this stuff?"

"Hell, Coop, I worked in the oil field for over twenty years." He pushed back in the chair, long legs straight out, hands clasped behind his head. "Hear all kinds of crap."

"Alice give you any grief about being taken off dispatch?"

"You know how she is. Likes to be in the center of things. I told her not to get her panties in a wad. It's temporary."

Coop raised a brow.

"Okay, so maybe I didn't use those exact words, but I told her to be patient, and she'd have her pipeline back in no time."

"Speaking of pipelines, how's things in the oil world?"

"Same ole same ole." His square jaw visibly tensed, dark brows creating lines across a wide forehead. "A few rigs starting up here and there, but nothing to hang your hat on." The chair gave a protesting squeak as he shifted to sit up, his stare direct and sincere. "I can't thank you enough for this job, man. If you hadn't put me on last year…"

Coop waved aside his friend's gratitude. "You'd do the same for me. Besides, you're good at the job. Being a jailer isn't easy and you have a knack for getting along with folks. Plus, your knowledge of the county is useful on dispatch."

"All the same, I appreciate you having my back." A faint light twinkled in the depths of his coffee-colored eyes, and a smirk found its way through the cloud of melancholy. "Remember back in high school when the Bennett brothers wanted to kick my ass for kissing their sister."

"If I remember correctly, you did more than kiss."

He ducked his head. "Yeah, well, despite what she told them, I never got past second base."

Coop smiled at the long ago memory of best friends standing up together. "Hell of a fight, wasn't it?"

The jailer's voice dropped lower. "Yeah. Probably the only time my old man was ever proud of me."

Coop didn't know how to respond. Billy's relationship with his alcoholic father was tumultuous at best, and he spent more time with Coop's family than his own. After the old man died ten years ago, Billy's mother left town to live with her sister in Dallas. He didn't think they had spoken since.

Billy Ray tapped the folders on his desk. "I best get back to work. My boss is a real hard ass and wouldn't like me chit-chatting with the worker bees."

"Let me know if you need anything, Bill. Anything at all."

"I will. Thanks, Coop."

Back in his office, he powered up his computer and stared at the screen, images of Sam dancing through his mind. How was it possible to be so attracted to someone he just met? The vibration of his cell phone interrupted his revelry. He glanced at caller ID as he picked it up. "Hiya, Doc."

"We're going to have to postpone our date."

Her breathless voice set off warning bells. "What's wrong?"

"I found another body."

CHAPTER NINETEEN

She found me.

Coop tried to ignore the voice as the squad car slid to a stop. In his haste to get out, he missed the door handle the first time he grabbed for it. He hurried to where Sam waited. "You all right?"

"Yeah." She rubbed her arms, inclined her head toward the walking trail. "Maybe a hundred yards in. Trail hooks right. Look for two limbs propped against a pine tree. She's off to the left toward the lake. You can't miss it."

She inhaled, letting it out slowly as though struggling for control.

"How do you know it's a she?"

"Shallow grave." She shuddered. "I guess the rains washed some of the dirt away. I saw her face. She's been there a while."

"Stay here. JD's on his way." He purposefully hadn't told anyone other than his chief deputy about the call. He wanted to see things himself without interference. He skimmed the ground as he headed toward the trail. A popular destination, many people hiked it every day. *Why had they not found this body?*

When he saw the limbs against the tree, he turned left, steps slow and precise, studying the terrain carefully. A few yards further, he saw it.

A small mound, not much more than leaves and debris, and the recent heavy rains had washed a lot of it away. He approached with care, trying not to disturb things any more than they were.

A muscle flicked in his jaw, anger increasing as he stared at the remains. Pale blonde hair, matted with dirt and leaves covered part of her face. Sam was right. The woman died several weeks ago.

Maybe even about the time he began hearing the voice in his head. *Is this what you wanted me to find?*

He made his way back to the parking lot as JD arrived.

"Crime unit's on the way, Sheriff." The deputy's solemn voice was ringed with tension. "What do you want me to do now?"

"I'll get the perimeter secured. Call Billy Ray on his cell. Don't use the radio. Have him pull everyone out here. See if Bakersville PD can spare a couple of folks, too. This area is going to be swarming with gawkers, and I need everyone to secure the scene for the Rangers."

Within an hour, the area was crawling with law enforcement personnel as well as a few townspeople who saw all the activity and came to investigate.

Nothing wrong with the rumor mill.

Coop looked up and noted Sam remained where he left her so he walked toward her.

He wants her.

Sam watched Coop approach, her arms crossed in front to

ward off the chill that would not abate, despite the balmy day. He was in full-on cop mode, and she prepared herself for the interrogation to come.

Two bodies in one week. Both found by her. Even she would question the coincidence.

"What were you doing out here?"

The harshness in his voice made her stomach churn with anxiety. She hugged herself tighter. The truth wasn't an option. "I found the trail yesterday, but didn't have time to explore."

His stare drilled into her, causing her voice to shake, and she focused on a red fiber clinging to his left shoulder. "Eva told me this was a good walking trail, and I wanted to check it out." She paused. "Jack heard something, saw something, I'm not sure. Anyway, he took off. It caught me by surprise, and I lost his leash." She glanced up and away.

He knows I'm lying.

"I ran after him. He was barking and pawing at - at her face." She sucked in air, and blew it out slowly, immense self-control the only thing holding her together. "I pulled him back and we left." She finally met his chilly gaze. "And called you."

He made no comment, just watched her closely. "Your knees are dirty. So are your hands."

Face flaming, she snapped, "There's nothing like finding a body that's been buried in a shallow grave for several weeks to test your composure. Mine failed."

"Where?"

"Where what?"

"Where did you *fail*?"

Inner turmoil masked by a deceptive calmness, she replied, "Head of the grave. The ground is still damp enough my handprints are probably visible."

"Is that all?"

Sadness overwhelmed me, and I fell to my knees, unable to move until it passed.

"Yes."

"Did you throw up?"

"No."

Arms folded across his chest, feet planted apart, tension bounced off him in waves. "It's more than fifty feet off the trail, almost to the lake. How did you find it?"

She pulled me there. "I told you. Jack got away from me, and I chased after him."

"Jack is the reason you found the last one." The statement sizzled with accusation.

Body stiff, she met his frosty glare head on. "That's right, Sheriff Delaney. Jack is the reason I found the last one, too."

"One of the Rangers will be over to talk to you. I have some sweats and a tee shirt in the back you can change into. They won't fit but it's all I got."

"Change?"

"You fell at a crime scene. Your clothes are now evidence."

"Oh. Of course."

The afternoon drug on to early evening. She changed in the crime van with a female trooper in attendance, gave her statement to a Ranger, and waited to be allowed to leave.

As she watched the activity around her, a sensation of growing anxiety replaced the sadness, though she couldn't explain why. Coop was brusque, even sharp at times, but that wasn't the reason.

While the exact cause of her unease remained unclear, one thing was certain; it involved the woman in the grave.

After finally being allowed to leave, she couldn't get home fast enough. A hot shower and strong coffee topped her to-do list.

Eva met her at the back door, face once more etched with concern. "Oh my dear, are you all right?"

The last thing she wanted was to discuss the events of the afternoon. "I'm fine, thank you. But I really need a long, hot bath, and some of your wonderful coffee."

"Of course, my dear. Of course. I'll keep your dinner on the stove to stay warm."

"Is Dad okay?" Jason sat at the table, his face a cool mask.

She squeezed his shoulder. "I know you're concerned, Jason, but he's fine. This is part of his job."

"They say she was partially buried." The older woman's hushed voice proved the rumor mill hadn't missed a lick.

Sam chose not to reply as she reached for the coffee pot. "Coop will likely be late getting home if he has to accompany the remains to Dallas."

"Two bodies in one week." Eva twisted the towel she held in her hands. "I just can't believe it."

"How did you find this one?" Jason's question held no censure. In fact, his voice showed no emotion at all.

Like father, like son. She saw no harm in relaying the essence of the story she told Coop. "Jack got away from me and found her." She turned for the door, the dog on her heels. "Don't worry about keeping anything warm for me. I'll find something later if I'm hungry."

As she reached the top of the stairs, the scent of gardenias made her hesitate.

Oh Granny, what's going on? Am I crazy?

CHAPTER TWENTY

"I appreciate you letting me come along to the morgue, Sheriff." JD focused on the dark road ahead. "Only time I ever went there was during the academy."

Exhaustion weighed Coop down in the seat. Two bodies in one week. And he couldn't ignore the fact there could be more because The Voice insisted he wasn't done yet. "Hindsight being twenty-twenty, I should have let you come along for the last one. You need know these things."

"I know it sounds bad to say this, but it's kind of exciting to see how all this works for real, not just in the books."

Coop hoped the deputy never got another chance to use what he learned today.

Lost in thought, neither spoke as the white lines on the highway raced by.

"You think it's the same guy?" JD's question sounded more like a statement.

"Yeah. Preliminary cause of death is strangulation, and her right index finger is broken, so, yeah, looks like the same guy."

"You think he's local?"

A light shrug preceded his reply. "I hate to think so, but it's possible. Could be someone who comes this way on a regular basis, but it doesn't feel right to me."

"How so?"

He hesitated, choosing his words carefully. "Both bodies were found in out of the way places a stranger wouldn't know about."

"True."

"Both in high traffic spots. Lots of people in and out." Coop rubbed the tight muscles in his neck with one hand. "I haven't had to think like a killer in a while, but consider this. He took the time to more or less bury the first one. Maybe he didn't want her found. At least, not right away. The next one, he expected to be. Or got careless."

Jimmy shook his head, features tight. "He seems pretty slick to me. I mean, we got nothing on him up to this point."

"Cocky guys make mistakes."

JD nodded. "You'd know." He snapped his head toward Coop. "I mean, with your experience and all. Not that I think you're cocky or anything like that."

Coop smiled at the younger man's unease. "I know what you meant."

JD broke the lengthy silence that followed. "I think about folks in town, people I've known for years, and I can't think of a single person who might do such a thing."

"I know."

"How long do you think it will take to find out who she is?"

"Death was at least four to five weeks ago, so she'll be on a missing persons' report somewhere. And her dental work is extensive and expensive so records shouldn't be hard to match."

"You can't really think Sunshine is involved with this, do you?"

Coop leaned his head back and rolled his head

side-to-side. "No. Her finding both bodies is a strange coincidence but no, I don't think she's involved."

"Me neither."

The eastern sky showed the faintest tinge of pink as JD dropped Coop off at the house. Though it was Saturday, he would be back in the office as soon as he showered and changed.

Miss Eva wouldn't be up yet, but she would have left the coffee pot ready to go, and food in the fridge, which gave him a small surge of energy.

Jack greeted him at the back door as did the smell of fresh-brewed coffee.

And Sam.

She stood at the sink, hands behind her back, dressed in sweat pants and a faded football jersey, her ebony mane pulled up in a haphazard ponytail that left several strands flying around her face. The deep shadows under her eyes and fatigue clouding her features said she hadn't slept much.

But she was beautiful to him.

He stopped within arms-reach, and noted the rapid pulse at the base of her throat, the jerky rise and fall of her chest.

"Are you okay?" Her voice quivered as she searched his face.

He didn't give himself time to second guess his decision. He stepped forward and pulled her into a gentle embrace. "I am now."

She stiffened, then wound her arms tightly around his back, her breath warming more than his skin when she exhaled.

Sam relished the tenderness of the arms around her, amazed to realize something as simple as an embrace could be so satisfying.

He pulled her more snugly against him, her curves molding to the hard contours of his body.

"I'm sorry if I was hard on you yesterday," he murmured against her ear, "but a second body…"

She rubbed her hands over the solid plane of his back, easily detecting the muscles tight with tension and weariness and knew, without a doubt, she was about to make a big mistake. Again. And didn't care.

Whatever happened from now on happened, and she would deal with it. This was where she wanted to be. In his arms.

She rubbed her cheek against his chest, crinkling her nose at the light odor of antiseptic clinging to his shirt, then tilted her head back to look at him. "I'm liking this friend stuff."

His smile developed slowly, but when it did, her heart turned over as certainty dawned.

Love at first sight was not a myth. It was real.

I'm in love with a man I just met. The chances of ending up hurt again, were high. Until then, she would cherish whatever time they were given.

"Me, too." After a chaste kiss to the tip of her nose, he stepped back. "But I need to get a move on."

She pulled his cup from the cabinet and filled it with coffee. "Take this with you. I'll have something for you to eat when you come down."

"Beautiful and cooks, too."

"Yeah, well, it won't be anywhere close to Eva's efforts but I can scramble eggs with the best of them."

He sipped his coffee as he turned to let Jack out.

"Oh, did anyone find my gold hair clip after I left?"

"Not that I know of. Why?"

"I had it on when I changed in the van. I guess I left it there." She brushed her hands on her thighs.

"I'll ask the trooper who took your clothes if she saw it."

"It's no big deal. Just a cheap hair clip I picked up somewhere."

He nodded and headed for the door. "By the way, no running alone."

She started to argue, but reconsidered. There were too many unknowns about this case, and the killer could still be around. "Do I need to come down and give another formal statement?"

"Yeah."

"Okay. I'll be there by ten." She folded a towel and lay it on the counter. "Will you be able to come home and rest soon?"

"Not sure. Lots of paperwork yet."

She watched him walk out, heart heavy and light at the same time.

I love him.

CHAPTER TWENTY-ONE

Coop studied the gruesome images on his computer screen, unable to focus. He muttered a curse, and swiveled his chair around toward the window.

Instead of the tall pecan tree on the southwest corner of the courthouse lawn, his mind's eye saw cornflower blue eyes, full of life and laughter, a smile bright as the Texas sun, and lips that tasted of everything good in the world.

His thoughts drifted back to breakfast this morning, cooked for him by Sam. A no-frills plate of bacon, scrambled eggs and toast but the company, the atmosphere, was priceless. When Jason and Eva joined them, the comfortable familiarity resounded of family.

Prior to Sam's arrival, he considered his life complete and happy. *Mr.-I'm-not-in-to-permanent-relationships* suddenly found himself wanting one. With her. The shock of discovery hit him full force and promptly scared the hell out of him.

He gave himself a mental shake and turned back to the computer. Eyes dry and tired, he blinked several times in quick succession in an effort to moisten them, to no avail. "Dammit." He rummaged around his desk for eye drops.

"You look like death warmed over." Billy Ray stood inside the door, arms folded across his chest.

Coop cast a quick glance at his friend. "I thought you were off today?"

"I am. Saw you come in earlier, and thought I'd check on you." His rangy, wide-shouldered body moved with an easy grace as he entered the room. "Heard your girlfriend found another body."

"Yeah." He stood and walked toward the door. "Alice got any eye drops in her stash? She's practically a walking pharmacy."

"Probably. She prides herself on being prepared." He chuckled as they headed down the hall. "I've seen her pull out a hammer and some duct tape before." Billy opened the bottom drawer and pulled out what everyone termed *the medicine bag*. Finding what he sought, he passed the small bottle to Coop with a grin. "You know she's picky about people messing with her drawers."

Coop added drops in each eye. "Yeah, well, tell her I said it was okay."

"So, you're okay if I play with stuff in her drawers?"

He tossed the vial back to Billy. "Long as it doesn't break any rules, Champ, you can play with whatever she'll let you play with."

Billy's whiskey-colored eyes crinkled at the corners when he grinned, before he sobered. "Anything new on the last body?"

"Not yet. Probably won't know anything until next week."

"How about you go home and get some sleep? You know they'll call if anything comes in."

"I will. Have a few things to finish up."

"Take care of yourself, Coop. I'm too old to train a new boss."

The hum of the air conditioner coming on coincided with the opening of the lobby door as JD sauntered in. "Hey, Billy Ray. How's it going?"

"Can't complain. You?"

"Could be worse, I guess."

Billy nodded toward Coop. "Make him go home. He's toast. And you ain't much better." He turned and left, not waiting for them to reply.

Coop headed back to his office, the deputy at his side. "Sam will be here shortly to give her statement. Once you're done, go ahead and take off."

"I need to update the teletype first. Maybe we'll get lucky, and get an ID soon."

"Okay. Get her statement then go home."

"What about you?"

He dropped into his chair and sighed. "I feel like I've missed something." He shook his head as he shuffled the photos Sam took. "I have looked at these and the crime scene ones till I'm cross-eyed."

JD nodded toward the photos. "You think something's there?"

"I don't know what I think anymore."

A light tap on the door caused both men to shift their attention.

"Sheriff?" Arlis, the kid from Teddy's stood there, a large envelope in his hand. "Teddy said for me to bring this by." He shuffled forward, hand shaking slightly as he passed the envelope. "It's the other DVDs from Sunday night. Said tell you they don't show much other than the cash register and a small piece of the dance floor."

"Thanks," said Coop as he took the envelope.

"Yes sir. Um, you're welcome, sir." The red-faced young man turned and made a hasty exit.

Coop fed the first DVD into the computer and watched the grainy, black and white footage of the cash register area, which revealed nothing. The second one showed more of the bar and a small portion of the dance floor.

"Wait…is that Alice?"

Coop, surprised at JD's question, paused it for a closer look.

"Dang. She's got some moves." JD shook his head. "Didn't know she ever went to Teddy's."

"Well, it was Ladies' Night," said Coop, "and Alice is a lady. Sort of."

A snort was the only reply as Coop hit play again.

"Wait, stop. Back it up." JD tapped the screen. "There… with her back to the camera. It's our vic, isn't it?"

Coop hit reverse, then slowly scrolled forward until the woman appeared again. "You're right. I'm so fricking tired, I missed it." Coop leaned forward to study the rough image. "Looks like she's talking with someone, but I can't get a look at him." He glanced down at the time stamp. "Ten forty-five." He inched the tape forward, eyes focused on the man. "Dammit. All I can see is part of his left shoulder. And with this black and white film, can't even tell what color the shirt is other than dark."

JD huffed out a breath. "Can't even see enough to judge his build."

"Her head is tilted up, so he's tall," said Coop, "and judging by the smile, attractive enough to get her attention."

"You want me to go to Teddy's and look for tall, good-looking men?"

JD's heavy sarcasm wasn't lost on Coop who chose not to respond. "A few people around I recognize." He scrolled forward slowly till the woman left the screen, her arm presumably in the crook of the unknown man. She came in camera range twice during a line dance, then disappeared. The remainder of the video provided no useful information, but they ran through it one more time to be sure.

Coop lifted a pencil from his desk, tapping it against the chair arm as he thought out loud. "At ten forty-five, she's having a conversation with some guy at the bar. The bartender isn't in sight so I'm assuming he or she won't be much help but we'll try anyway. At eleven-ten, she's line dancing." He paused, chewing on his lower lip. "Find out who worked the bar Sunday night and when can we talk with them. I'm going to run through the parking lot stuff one more time and see if anything pops out at me."

"Copy that."

"And go get some rest as soon as you finish Sam's statement. If the bartender is working tonight, I want you to talk to them."

"Yes sir."

Coop pushed the other DVD into the drive.

He's watching her.

CHAPTER TWENTY-TWO

Sam stood beside the door of the Bronco after giving her statement and debated what to do next. Even though Barbara would be here soon with her truck, Coop insisted she keep the Bronco to use, and had Jason bring him to work so she wouldn't have to drive Ethel. *Add thoughtfulness to the growing list of things I love about him.*

It was almost noon and there really wasn't much point in house-hunting now, even if she wanted to. The urge to bake something gave her an idea, so she cut across the street to the grocery store.

Inside, the narrow aisles were stacked with every conceivable item. Farm tools and implements lined the wall on the right while a meat counter off to the left offered hand-cut steaks and fresh shrimp when available. Long rods held antique ceiling fans, their oversized blades stirring the heavy air liberally scented with cedar, leather and fertilizer.

"Morning, ma'am. Anything I can help you find?"

Sam immediately liked the pleasant-looking man wearing a red apron proclaiming *If Arnolds ain't got it, you don't need it.* "I like your apron."

"My wife's idea. Wasn't too sure about it, but folks seem to like it."

"This place is wonderful. Like a general store from the old days. You really do have everything here."

"We try. Ain't you the new doctor taking over for Doc Harper?"

She held out her hand. "Samantha Fowler."

"Frank Arnold."

"So you're the owner?"

"Yes, ma'am. This place has been in our family since 1880." He looked around, pride and concern evident in clear, blue eyes. "We try to change with the times, but it's getting harder to keep up." He rubbed his hands together, eyes bright with interest. "Now, how can I help you today, Dr. Fowler?"

She listed the items needed, as he led her around the store, ending in the back at an old-fashioned soda fountain boasting a sign for root beer floats. "I've never had one of those."

"What? You've never had a root beer float?" He grabbed his chest as though in pain. "Why, that's plain un-American." He turned to the young woman behind the counter. "Josie, please fix this lovely lady one of your famous root beer floats."

Her mouth began to water in anticipation as she watched the young woman pull a tall frosted mug from the freezer and add two scoops of vanilla ice cream. Next, she slowly added the soda from a spout until the foamy head spilled over the top. A straw and long spoon were inserted as she passed it over to Sam.

The first sip of the sweet, carbonated drink slid smoothly down her throat. "Oh my goodness," she said, "this is delicious."

She spent the next half hour chatting with the proprietor and others who stopped by while she enjoyed the syrupy concoction, and vowed to herself this would be a frequent treat.

The straw made a slurping sound as she finished off the drink. "That was so good."

"Frank." The sharp command came from a woman stalking toward them from the back. "You have other customers you need to see to."

Sam fought the urge to step back.

The woman's resentment was obvious. A deep flush raced across her pale face like a fever. She might have been pretty at one time, but anger transformed her features into an ugly mask. Thin lips formed a tight line across a narrow face, and her dark eyes gleamed like volcanic rock.

Arnold did step back, shoulders drooping, his once jubilant expression gloomy as he faced the woman. "Um, Sweetheart, this is –"

"I know who she is." She glared at Sam. "Are you finished?"

Sympathy for her new friend overrode Sam's better judgement. She glanced at the woman who she now assumed to be Mrs. Arnold. "I was just leaving." She turned to the man and extended her hand. "Thank you, Mr. Arnold for your kind hospitality. And the company."

He glanced at his wife as he shook Sam's hand, squeezing a little too tight. "My pleasure, Doc. Drop by anytime."

The low harrumph from the woman followed Sam down the aisle.

At the door, a man juggled two bags of groceries as he grabbed at the door handle.

"Here. Allow me." She reached around him, and he stepped aside so she could open the door.

He waited for her on the sidewalk. "Thanks. I was about to lose my grip on this stuff." Brown eyes glittered with self-deprecating humor. "But I rather like being rescued by a beautiful woman."

She quickly sized him up. *A shameless flirt.* Sun-bleached chestnut hair, wind tossed and a little longer than normal, curled over a wide forehead. He stood around six-one or two, with an ingenuously appealing face. Bronzed skin proclaimed a life outdoors and made perfect, white teeth sparkle. A knowing smile tipped up one corner of his mouth.

Apparently, he was accustomed to women appreciating his impressive physical attributes.

Sam wasn't in the market and gave a short, "You're welcome," as she turned to leave.

"I'm sorry. I didn't mean to embarrass you, Dr. Fowler." He extended his right hand, but unbalanced his groceries and pulled it back. "I'm Billy Ray Thomas. A friend of Coop's."

"Oh. Right. One of the deputies. I saw you…the other day."

He rolled his head side-to-side, causing a dark brown curl to flip over one eye giving him a compellingly rakish look. "Not deputy. Jailer, slash dispatcher, slash chief cook and bottle-washer."

She relaxed a little. He was merely being friendly. Okay, a flirty kind of friendly. She could deal with flirty. "Samantha Fowler."

"I saw you talking to Frank and Miriam. Wanted to say hello but didn't want to interrupt."

"Miriam? Mr. Arnold's wife?"

He nodded. "She's a piece of work."

Sam couldn't think of anything nice to say, so kept silent.

"Never understood the attraction. Leads him around by his…nose. Been that way since they married right out of high school."

"They say opposites attract."

"I could never be so…docile." His expression went somber a split second before the attitude ramped up from casual to flirty. "You're staying at Miss Eva's, right?"

"For now. Until I find something permanent."

"There's some new condo-type rentals south of town. One and two-bedroom units around this nice courtyard area with a small pool. I live in one of them. Coop can tell you how to get there."

"Thanks. I appreciate the information."

"No problem. See you around."

He sauntered away, whistling some undecipherable tune.

She had to admit he was engaging, devilishly handsome with a perfectly portioned body and a sensual smile, but…he wasn't Coop.

After putting away the items she purchased, she helped Eva with the noon meal. By the time it was ready, Barbara and her husband arrived with her truck, and some items she asked them to include. They departed mid-afternoon and Coop had yet to return home.

"There's a dinner at church tonight," said Eva as she wiped off the counter top, "to raise money for a new stained-glass window to replace one broken in a storm this summer. You're welcome to come if you like."

Before she could fashion a reply, her hostess continued.

"Of course, you and Coop may want to have your date tonight since it got cancelled last night."

"I'm sure he's going be exhausted, but I'll see when he gets home."

"Well, there will be plenty of leftovers for y'all and Jason, too, if he comes home in time. Just make yourself at home."

"Thank you. Um, I wondered if you would mind if I baked something."

"Of course not, dear. You're free to cook whatever you like."

"Well, I'm not much of a cook. I mean, I can follow a recipe, but I'm not very imaginative. With work and all, I seldom had time. But I do love to bake. My other creative outlet, along with my photography." As an afterthought, she added, "Could you by chance use something sweet at your dinner tonight? I mean, if you could, I'd be happy to contribute."

"How thoughtful of you, dear. Dinner is pot luck and afterwards, we auction off the desserts as a fundraiser. Did you have something in particular in mind?"

"Granny made this sheet cake she called Chocolate Candy Cake. It's pretty rich, but so dang good. Or maybe Pecan Pie Muffins? I'm thinking the cake would probably be better. I can do the muffins for here."

"You had me at chocolate candy."

"I bought what I needed in town this morning. What time will you be leaving?"

"Mavis is picking me up about four-forty-five. We have to help get things set up."

"Perfect. I'll have it ready for you."

Time flew by and the constant activity kept troubling thoughts at bay. She pulled the last pan of muffins from the oven when Coop walked in.

"I don't know what you're cooking, but it smells wonderful in here."

"The cake is for Eva's social tonight. But we have pecan pie muffins."

He stopped at the stove and eyed the small morsels on the

plate. "Can I have ten now? I'm starved." Even as he asked, he plucked two and popped one in his mouth, quickly followed by the second. "You made these?"

"I did."

"They're really good." He grabbed another. "You can't eat just one."

She handed him a mug of coffee. "Sit. You need real food, not muffins."

"Yes ma'am." He sat down and cradled the cup in his hands. "What brought this on?"

"Needed something to do. I'm not very good at sitting around twiddling my thumbs."

He eyed the plastic-wrapped sheet cake on the counter. "I love chocolate cake."

She set a plate of meat loaf, glazed carrots and green beans in front of him. "I'll make another tomorrow."

He forked a hunk of meat. "Promise?"

"Promise." She paused, then sat down across from him, placing the plate of muffins in the middle. "You need some rest."

"Yeah. I'm beat." He continued eating with fervor.

"Maybe you can get to bed early tonight."

As soon as the comment left her mouth, heat crept up her neck as visions of him in bed—with her - danced around the edges of her mind.

His smirk said he knew where her mind drifted, but he kept his thoughts to himself.

In no time at all, his plate was empty. He pushed it aside and reached for the muffins. "These are really, really good." He stuck one in his mouth and grinned. "I bet it's not as good as that cake, though."

His obvious enjoyment gave her self-esteem a much-needed boost. "Thanks."

"Mavis is here, dear, and—oh, Coop," said Miss Eva as she rushed into the kitchen like a white-haired tornado. "I'm glad you finally made it home." She turned to Sam. "I doubt I'll be home till at least ten, so unless you two go on your date, you should have the house to yourself."

The woman was subtle as thunder.

"Um, okay."

"This cake looks delicious. I might have to bid on it myself." She rushed around, grabbing up things she needed and disappeared out the back door.

Alone with Coop, conversation came to a halt.

Sam finally broke the prolonged silence. "How about I take a raincheck on our friend-date? You need rest."

"Rest is overrated."

"No. It isn't. You can't perform at your best when you're exhausted."

His sexy smile made her belly tighten.

"I can perform just fine. Care to test me?"

Cheeks so hot she expected them to combust at any time, she glared. "You're hopeless."

He winked.

The man was incorrigible. And adorable. "How about we compromise?"

"I'm all ears. Well, not *all* of me."

Her shoulders slumped a little. He had a one-track mind. "Why don't you shower and lie down for a couple of hours? We can vegetate tonight; maybe catch a movie on television. We'll call it a practice date."

His yawn said it all. "Okay. Wake me up at seven."

"Eight."

"Fine. Eight."

He walked to where she sat, bent down and kissed her upturned forehead. "I'll be waiting for you to wake me."

Wait…Why should I wake him? Doesn't he have an alarm?

On the heels of those questions, came images that sent her heart rate through the roof. Coop naked in the shower, then lying on his big bed…waiting for her to wake him. And do what?

"Holy mother of pearl. I am in so much trouble here."

CHAPTER TWENTY-THREE

Coop relaxed on the couch sipping a glass of wine of all things, not beer, watching some chick flick set in England back in the old days on TV.

Jack wandered in, glanced at the screen, and went back to the kitchen.

Coop hid a smile by taking another drink. *Smart dog.*

When Sam came to his door half an hour ago, he was already awake, anticipating the remainder of the evening. Her choice in movies notwithstanding, he was enjoying himself.

"What about the last victim? Any progress?" Sam lounged beside him, long legs curled up beneath her, slender fingers wrapped around the delicate stem of her wineglass.

The flowery fragrance she wore reminded him of sunshine and roses. He really liked sunshine and roses. "No ID yet. I'm hoping the dental records will help. Basically, I got squat for evidence on either of them."

"Is it...could it be the same killer?"

"...I think it is." He rolled his head to look at her. "I believe he's either local or comes through on a regular basis. That's why I said no jogging alone till I catch him. I don't want you taking any chances. I'm glad Eva had someone to drive her to the social tonight, or I would have taken her and brought her home."

"I just can't imagine someone doing something so vile."

The statement didn't really need an answer so he turned his attention to the program as a meddlesome, shrill-voiced woman plotted to get one of her daughters married off to some rich dude.

He tried to ignore the warmth of Sam's knee where it pressed against his thigh. More than anything, he wanted to run his hand up her leg—he gave himself a mental shake and focused on the unpleasant woman again, a mood-killer if ever one existed.

"What about the other girl?"

"Joyce Ayers. From Dallas. All indications are she was just passing through." He didn't offer more since the evening news would provide that much, and she didn't ask for particulars. It suddenly dawned on him how much he missed having someone to talk to; someone to share a glass of wine with or watch a bad movie. Life before Sam wasn't much fun.

She drained her glass as the program broke for commercials. "You hate this movie, don't you?"

He didn't have to be a cop to recognize a trick question when he heard it, so opted for a neutral answer. "I don't *hate* it. But, that mother is a piece of work."

"Back then, few marriages were love matches. Most were arranged by the families for one reason or another, and the woman rarely had a say in it."

He grinned. "Can't see you letting anyone order you around."

"Yeah, well, I take suggestions under advisement. Orders…I tend to ignore."

"So, you wouldn't consider one of those marriages of convenience?"

"No," she said firmly. "It's love or not at all."

Their gazes locked and his heart hammered. She was the most beautiful woman he'd ever seen. From the very beginning, she affected him in ways no woman ever had, which alternately scared and fascinated him.

He felt like he was drowning, flailing about as he treaded water, and she was a lifeline.

He leaned over to place his empty glass on the table beside hers. He could have more easily reached to his right and set it there, but he wouldn't be in a position to entice a kiss. And he wanted a kiss. Desperately.

Her chest moved in rapid, uneven motions as he took his time putting the glass down, then pulled back until they were face-to-face.

"You make me crazy, Doc," he whispered, as he cupped her neck and brought his lips down to hers. The kiss was slow and methodical as he explored the luscious recesses of her mouth, tasting the tartness of the Bordeaux along with the sweetness uniquely Sam. Her soft moan of pleasure as her arms encircled his waist nearly undid him.

She returned his kiss with enthusiasm, fingers digging into his back as she melted against him. With little effort, he could have her beneath him on the over-sized couch. He considered following the primordial instinct blazing inside him.

He wanted her. She wanted him.

There was nothing to stop them from taking what they wanted.

But suddenly, it was more than physical need driving him. Some indefinable emotion intruded, and he pulled back, bringing her with him so she lay against his side. He slid his hand up and down her arm. "I want you, Sam. You know that," he whispered against her hair. "But I want to know you, too. I want to sit here and watch this movie if that's what interests you. I want to know about your life, things you like and don't like, whatever you want to tell me."

She craned her neck to look at him, and those azure depths sucked him in, body and soul.

"I want that, too, Coop." Her face glowed brighter than the noonday sun. "But I won't make you watch any more of this movie. It's just where the channel was when I turned it on."

"You'll still make me a chocolate cake tomorrow, right? Even if I don't watch your movie?"

She nestled against him. "Yes, I'll make you a cake. The remote is on the coffee table. Put it wherever you want."

The screeching woman was gone and two pretty girls were discussing some wealthy bachelor their father went to see… or planned to see…or something. Nothing he couldn't handle.

"If this gets me brownie points, I'm in for the duration." He put his sock-clad feet up on the coffee table, and relaxed against the back of the couch, with Sam nestled beside him.

"So," asked Coop, "what's your favorite color?"

Distracted by the spicy mixture of sandalwood and cardamom emanating from him, Sam took a moment to reply. "Purple."

"Favorite food?"

"Mexican."

He angled his face toward her, dark brows slanted in a frown. "This is really important. Can you Two-step?"

It was difficult to remain serious as she matched his grave expression. "It's been a while, but, yes. And Schottische and waltz, too."

He grinned like Cheshire cat as he relaxed against the couch again. "Good. Favorite hobby, other than photography?"

"How did you know I liked photography?"

"You told me so at the first crime scene."

Thoughts of the dead woman caused her throat to tighten with sorrow and she ducked her head.

Coop jostled her shoulder. "No sadness, Sam, not tonight." He paused. "Hobby?"

"…Baking. My turn. Favorite color?"

"Your eyes."

"Um…okay. Favorite food?"

"Steak. And chocolate cake. Not necessarily together."

"Favorite hobby?"

"Fishing."

"I saw some folks fishing at the lake the other day. Thought I might invest in some gear and give it a try."

"I have more than you'll ever need in the shed out back. Maybe we'll go drown a worm tomorrow for another practice date."

She snickered. "Drown a worm?"

"Just another way to say go fishing."

"Ah. Let's see…favorite sound?"

"Your laughter."

"Favorite smell?"

"Your shampoo."

She pushed back and looked at him. "Am I detecting a pattern here?"

"I hope so."

His sensual voice dropped an octave and gooseflesh peppered her arms. When his head bent down, her heart did a little flip-flop.

The chirp of a cell phone stopped his motion. "Hold that thought," he whispered as he pulled the phone from his pocket. "Delaney. Damn. When does he come on duty? No, you've done enough. Go home, get some rest. I'll go out there tomorrow and talk to him. And Jimmy? Good job." He jammed the phone back in his pocket.

"Bad news?"

"We still need to talk to the bartender on duty Sunday night, but he called in sick again. The other one is out of town until tomorrow night." He pulled her in his arms. "Where were we?"

"We were discussing a pattern."

"I thought we were doing this," he murmured.

His lips were surprisingly gentle, yet sent the pit of her stomach in a wild spin. Each time their lips touched, she experienced a new sensation as her emotions whirled and skidded, the gentle massage sending currents of desire through her.

When he broke contact, her senses reeled as if short-circuited.

His voice oozed an underlying sensuality. "We're missing your movie."

"It's overrated."

"I promised to watch it with you, and so I shall."

Time went unnoticed as they absently watched the movie and talked about whatever topic came up.

He told her of Jason's impending marriage, the job offer in Houston, and his mixed feelings about it.

She told him about her life-long desire to be a doctor, and

of growing up the only girl in her family.

They skimmed over the especially hard pieces of their past to focus on who they were today. And, snuggled together on the couch, movie all but forgotten, they discovered the past wasn't important at all. The here and now mattered most.

As the final credits began to roll, she heard Coop's light snores and debated waking him. Since she liked cuddling, she opted to indulge herself a little longer.

Sunlight streaming through the front window coupled with the smell of bacon frying and coffee, woke her the next morning.

She jerked upright, startling Coop, who struggled to sit up, reaching for something on the end table, nearly dumping her to the floor.

He pulled her on top of him as Jason walked in.

"Morning, sleepy-heads." He sauntered into the room, a cup of coffee in each hand.

"We fell asleep watching a movie." Sam stammered like a teenager caught necking by her parents. She glanced at the darkened screen, then back to Coop.

"I didn't turn it off," he said around a prolonged yawn.

"I did." Jason passed steaming mugs to them. "Y'all were out like a light. Never even budged when I threw the afghan over you." His eyes sparkled with humor. "Though I doubt either of you were very cold."

He headed back toward the kitchen. "Breakfast in ten minutes."

Sam ducked her head. "Oh, my God. What on earth must he think of me? Pawing you on the front porch, and now this."

Coop took a cautious sip from the cup. "He likes you."

"I was spread over you like a blanket!"

"I didn't properly thank you for it, either."

"This isn't funny. He's your son, and he saw us...like that."

"We were fully clothed and sound asleep." He took another sip from his cup. "It's not like we were having wild monkey-sex or anything."

Her mouth opened and closed but nothing came out.

"I'm sorry if it embarrassed you, Sam, but the fact is, we're adults. Adults cuddle on the couch, and fall asleep together, and, hopefully, eventually, have wild monkey-sex."

She blinked several times in rapid succession, the images those words provoked robbing her of speech.

The gentle pressure of his hand on her knee brought reality back.

"We have a connection, Sam. Something special." He regarded her carefully. "Or am I the only one who feels it?" His whispered voice was cloaked in uncertainty.

She reached out and covered his hand with her own. "No. You're not."

He visibly relaxed, and set his cup on the end table. "Jason likes you, and he's glad we're together." His mouth curled up in a sexy grin. "And he knows about the birds and the bees." He pushed himself from the couch, and pulled her up. "Come on, I'm starved."

"Eva!" Heat scorched her cheeks as she thought about her hostess. "I don't want her...them to think I'm some kind of...of scarlet woman."

"Scarlet woman?" Grey eyes crinkled at the corners. "You do know this is the twenty-first century, don't you?"

"I really care what they think of me, Coop."

He rubbed her arms. "I honestly think you're making too

much of this. We fell asleep together on the couch. Big deal. I won't lie and say I didn't enjoy it because I did." He lightly fingered a loose tendril of hair on her cheek. "I haven't slept so sound in weeks. And I look forward to a time when we do more than sleep. But not on that lumpy couch."

Her breath hitched and she gave his chest a playful tap. "You have a one-track mind."

"Guilty as charged where you're concerned."

He led her toward the door.

"What do I say to them?"

"You say good morning and eat your breakfast."

Sam followed behind, dreading the encounter.

"Good morning," chirped Eva as they walked in, "breakfast is almost ready."

Cheeks burning, Sam moved to her chair and sat down.

"Your cake brought fifty dollars at the auction," said Eva. "Thank you so much for donating it."

"Fifty dollars?" echoed Sam. "Really?"

"Yep. Highest one in fact."

"Who on earth bought it?"

"James Puckett from the bank. He and Billy Ray duked it out, and James won. Though to be honest, I think Billy Ray egged him on to get the bid up."

Coop snorted. "I'm sure he did. They've been competing against each other since high school."

"I hope he thinks it's worth the price he paid," murmured Sam.

"Oh, he did. So did everyone else. In fact, it was all gone by the time he left."

Sam couldn't hide her surprise. "He paid for it, and gave it away?"

Eva shrugged as she placed biscuits and sausage on the table. "Most people did. Though I must say, yours got the most attention. I lost track of the people wanting the recipe." She retrieved eggs from the stove. "If you don't mind sharing it, I mean."

"Of course not. I'd be glad to."

"Wonderful. Just write it out, and I'll make copies."

"Now, I really want that cake," said Coop as he filled his plate. "Can you bake it after we go fishing?"

"You fish, too?" asked Jason with a playful grin. "No wonder Dad's in hog heaven."

There was no use pretending he hadn't seen them. Taking the old if-you-can't-beat-them-join-them approach, she arched one brow and grinned as she plucked a biscuit from the pile. "I'm a woman of many and varied talents."

He nodded at her and winked. "You go, girl."

"I have work to do this afternoon, so we're going after breakfast," said Coop. "Wanna come along?"

"Another time," said the young man. "I'm spending the day with Laurie and her folks." He sat up straighter and cleared his throat as he slid his plate to the side, not looking at anyone.

Sam found his demeanor intriguing. Gone was the jovial, carefree young man who delighted in teasing her. This Jason fidgeted in his seat and toyed with his food. Thanks to her recent conversations with Coop, she suspected the reason why.

He looked at his father who gave a slight nod. "Um, Miss Eva, Sam. I, um, have an announcement." The words ran together when he blurted out the news. "Laurie and me are getting married."

Eva clapped her hands, then popped up and pulled him into a heartfelt hug. "How wonderful! Wonderful! About time, too." She looked at Sam, face beaming with happiness. "We have a lot of work to do!"

"Congratulations, Jason," said Sam. "I wish you both all the best."

"Thanks. We haven't told her parents yet. We're springing the news tonight, but I wanted my family to know now." His exuberant gaze took in the small group.

My family.

The lump in her throat made words impossible. She reached for Coop's hand and squeezed.

His smile said it all.

Family.

He plucked a petal from the pale-pink rose and watched it float on the morning breeze. He loved roses. So beautiful to gaze upon, but possessed the ability to hurt if you weren't careful. And he was always careful.

Eyes closed, he sniffed the fragrant bloom, recalling how it looked as he drew it across her creamy skin. She didn't appreciate the symbolism of beauty and pain in one object and protested loudly when he pricked her with a thorn.

He grimaced. She did serve a purpose, though, and quenched a thirst. Until she ruined everything and pissed him off. Bad move on her part.

Sam. Now there was a woman who inspired. She possessed such fire, and a passion he craved from their first encounter. But, he must be patient and wait for the perfect time. Anticipation made the event so much more enjoyable.

He pulled another petal and watched it fall.

CHAPTER TWENTY-FOUR

Monday morning

Coop sat at his desk, mood upbeat despite the lack of leads in two murder investigations. The interview with one of the bartenders provided nothing helpful. He claimed he was so busy last Sunday, he wouldn't know if his own mother walked in. They had yet to talk to the one who left ill last Sunday.

Coop spoke to most of the patrons on hand that night with similar results.

Still, he remained in a decent mood. Because of Sam. Their second practice date, fishing at Baker Lake yesterday morning, was a definite success. She hadn't fished since childhood and listened attentively to his instructions. She didn't shy away from baiting her own hooks or removing fish. She possessed an off-beat brand of humor that sometimes caught him off guard, but never failed to make him laugh. How strange to discover at this point in life he really liked to laugh.

He switched on his computer and pulled his notes together while it booted up.

"We got an ID on the last vic, Sheriff." The anxious deputy passed him a folder. "Peggy Wallace. Age thirty-three, a school teacher from Austin."

Coop glanced at the driver's license photo, and leaned forward. "I think I've seen her before." Thick brows drew together in a tight line as he racked his brain for information. "It's the hair. You don't see that white-blonde color very often." He tapped the photo. "I'm pretty sure she's been a guest at Eva's."

He reached for the phone on his desk, but stopped. "I'll be back shortly. If she was a guest at The Grove, Eva will remember. Maybe help us piece together a timeline." He grabbed his hat on the way out. "In the meantime, see what else you can find out about her. Where she was going, anything."

It's me.

The Voice's pronouncement followed him to the car. Once behind the wheel, he vented his frustration. "These damn cryptic messages are driving me crazy! What do you want from me? And why the hell can't you say more than a few words at a time?"

Silence answered him.

Ten minutes later, he pulled into the drive.

Sam swept the front porch while Jack lounged on the steps. "Hi there. Didn't expect you home so soon." Her smile of welcome quickly vanished. "What's wrong? Not another body?"

"Where's Eva?"

Her brows drew together in a tight frown. "The front parlor, working on the books."

He headed for the door, and stopped. "Maybe you should come, too. I'm not sure how she'll handle this."

Color drained from her face. "Oh my God, Coop, what's wrong?"

He held up the folder. "ID on the last victim. Might have been a guest here. One of those women Eva wanted to set me up with."

Silent, they entered the parlor.

"Coop wh –" Eva stopped and looked from one to the other. "What's wrong? Is it Jason?"

"No, no, nothing like that," said Coop. "I need you to look at a photo and tell me if you recognize it."

"…Okay."

Coop pulled the picture from the file and passed it to her.

She gasped and put a hand to her throat. "Peggy Wallace. She was here last month. I remember because of the hair. And her personality…such a lost and lonely soul." She looked at Coop, eyes filled with sadness. "She's the other one, isn't she?"

"I think so. I need anything you might remember about her; when she arrived, how long she stayed. All of it."

Eva pulled a ledger from a desk drawer and thumbed through it. "Here it is. Told me this was her last week of freedom before school started again. She booked August third through the ninth, but, checked out a day early."

"Did she say anything about people she met here?"

Eva's cheeks turned a bright rosy-red as she glanced back and forth from him to Sam. "Only you. Which is my fault." The older woman squirmed in her chair, obviously uncomfortable with the topic. "I had high hopes when I first spoke with her on the phone. After we met, though, I knew it would never work, so didn't encourage her."

Thrown off by the admission, he asked. "Why? I thought that was your number one priority."

She closed the ledger and looked at him, blue eyes full of compassion. "I hate to speak ill of the dead, but," she huffed out a breath. "Bless her heart, she was a hot mess, as they say today."

"In what way?"

Her gnarled fingers slid over the ledger's rough exterior, eyes downcast. "She seemed to be, um…I think the term is a party girl." Faded blue eyes softened as she looked at him. "She said she just wanted a good time, but down deep, I think she was a terribly lonely woman. She had just broke up with a long-time boyfriend." She glanced between them, cheeks coloring again. "The night you joined us for dessert meant a lot to her. She said you treated her like she mattered." She paused in thought. "Let's see…that was Thursday night. You left for Austin the next day for your sheriff's meeting. She left on Saturday."

"She didn't say anything about where she went or who she saw?"

"No, not really. She mentioned sightseeing, shopping on the square, ate at Bub's. She did go to Teddy's on Friday night and was late getting home. Then late Saturday afternoon, she came down with her luggage. She said her plans changed, and she checked out."

His pulse quickened. *Teddy's. The first victim went there, too. Was that the connection?*

"Did she seem upset or anything?"

"No. In fact, she seemed quite happy, like the change in plans was a good thing."

He gave her a light kiss on the cheek. "Thanks." He stuffed the photo back in the file and took Sam's hand. "No leaving the house alone until this is settled. Please. And Jack doesn't count as company."

Twin lines of worry appeared between her eyes, but her voice remained light. "Well, since you said please…oh wait. I'm supposed to meet with Doc and his attorney this afternoon at the clinic."

"What time?"

"Four."

"I'll pick you up at three-thirty."

"I hate to bother you. I can drive myself. Jack will be with me."

"Sam –"

"You know how Jack is. He won't let anyone near me."

He hesitated, mulling over the long list of things he needed to do regarding the investigations. "Fine. Drive yourself, but call me when you leave here, and when you get there."

"I will."

"And call me when you're done. I'll follow you home."

"Coop –"

"Call me."

"You know you're really bossy, right?"

"Part of my charm." Satisfied she would follow his dictates, he turned to leave, swiveled around, and kissed those luscious lips because he couldn't resist the temptation any longer. "I pick the movie tonight."

Teddy's had to be the key.

CHAPTER TWENTY-FIVE

Sam took the chair beside Doc Harper as the attorney, Anson McElroy, strode to the chair behind the desk. Younger than she expected and all business, he had striking whiskey-colored eyes, chiseled features, and perfectly coifed, dark-brown hair. He carried himself with a commanding air of self-confidence as he sat down and placed his briefcase on the corner. His woodsy cologne reminded her of pine trees and lemons.

Sam watched in morbid fascination as he methodically pulled out a dark blue folder and positioned it squarely in front of him. Next, he tugged a white handkerchief from the inside pocket of his dark suit. He blew on each lens of wire-rimmed glasses and rubbed them with a hankie before stuffing it back in his pocket.

All without saying a word to them.

He adjusted the glasses on his face. "I think I have everything in order." A strong velvet edged voice. A lawyer's voice. "Of course, Dr. Fowler, you will want your own attorney to look them over."

"He's expecting the documents this week."

He nodded. "I'd like to go over the particulars in detail, then we can discuss any changes."

By five-thirty, her brain was fried.

A stickler for details, the attorney insisted on going over every one of them. Twice. But, in the end, all parties were in agreement.

McElroy clicked his pen a couple of times as he read over his notes, then put it in his breast pocket, and stood. "It's been a pleasure working with you, Dr. Fowler. I'm delighted someone such as yourself decided to become part of our little town."

A subtle change in his voice showed the shift from lawyer mode to interested male. Determined to retain the client-attorney relationship, she stood. "Thank you, Mr. McElroy. I'm looking forward to setting up my practice here."

"Anson here is a third-generation lawyer," offered Doc. "His father and grandfather both practiced in the same office he uses."

"I'm sure they're very proud of you carrying on the family tradition."

"They were. Both gone now," said Anson. "What about you? Are you carrying on the tradition?"

"Afraid not. I'm from a family of cops."

"Really?" He returned the document to the briefcase and snapped it shut. "What made you decide to become a doctor?" His cheeks flushed. "I'm sorry. That was a bit too personal."

"It's okay. I've always wanted to be a doctor." Her voice grew bubbly as memories flashed through her mind. "I can remember as a child lining up all my dolls and stuffed animals and doing check-ups and operations on them. I even practiced on my brothers."

"How many brothers do you have?"

His heavy cologne now permeated the stuffy room, and she needed fresh air soon. She slipped her purse strap over her shoulder. "Two. Both older. Both cops."

He picked up the briefcase and came around the desk. "And they live in Dallas?"

"Yes." She turned to Doc Harper who barely managed to stifle a yawn. "You mentioned me coming by to spend some time getting to know the patients. Do you think I could do so this week? Maybe Wednesday or Thursday? I could come for some or all of the day."

"How about Thursday and Friday? I only work till noon on Wednesdays."

"Works for me." She turned to the attorney and extended her hand. "Thank you very much for all your hard work on this, Mr. McElroy, and for the expediency of it as well."

"My pleasure. And please, call me Anson."

His grip was firm, his fingers cool, making the old adage *cold hands, warm heart* pop into her head. He held on a fraction longer than necessary, and his steady gaze was discomforting.

She pulled her hand away and resisted the urge to wipe the palm on her leg. "Thank you." The omission of his name wasn't an accident.

"I'll get the changes made tomorrow and have copies sent to both of you. I'll also overnight copies to your attorney." He reached for her hand again, dark eyes intent as they connected with hers. "Let me know if I can do anything…*anything* at all for you."

Female spidey-sense kicked into overdrive and her initial opinion morphed from straight-forward attorney to slimy bastard. Pretty to look at, but darkness lurked inside.

He turned his attention to Harper. "Let me know if you need something else, Doc."

"I will, son, I will." The old man grunted as he pushed

himself from the chair and extended his hand. "I appreciate everything you do for me."

The look he gave Sam could best be described as a leer before he turned and strode out the door in long purposeful strides.

"Give me a few minutes to lock up, Sam, and I'll walk you out."

"Thanks, Dr. Harper. I need to call Coop, and let him know we're done."

"Ever'one calls me Doc. You do the same."

Coop answered on the first ring. "Why didn't you take Jack inside with you?"

"Hello to you, too. Yes, the meeting is finally over, and it went fine."

She heard him grind his teeth.

"Jack needs to be where you are. All the time. Period."

"He needed to go outside."

"All the time, Sam."

"Fine. I'll keep him with me in the office when I come back."

There was a short pause on the other end as she visualized him counting to ten.

"I was beginning to wonder if Anson would keep y'all all night."

"You know how long-winded lawyers are."

"I know how Anson is. Especially around pretty women." Something in his voice said he didn't much care for the attorney.

"I'm parked out back where the staff parks. Doc is locking up. We'll be out in a minute."

"I'm out back with Jack now. He's pissed cause you didn't

let him come back inside."

It was her turn to count. No point in both of them being mad. "I'll be right out."

Doc met her in the hallway. "Coop is outside, Doc, so I'm leaving now. I'll see you Thursday about nine?"

"Nine is good."

They exited the building together.

"Howdy, Sheriff."

"Doc."

"Y'all have a good evening," said Doc as he stuffed himself inside his SUV.

Sam didn't need a degree in psychology to recognize the alpha male stance of the man who frequently invaded her every thought.

He stood beside her truck, both feet planted firmly on the ground, arms folded over a broad chest, eyes hidden by dark shades.

Jack lay on the ground at his feet like some adoring fan.

A spark of annoyance flashed. Jack was her dog. Hers. And then it dawned on her. Jack hadn't abandoned her or tossed her over for someone else. He merely added Coop to his extremely small circle of friends. Family.

Like a caffeine buzz, happiness coursed through her. A man she barely knew had managed to unlock the bars around her heart which now pounded with new-found life. She gave up trying to convince herself it was nothing. It was everything. *He* was everything.

She loved him; with every fiber of her being, she loved him.

Coop fully intended to read Sam the riot act for not keeping Jack with her, but the minute she stepped out, his mouth went dry, and the words lodged in his throat.

She moved toward him slowly, like a model or a dancer, hips swaying, her sinfully delicious mouth edged up in a mysterious half smile. Wind tossed ebony tresses shimmered like polished glass, and blue eyes flashed azure fire.

She had him by the short hairs. And knew it.

One brow arched up when she stopped a few feet away. "Did you have something else to say?"

He did. He was sure of it. He just couldn't remember what.

Streaks of summer lightening filled the eyes staring at him. She uncrossed his arms, and slid her hands up his chest. "Well?"

How could one word, spoken on a breathless whisper, be an utterly sensual experience, and an absolute turn-on?

Suddenly thankful for the secluded parking lot, he pulled her to him, rougher than he should have, but unable to tamp down the white-hot desire inside, and devoured her mouth with deep, sweeping strokes of his tongue.

She returned his kiss with reckless abandon as his hands explored the length of her back, dropping down to cup her bottom, pulling her against his hardness.

A soft moan escaped as she molded herself against him.

The undeniable magnetism surged between them and he gave up fighting the inevitable. Love? Lust? He didn't know. All he knew for certain was, before Sam, his life was an empty, meaningless shell. Without her, the dark chasm of loneliness would engulf him again.

The shrill blast of a train whistle behind the lot brought an abrupt end to their unintentional foreplay.

Please let it be foreplay.

They pulled apart, foreheads touching, chests heaving as they gulped air.

"Good God, woman, you're going to be the death of me."

Her finger lightly traced the outline of a button on his shirt. "I'm really not in a movie mood tonight."

His heart pounded at the implications in her words.

"…Did you…have something else in mind?" Even to him his voice sounded rough.

"Uh-huh."

When she met his desire-clogged gaze with one of her own, the world tilted on its axis, causing his head to spin.

"Jason is back at school. Eva has bridge tonight."

She glanced at him through lowered lashes, the image so seductive, his mouth went dry as the West Texas desert in July.

"I could cook for us—or something."

Only a fool would go with option one.

Cooper Delaney was a lot things; a fool wasn't one of them.

CHAPTER TWENTY-SIX

A myriad of thoughts congested Sam's mind as she drove home. Never one to deceive herself, she reasoned the thing between them may be nothing more than physical need, which could prove disastrous.

But her heart believed otherwise. The last few days spent getting to know each other reinforced her belief that it went way beyond the physical.

She pulled into the drive and stopped, thankful Eva had already left for her bridge game.

They walked in silence into the kitchen, Jack on their heels, seemingly ignorant of the violent tangle of emotions ripping through his mistress.

They stood by the counter where a note from Eva caught Sam's eye. She picked it up for something to do. "Um, she left food on the stove, so I guess I don't have to cook."

She didn't look at Coop, who cleared his throat but didn't comment.

The silence became uncomfortable, and she groped for words. *I practically gave him an engraved invitation, so the next move is his. Right?*

Since playing the saucy seductress wasn't her strong suit, she opted for the straight-forward approach. Sam drew in a deep lungful of air and turned to face him. The smoldering look in those storm-cloud eyes derailed her train of thought.

His hungry gaze drank in her face, her lips and lowered to her breasts, causing the tips to become painfully tight. His nostrils flared when he inhaled deeply, his stare bold and relentless as it traveled down, then back up her body.

In a flash, the path became clear. She wanted him more than the air she breathed. Her love grew with each rapid beat of her heart. Tomorrow wasn't promised to anyone. There was only today. Now. This moment in time.

Without regret, she yielded to the firestorm of need building from their first glance. One step closed the distance between them. His heart pounded out a staccato beneath her palm on his chest.

"Are you sure about this?" His words, ground out through slightly parted lips, were gruff and thick with emotion.

He stood rigidly in place as she kissed the base of his neck, his chin. Standing on tiptoes, she nibbled his lower lip. "I'm sure."

He moaned deep in his throat. "Sam." The touch of his hands was unbearably tender as he cupped her face. His lips pressed against hers, urgent and exploratory.

She raised up to meet his kiss with a hunger that belied her outer calm.

His mouth scorched a path down her neck, her shoulder, before recapturing her lips, more demanding this time, setting her body ablaze.

Suddenly, he pulled back and swept her into his arms.

Jack snuffled and Sam twisted to look at him.

"Stay," she said sharply and the dog went to his spot under the table.

She looked into the eyes of the man who owned her heart. "You're going to carry me upstairs?"

"You don't think I can?"

She slid her arms around his neck. "I think you can do anything you put your mind to."

"Your place or mine?"

"Your bed is bigger."

By the time he kicked the door shut behind them, Sam was on fire.

He set her feet on the floor beside the bed and proceeded to do carnal things to her mouth. His tongue caressed and coaxed as his hands gripped her hips, anchoring her snugly against the evidence of his excitement.

She gripped the edge of his shirt and yanked it from his jeans, fingers fumbling with the western snaps.

Hands on top of hers, he stilled their progress. "I want you to know something, Sam." His gaze bored into her. "There's never been a woman in here." His head rolled side to side as though amazed at something. "I've never felt this way about anyone before. I don't know what it is, but I want to enjoy every moment of it." His grip tightened as he spoke. "I want you so bad, I can't think straight. But, I'd like to take this slow." He kissed the tip of her nose. "To savor every moment." He brushed his lips across her forehead. "I want to remember exactly how you look standing here." His hands slid down her arms to her waist, coming to rest on her hips. "How it feels to undress you, one button at a time until you are naked, lying in my bed. Waiting."

Sam couldn't get enough air. Those softly spoken words were more powerful than any aphrodisiac, skyrocketing her desire and cementing her love.

A shiver ran though her as she basked in the passion flowing from those grey orbs. "Slow is over-rated."

The sensual upturn of his mouth made her knees weak.

"Not if it's done right." He took one of her hands and stepped back to give her space. "Kick off your shoes. Slowly."

Anticipation hurried her along as first one, then the other ended up across the room.

"That wasn't slow."

He moved to the chair beside the bed and sat down. "This is slow." Eyes locked with hers, he toed the heel of one boot off and placed it beside the chair. The second one soon followed. "Come here."

When she stood in front of him, he skimmed his hands over her hips, leisurely pulled the blouse from the waistband of her slacks, and slid his hands underneath to cup her breasts before he slid his hands down her sides to her hips, and let the shirttail fall. With deliberate care, he opened each button of her blouse. One. By. One.

She gasped when his warm breath touched her skin, followed by the lightest touch of his lips. Hands fisted in his hair held him in place as his tongue slid over her body.

Her stomach clinched, and her knees threatened to give way when he licked the exposed flesh with agonizing precision.

A gentle nudge and the silky fabric pooled on the floor behind her. Callused hands once again cupped the laced-covered fullness of her breasts, thumbs rubbing the hard peaks until she squirmed and pressed against them.

"Still think slow is over-rated?" His mouth traced the path of his thumbs, teeth scraping across each sensitive point, muffling his words.

"Wh-who c-can think?"

He undid the leather belt on her slacks and released the button. The raspy slide of the zipper turned her knees to Jello and reduced each breath to a jerky gasp.

The only thing preventing her from melting into a puddle on the floor was a firm grip on his shoulders. Every nerve in her body tingled with anticipation as the material slithered down her hips. Heat rippled under her skin as a rush of desire unlike anything she'd ever known coursed through her.

His lips seared a path down her ribcage to her stomach while one hand explored her soft, inner thigh. "Coop…"

He stood and crushed her to him, the hunger of his lips sending her to new heights of ecstasy. He showered moist kisses along her jaw, to the base of her neck and across her shoulder. In a heartbeat, her bra joined the growing pile on the floor.

She swooned and gripped the front of his shirt. "I need to touch you." Slender fingers shook as she pulled the edges of his shirt apart, the snaps making it easy to rid him of it. His tee shirt followed in rapid succession. She ran her fingers through the thick mat of curls, before leaning in to nip at one tight nipple.

His tormented groan proved a heady invitation, and she repeated the maneuver on the other one. She tugged at the buttons on his jeans, fingers pressing against his hot center, producing another groan of pleasure.

She ran her hands up his chest, raking her nails over the dark nipples, enjoying the way his muscles tightened and jerked when she rubbed her cheek against him before teasing the taunt nubs with her tongue.

"Damn, Sam."

She raised up and kissed him, gasping when her pebble-hard nipples scraped against his hair-roughened chest, then slowly skimmed his jeans past his hips. Her cheek grazed him as she pushed them past his knees to the floor, taking his boxers, too.

"Shit!"

The touch of skin against skin as he eased her back on the bed stoked the fire inside.

"You take my breath away."

The words, spoken with whispered reverence, went straight to her heart.

His kiss was achingly tender as one hand explored her body. He fondled each smooth globe, rolling the marble-hard tip between his thumb and index finger until she squirmed and moaned.

She arched up to meet him when his warm mouth covered her breast, his tongue rolling over the peak, teeth scraping against the responsive tip before he suckled each one. Her stomach convulsed when his fingertips skated around her navel. She held her breath as they teased the soft skin of her inner thigh, edging upwards to palm her femininity, fingers playing around the edges of the scrap of lace, before dipping inside.

Her nails dug in to the hard tendons of his back and neck as he delved into her delicate softness, making her buck forward. "Coop!"

He found her center, stroking it until she cried out again. When the bit of lace disappeared, and his mouth replaced his fingers, she couldn't control an outcry of delight.

Coherent thought shattered as his hands and lips continued their greedy exploration of her body until it convulsed in a crescendo of pleasure so intense, she whimpered and shook head-to-toe.

He poised over her, body glistening with sweat, eyes

focused on hers. "What have you done to me?" he whispered.

She raised up on her elbows and kissed him. "Nothing more than you have done to me."

Restraint vanished as he pushed at her entrance. Strong arms trembled as he held back, until finally, with a guttural groan, he buried himself in her softness.

Ankles crossed over his back, their bodies in perfect harmony as, gazes locked, they found their tempo.

Slow and steady became fast and furious as they soared ever higher until the ultimate peak was reached and they exploded in deluge of fiery sensations.

Surges of ecstasy throbbed through her as she surrendered to the numbed sleep of a satisfied lover.

CHAPTER TWENTY-SEVEN

Coop woke to the warmth of Sam snuggled against him, her head resting in the hollow of his neck, their legs entwined.

He ran his hand down her arm to rest on her waist, his body already gaining momentum for round three, the corners of his mouth edging up in a self-satisfied smile.

Sam sighed and nestled closer, one hand splayed over his chest, her knee brushing against him.

A deep sense of peace settled over him as realization dawned; the huge chunk missing from his life slept beside him.

But how did she feel about him? She desired him to be sure, but did it go beyond the physical?

He's watching her.

Coop flinched at The Voice's intrusion on this special moment. *Not now,* he mentally pleaded, *not now.*

He's watching her.

Who's watching who, dammit! Give me something more to go on!

"Coop? What's wrong?" Sam leaned on her elbow, and peered at him with anxious eyes.

He blinked and wondered if he'd spoken out loud or perhaps she heard the voice as well. "Nothing's wrong."

"You're tense all over and your face looks like you sucked a lemon."

He pulled her on top of him, not ready to talk about it, or willing to give up this time with her. "Maybe I was disappointed you fell asleep on me."

She settled herself along the length of him, one hand brushing aside his hair, those deep blue pools piercing his soul.

"Something's bothering you." She chewed her lower lip. "I hope it's not me."

He opened his mouth to protest, but she covered his lips with her fingers.

"I don't sleep around, Dee. Something about you got to me the first time we met, and it's grown stronger every day since."

She squared her shoulders and inhaled deeply as though preparing herself for some unpleasant task.

"I never thought it would happen to me, but –"

He turned his head to remove her fingers from his mouth, joyful heart anticipating her words. "You rocked my world from the get-go, Sam, and it's been rocking ever since." His thumb caressed her lower lip. "I think it's safe to say the feelings are mutual."

Something brilliant and earth-shattering flashed in her eyes. She leaned forward, her breasts brushing against his chest, and covered his mouth with hers in a savoring, lingering kiss.

Rational thought vanished.

More than sexual desire, it signified a blending of hearts.

When she straddled him, the pleasure was pure and explosive; a raw act of possession.

He belonged to her. She belonged to him.

Hypnotized by the love flowing from her like warm honey, he surrendered completely to her slow, deliberate seduction.

The slide of her sweat-coated body against his was exquisite torture. He couldn't get enough. His neck arched and he gripped her hips, thrusting upward.

She pushed at his hands. "Slow is good, remember?"

He groaned in sweet agony as her raw sensuousness carried him way beyond anything he could have imagined.

Their moves gained momentum until they shattered into a million points of light, their breath coming in long, shuddering moans as currents of pleasure pulsed through them.

Gasping for air, Sam collapsed on his chest. It was some time before she slid off, and snuggled by his side.

"Wanna talk about it now?"

Her quiet question pulled him from the edge of exhausted sleep. "About what?"

"Whatever troubled you earlier. And don't try and tell me it was nothing."

For a moment he considered the old *just work stuff* answer. But he didn't want to start their relationship off with a lie. On the other hand, he didn't want her to think he was crazy, either.

She believes in ghosts, thinks her grandmother talks to her. Maybe she won't think I'm crazy. "It's…complicated."

"I'm a doctor. I deal with complications all the time." She rubbed a circle on his chest. "But I understand if it's something you'd rather not talk to me about."

"It's not that I don't want to."

She raised up to look at him. "Then what is it?"

He clamped his jaw tight, released it. "You'll think I'm crazy."

"Try me."

His heart pounded as he read the understanding in her eyes. And he told her. All of it.

She never even flinched.

"And you think the voice is Peggy?"

"Yeah. Maybe." He looked away. "I told you it was crazy."

"I don't think it's crazy at all." She waited for him to look at her. "Like I said before…I believe there are things in this world science and logic can't explain." She paused. "Why do you think she speaks to you? Did you…know her well?" She failed to cover the other unspoken question in her voice.

"No. I only talked to her a time or two here. I did my best to hide when Eva started having single women as guests."

Her fingers rubbed absent circles on his chest. "I read somewhere that spirits can sometimes attach themselves to someone for no apparent reason."

"To be honest, I felt sorry for her. She seemed, I don't know, lost maybe. She and Eva were having a late dinner one night when I got home. I had dessert with them and left as soon as I could." Those grey orbs held hers. "I meant what I said, Sam…no other woman has been in here."

She kissed his nose. "I know." She looked away, then back to him. "…I found her body because something called me there."

His brow furrowed. "What do you mean, called you there?"

She couldn't meet his fierce gaze as she told him about her first trip to the lake, the cold air around her, and the feeling of being pulled toward where the body lay buried. "That's why I went back. I had to know if it was real or imagined." She sat up, oblivious to the fact she was naked in his bed. "It was worse the second time." She wrapped her arms around her middle as she recalled finding the grave, the crushing sense of loss. "The sadness was overwhelming."

"So…you're a psychic?"

The way he said the word psychic bothered her, and she paused. "Not psychic. I just sometimes sense strong emotions in other people, though it doesn't happen very often. And never like it did with Peggy."

"How does it work? This sensing thing?"

Unsure of his reaction, she hesitated.

"I'm trying hard to understand, Sam. I am. I'm way out of my comfort zone with this crap." He reached for her hand. "I'm sorry. I didn't mean it to sound like I thought what you said was crap. I meant…hell, I don't know what I meant beyond I'm just trying to understand some really weird stuff."

"…I don't know. It…just happens sometimes." She rubbed the top of his hand. "It happened a little bit with the first body. With Peggy…it was so much more intense." She lifted a shoulder, didn't look at him. "Like I said, there's no rhyme or reason to it. It just happens."

They remained silent for several heartbeats, each trying to process something way beyond their ability to interpret.

"Okay," she said at last, "let's just agree some things can't be explained away and go from there." She glanced at the clock on his night stand. "Oh my goodness! It's after midnight. Eva came home hours ago. What if she heard us?"

He pulled her down beside him. "Let's get some sleep. You wore me out."

"I can't stay here all night. And besides, I need a shower."

"Why can't you stay?"

"Duh. She'll know."

His devilish grin made her heart jump. "You're noisy. I'm betting she already does."

Face burning hot, she slapped at his shoulder. "I am not."

"Are, too." He pulled the sheet up over them and kissed the top of her head. "I need sleep. We can shower in the morning."

Common sense urged her to argue, to get up and retreat to her own room, but common sense was no match for the rightness of lying beside him, and she snuggled closer.

One thought danced around her head as exhaustion claimed her: *I love you Cooper Delaney. Ghosts and all.*

CHAPTER TWENTY-EIGHT

Tuesday morning

Coop threw his hat toward the rack in the corner and fell into his chair. His day got off to a great start with Sam in his bed, but took a decided downward turn when he entered the office of Ruby's Diner a few minutes ago. He had avoided the place for weeks, but since rumors would fly, he needed to tell Ruby once again, they could never be more than friends.

She didn't seem surprised by the news, even wished him well, but the hurt in her eyes made him feel like the devil incarnate.

"You never made your feelings a secret, Coop," she'd said, "I hoped things might shift, of course, but we've been friends a long time. That will never change."

The trek back to the office allowed him a few minutes to work off the anger he held against himself. He disliked hurting innocent people. And he did care about Ruby, just not like she wanted.

He caught a whiff of Sam's perfume when he reached over to power up the old computer, and more pleasant memories interrupted his concentration. Sam, last night in his bed, and this morning in the shower.

Pleasant company and good-humored conversation at breakfast, and then a kiss goodbye as he left for work. Everything absent from his life, suddenly there.

It was a lot to take in.

"Sheriff?"

JD's voice jerked Coop back to the present. "Yeah. What's up?"

"Something kept calling me back to the video from Sunday night." The deputy opened a folder in his hands. "I went back over it practically one frame at a time." He passed Coop a DVD. "Run this to time stamp 10:33:22."

Coop did as he requested. "What am I looking for?"

"Maybe nothing. Just thought it was interesting."

After reaching the designated spot, he hit pause. "Okay. 10:33:22." He peered at the screen. "What did you see?"

"Upper right hand corner. Who do you see?"

Coop rubbed his eyes and looked at the fuzzy image again. "Is that—Anson McElroy?"

"Who's he talking to?"

"Sonofabitch!"

"You can't get a good look at her face, just her blouse and the hair, but I believe that's our vic."

Coop's heartrate accelerated as he inched the DVD forward. A slightly distorted profile view showed Anson definitely talking to a woman who could be Joyce Ayers before they move out of camera range. "Hard to tell if he's the guy we saw her with later at the bar. Shirt is dark, so could be. I'm just not sure."

"Yeah. And look here," said the deputy as he pointed to another partial image near the corner of the screen. "Mr. Puckett from the bank. Is he following them?"

"...I don't know." Coop glanced up. "I saw him in the parking lot on the other surveillance video getting it on with one of the waitresses."

"Yeah. I saw that, too." JD shook his head. "I always thought of him as a pretty-boy type. Never pictured him as a player."

"Me neither. I'll go back and look at it again. I think it was later, but not sure." Coop blew out a long breath. "Can't believe I missed both of those."

"I looked at this thing three times before I saw them. And if I hadn't been looking at it really slow, wouldn't have seen it then cause they are in and out of the frame so fast. Teddy needs to invest in better equipment. The quality sucks."

Coop stood and reached for his hat. "I'm going to talk to Anson. You talk to Puckett." He looked at the clock on the wall. "Sam is probably at the bank with Puckett right now. Give them half an hour, then call and have him come by the office. Show him pictures of both women. We'll meet back here after lunch."

"Roger that."

Sam's ring tone caught him at the door. "Delaney."

"Hey."

Sam's voice instantly lifted his sober mood. "Hey. You through with Puckett already?"

"He moved our appointment to this afternoon. I'm headed over to Mr. McElroy's instead. My attorney approved the paperwork, so I'm going to his office and sign my life away."

Coop paused. "You're headed there now?"

"Yeah. I just called and he's expecting me. He has court in an hour and wanted me to come on now. Is something wrong?"

"What? Oh no. Lot on my mind this morning." *Like whether I need to be there with you or not.* "Actually, I need a favor."

"I just happen to be in a favor granting mood this morning."

"Would you mind putting off seeing Anson till later? I need to bend his ear on some work stuff that really can't wait."

"Of course not. Eva wanted me to pick up some things at Arnolds anyway. I'll call him back and set it up for later."

"I'll take care of it. I'm almost there and I'll let him know. Any particular time you want to see him?"

"No, just whatever works for him."

"I'll let you know what he says."

"Thanks. I'll call you when I get back to the house."

"Sounds good."

He saw JD coming out and motioned him over. "Puckett won't be in till later."

"Yeah. His secretary told me."

"Sam was headed to Anson's to sign the papers on Doc's place. I asked her to put it off till later so I could talk to him first."

"So, what's the plan?"

"I'll talk to Anson." He chewed his lip as his mind raced. "Call Puckett at home or on his cell and ask him to come by the office. He's on the council so no one will think anything about it. If we go to him, folks might talk."

"Copy that."

Ten minutes later, Coop sat opposite the lawyer who appeared aloof and disinterested. Perhaps too aloof, pushing his cop instincts to full alert.

"As I said, I have court in less than an hour. Judge Walker has no tolerance for tardiness in his courtroom."

"I appreciate you seeing me. I won't take up too much of your time."

"What's this about?"

"I'm investigating the deaths of two women. I'm sure you heard about it."

He glanced pointedly at his watch. "What's that got to do with me?"

"You were at Teddy's last Sunday night."

"So were half the men in the county." He squared the yellow tablet in front of him. "Ladies' Night, you know. Even saw your impertinent secretary there."

Coop ignored the comment. "What time did you arrive?"

"I didn't check the time."

"What time did you leave?"

"I don't remember."

"Did you leave alone?"

A muscle twitched in his jaw and his eyes narrowed slightly. "I can't see that as being any of your business."

Coop pulled Joyce Ayers' photo from the folder he carried and slid it across the desk. "Recognize this woman?"

A tic above Anson's left eye was the only visible reaction to Coop's question. "No."

"You were seen talking with her Sunday night."

"I talked with a lot of women."

"This one ended up dead."

Anson's faced reddened, and he sat up straighter in his chair. "I made the rounds, talked with a lot of women. I left alone. I don't know what time. Now, if you'll excuse me, I'm due in court."

Before Coop could respond, the lawyer stood holding the door open.

"I'll be in touch," said Coop as he walked out.

"Bring a warrant, or you'll be wasting your time."

CHAPTER TWENTY-NINE

"Thank you so much for shopping for me, Sam." Eva stirred a pot on the stove, then pushed a silver curl away from her flushed face. "I feel like I'm meeting myself coming back these days."

"I'm very glad to help in any way I can." Sam considered her next statement carefully, not wanting to appear rude. "I know you love what you do, but really, Eva, you don't need to do so much for me. I mean, I appreciate it, I really do, but you work much too hard."

She smoothed down the front of her apron, cheeks a rosy pink. "You sound like Coop. He tells me that all the time."

"At least consider letting me help out some while I'm here."

"You aren't thinking of leaving are you?" Eva's face wrinkled up in a frown. "We'd be so disappointed."

"No. At least not right away. I love being here, but I just don't want you to work yourself down doing too much." On impulse, she put her hands on Eva's shoulders. "I'll make a deal with you. I won't leave anytime soon if you let me help out. I can't cook as well as you but I can help in other ways, and I can certainly clean and do laundry."

Her head bobbed in agreement. "Deal." Eva covered one

of Sam's hands with her own. "I'm so glad to see you and Coop together. You have no idea what a difference you have made in his life."

"He's made a big difference in mine as well. As have you." She gently rubbed the older woman's arms. "You are a wonderful human being. Thank you for all that you do for me. For us."

Flustered, Eva waved a hand in front of her face. "Don't make me get all misty-eyed. We have work to do."

"What can I do to help?"

The rest of morning flew by as the two women worked together to complete necessary chores. At Eva's request, Sam put a note on the B&B website stating they were not booking rooms for a while, and later, she did something she hadn't done in a long time. Laundry. And loved every minute of the whole domesticated process.

After lunch, she gathered up what she needed for her appointment with Mr. Puckett at the bank, left a message for Coop on his cell, and drove to town. Anson would be in court all afternoon, but she was to drop by his office on the way home to sign the papers.

Outside the banker's glassed-in office, the dour-faced secretary barely glanced up when she told Sam to take a seat, and he'd be with her soon.

Her first impression of James Puckett wasn't so flattering, either.

He made a steeple with his fingers as he sat behind his desk like a king granting an audience to a subordinate. His icy smile held no mirth.

The man, dressed in bib overalls and boots, appeared nervous, constantly rolling a worn straw hat in his hands.

Suddenly feeling like an eavesdropper, Sam turned her

attention to the small lobby. People came and went with smooth efficiency, a few stopping to speak to her, which both surprised and pleased her, while others nodded or tipped their western hats in greeting. *I made the right decision. I belong here.*

A few minutes later, the door to Puckett's office opened. Sam recognized the farmer exiting as someone she had met at Bub's the other day, though his name escaped her at the moment. She stood, prepared to speak as he passed, but he went by so quickly, she didn't get a chance.

"You can go in now." The secretary's droll voice lacked any warmth or friendship.

Everything about Puckett shouted self-confidence and a cock-of-the-walk attitude. His stylish blue-grey suit fit to perfection, the color several shades darker than the eyes boldly giving her a thorough once-over.

"I can't tell you how much I enjoyed your delicious chocolate cake," he crooned as he grabbed her in a two-handed shake. "A beautiful woman who cooks like an angel is rare indeed."

The touch of his left hand as it cupped her arm gave her the creeps. "Thank you, Mr. Puckett." She pulled her hand from his too-tight grasp, and took a slight step toward the chair recently vacated by the farmer, but he retained his light grip on her upper arm. "I appreciate the kind words."

"Please, call me James, Sam. We're not much on formality around here." One finger skimmed over her skin as his hand slid down her arm. "Perhaps I could persuade you to make me another cake some time. One we could enjoy together."

Having seen the wedding ring on his left hand, his comment left her momentarily speechless. She straightened her shoulders and fixed him with an icy stare. "I don't think so, Mr. Puckett. Now, can we please conclude our business? I have several errands to complete this afternoon."

"Of course." Apparently undaunted by her rejection, he continued in a lower, huskier tone. "Just let me know when you change your mind."

The words, spoken with the absolute certainty of a man who fully expected her to succumb to his charm, infuriated her. *Not in this life asshole.*

He returned to his chair and opened a folder. "I have everything ready to set up the accounts you requested."

His intercom buzzed and he picked it up. "I told you I wasn't to be interrupted." His tone resonated impatience. "What does he want? Fine. Put him through." He looked at Sam. "Excuse me. I need to take this."

"Should I wait outside?"

"No, it's quite all right." He turned his attention to the caller. "Good afternoon, JD. Yes, I got your message, but I have a customer to take care of first."

His gaze found hers, then slid to her breasts. He licked his lower lip as he listened to the caller.

In the space of a few seconds, she pegged him as cold and calculating, like a wolf watching a fawn. A predator. The man had no morals. None.

"What's this about?"

She watched him stiffen as his expression faded from brazen to serious and perspiration popped out on his brow.

"I see. Of course. I'm almost done here. I'll drop by in a few minutes." He dropped the phone back in the cradle a little too hard, then shuffled the papers on his desk, visibly flustered and nervous. "Let's see. Where was I? Oh yes. I just need a signature on these pages."

In less than fifteen minutes, the paperwork was completed, and Puckett ushered her out the door to his secretary.

"I have a City Council matter to attend to, Mavis. Please finish up with Dr. Fowler. I'll be back shortly."

Sam looked at the woman as the banker hurried out the door. "He seems a little flustered doesn't he?"

She huffed out a breath and straightened her horn-rimmed glasses. "If you'll just look through this packet and pick out what style checks you what, I'll take care of the funds transfer. Do you have the routing and account numbers?"

Okay, then, let's just stick to business.

Over the next few minutes, several other people made a point to speak as she waited for Mavis to complete her tasks, and Sam decided her life could not be any more perfect. A town that felt like home, a new practice to focus on, and a man worth letting her guard down.

Yes, life was indeed, perfect.

CHAPTER THIRTY

He wants her.

"Who, Peggy?" muttered Coop, accepting the fact the voice belonged to the woman he deemed the other victim, Peggy Wallace. "Can't you give me more?"

The plea went unanswered, and his jaw clinched tight as he struggled for control. *I'm talking to a voice no one hears but me. I'm losing my fricking mind.*

Coop stopped in the act of getting up from his chair when JD tapped on the doorframe.

"You wanted to see me, Sheriff?"

He pulled his notepad forward. "Yeah. Spoke with the forensic guy from the Rangers today. They're still processing things. So far, though, nothing to report." He blew out a long breath. "Only odd thing was a couple of pink rose petals stuck to her back. That's it."

"What about under her fingernails? ME said she showed signs of fighting back."

"Bastard cleaned under them."

JD's eyes widened. "He had to know we'd check."

"Yeah. He's thorough. Used a condom and cleaned up after himself." Coop rubbed his temple, a headache slowly building. "They processed the car and got zilch. Still working on stuff from the site. Kids hang out there all the time, too, so a lot of trash to sort through."

"So we're back to square one?"

"Looks like it."

"What about the second vic? Any news on her?"

"Not yet. He said they are backed up, and will get to it as soon as they can." He rubbed his eyes. "But it's the same guy. I know it. Her right index finger was broken, too. Pretty advanced decomp so it's going to be hit or miss on anything useful. For now, we got nothing."

"I finished with Puckett."

"And?"

"The man was jumpy as a cat on a hot stove. Nearly choked when I told him we had him on camera in the parking lot and inside the bar."

"What about the women?"

"Recognized both right off. 'New meat' was how he described them." A muscle tensed in his jaw. "Pretty high opinion of himself. Claimed he sprung for a couple of drinks, hoped to get lucky, but didn't."

"What do you think?"

JD scratched his chin. "He's got the size, and about as conceited as they come. He could be the man at the bar, or it could be Billy Ray, or half a dozen others who were there that night." He focused on a spot in the ceiling, then shook his head. "I don't know. He's a cheating asshole more worried about his wife discovering his antics than being accused of murder." A shadow of annoyance crossed his face. "Seems whenever she makes her twice-monthly trip to Dallas to visit her mother, he heads over to Teddy's for some action." Jimmy shuffled his feet.

"What about Anson?"

"Smooth one. Didn't say much. We keep them on the person-of-interest list for now." Coop tapped a pencil on the corner of his desk. "Have we made contact with everyone who was there last Sunday? I know we had some travelers, but what about the locals?"

"We got everyone but Alice and Billy Ray." The deputy paused. "Did you know he was there?"

"Not surprised, but no, I didn't know. He likes the ladies. I talked to Alice this morning. She didn't remember either of the women. Said she talked some to Puckett, who she described as a sexist jerk, and saw Anson working the room. She didn't say anything about Billy Ray being there."

"Marla, she's the dark-haired waitress, is friends with Alice. Said she saw him in the corner with a woman she didn't know. Things got interesting when Alice saw them."

"Was she there with him?"

"Not that night. According to Marla, Alice has it bad for him. He's put her off for the most part. Said she's too young for him, but she keeps trying."

"What happened when she saw him with another woman?"

JD grinned. "She emptied a beer on his head and stomped out."

Coop sat up a little straighter. "What did he do?"

"According to Marla, he asked for a towel and wiped his head."

"He didn't go after her? Get mad?"

"Nope. In fact, Marla said he laughed and said something like *didn't see that coming*. The other woman left then. Marla got busy, and lost track of him." JD hesitated. "Want me to question him?"

Coop blew out a long breath and shook his head. "I'll do it. Is he here now?"

"Yeah."

"Thanks. I'll take care of it."

Twenty minutes later, Billy Ray stuck his head in the doorway. "You rang, Boss?"

Coop pushed the budget report aside and motioned to the chair in front of his desk. "Come in. Close the door."

Billy's smile vanished. "Sounds serious."

Coop waited until his friend sat down. "Why didn't you tell me you were at Teddy's last Sunday night?"

Tone even, Billy crossed his arms across his chest. "Why should I? It was my night off."

"A woman was murdered. You knew we were talking to anyone who was there, and yet, you never said a word."

He shifted in his seat, then uncrossed his arms. "I was there for a while. Talked to some people, danced a little and left."

"You were seen talking to the victim."

His chin rose a fraction of an inch. "I talked to several women that night."

Coop stared at him for a heartbeat, then pulled a photo from a folder, and passed it across the desk.

After a slight hesitation, Billy picked it up. "Yeah, I talked to her a few minutes." He tossed it back onto the desk. "She wasn't interested, so I moved on."

"What time did you leave?"

Bill's face reddened, and his lips formed a thin white line. "After Alice dumped beer on me."

"What time was that?"

Coop didn't miss the little tic above Bill's left eye or the thin bead of perspiration forming on his upper lip.

"Am I a suspect?" His voice tight and controlled, Billy glared at Coop. "Is that what this is about?"

Coop waited.

"Dammit, Coop." Bill swatted the air, and huffed out a breath. "You've known me all my life. How could you even think I'd be involved in shit like that?"

"What time, Bill?"

The strained silence lingered as Coop watched his friend struggle for control.

He sagged a little in his chair, then stared at a spot over Coop's right shoulder. "I don't know. Eleven or so. Didn't check the time."

"Were you alone?"

Bill's face flushed a deep red, and he looked away.

"Who was she, Bill?"

Coop thought for a moment he wouldn't answer and mentally geared up to push harder.

"Ruby," he snapped at last. "I left with Ruby."

Coop thought he hid his surprise well. Ruby was grown and free to make her own decisions, good, bad and otherwise. But, hook up with Billy Ray Thomas—the king of one-night-stands? No way did he expect that. He pushed personal feelings aside, and slid the other photo across the table. "How about this woman?"

Billy's eyes narrowed, and his jaw tightened before he snatched the photo off the desk. He glanced at it and shook his head. "I don't know. Something about the hair. I might have seen her before." He tossed the photo back onto the desk. "Anything else, *Sheriff Delaney?*"

Coop steeled himself against the raw hurt emanating

from Billy's hoarse voice. "That's all for now."

Silent, Billy stood in front of Coop's desk, hands on his hips, feet spread apart, face scrunched up in a heavy scowl. His mouth opened, then closed before he whirled around and stomped out.

Coop watched his best friend leave knowing he had shoved a huge wedge between them. But he had no choice. He had to find out who killed two innocent women. If it cost him Bill's friendship…well, he hoped it wouldn't come to that. But at the same time, he couldn't help but wonder why he had not come forward on his own. And did he have something to hide?

Coop rubbed the back of his neck, unable to ignore the instinct shouting Billy didn't give him the whole story. He pushed aside the worrying thought and stared at the phone on his desk, debating a call to Ruby versus in person to verify Bill's story. He gave a disgusted sigh and pushed up from his chair. It had to be in person. If he went now, he might have it over with before the lunch rush started.

Shit. Why did it have to be her?

Ten minutes later, he stared out the window of Ruby's tiny office waiting for her to return from the bank. The door opened, and she hurried in, a smile of welcome on her face.

"Hey, Coop. Two visits in one day. How did I get so lucky?"

He removed his hat and laid it on the desk. "I'll try and make this quick. I know you get pretty busy about this time."

She sat in the chair behind the desk and faced him. "My goodness. That scowl is serious. What's up?"

Warmth flooded his cheeks as he sank into an ancient straight-backed chair. "This is hard for me to ask, Ruby, but I have to."

Eyes guarded, she remained silent.

"Were you at Teddy's last Sunday night?"

She twitched, and drew in a deep breath. "Obviously you know I was or you wouldn't ask. But, if you need it official, then, yes, I was there. Marla convinced me I needed some adult time."

"What time did you leave?"

One shoulder rose, then fell. "Around eleven."

Muscles flexed in his jaw as he considered the next question, unable to avoid embarrassing his friend. "Alone?"

She gasped, and looked down, bright spots of red on each cheek. "Again, you know the answer or you wouldn't ask."

"Did you leave Teddy's alone Sunday night?"

"…No."

"Who did you leave with?"

Her head snapped up so fast a hair clip came undone and fell to the floor. She ignored it. Voice laced with humiliation and indignation, she stared him down. "So, just because you don't think I'm worthy of your attention, you think every man will feel the same way."

"That's not –"

Arms folded across her chest, her voice shook. "Then what is it?"

He heaved a heavy sigh. "A woman was murdered, Ruby, and I have a job to do."

She gaped at him. "You think I had something to do with that?"

"Of course not. I just need to know who you left with…. and what time you parted ways."

She clasped her hands on top of the desk so tightly, the knuckles turned white. "Fine," she snapped. "I left with Billy

Ray. We went back to my place."

He dreaded the hurt and embarrassment the next question would cause his friend. "I don't want to hurt you, Ruby. I don't. I know this is hard for you. It is for me, too. But I have to know. What time did he leave?"

The flush on her cheeks deepened, and her head bowed. "…I couldn't do it." She averted her gaze. "I thought I could, but I couldn't."

"Do what?"

She laced and unlaced her fingers. "…Sleep with him. I wanted to—to feel wanted. Special. But, with him, I'd be just another notch on his bedpost."

She looked up and he steeled himself against the hurt blazing in those amber eyes.

"I'm no saint, Coop. I've done my share of things I'm not proud of. Had some short-term flings, too. But I'm done with that. I want a home. A family." She inhaled deeply and continued. "I told him I was sorry, but he'd have to leave."

Cop radar jumped to high alert. Billy omitted all of that. "What happened?"

"Well, not surprisingly, he got mad, called me a few choice names, and left."

"Did he hurt you?" Coop couldn't keep the anger from his voice.

Ruby shook her head. "He grabbed my arm, but I've had my share of pissed off dates, too." She lifted a snub-nosed thirty-eight from a desk drawer. "I pulled this out, told him to leave, and he left."

"What time did he leave?"

"I'm not sure. Maybe eleven-thirty."

"Did he say where he was going?"

"Not really. Said he might go back to Teddy's. See if he could find a real woman."

Her stricken voice gashed at him because he knew he added to her pain. He stood and grabbed his hat, then looked at the woman he had called a friend for more than twenty years. "You're too good for the likes of him."

"But not good enough for you."

Before he could respond, she stood and waved a hand in front of her face. "I'm sorry, Coop. That was petty, and uncalled for."

He didn't know what to say, so he stuck to business. "Thanks for talking to me."

"Bill's a smooth-talking ladies' man, Coop. But he's no killer."

"Take care of yourself, Ruby." He hurried out, questions mounting with each step he took.

Why didn't Billy Ray tell me the whole truth? Why would he imply something more happened between him and Ruby when it didn't? He had to know I would check his story.

The friend side warred with the cop side as he wondered how a man who never had trouble getting a woman dealt with being rebuffed by two in the same night. Did he go back to Teddy's and find someone happy to be another a notch on his bedpost?

Or did something more sinister happen?

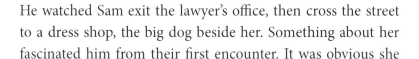

He watched Sam exit the lawyer's office, then cross the street to a dress shop, the big dog beside her. Something about her fascinated him from their first encounter. It was obvious she possessed great power, but at the same time, exuded a delicate vulnerability that titillated him. She would be the perfect accompaniment.

Suddenly consumed by a nervous energy he had not experienced before, it was difficult to remain focused. Everything must be perfect this time.

CHAPTER THIRTY-ONE

Sam headed back to her truck, arms loaded with packages, Jack at her side. She needed to get back to Dallas soon and retrieve more clothes, especially work scrubs. She juggled the bags, trying to reach into her pocket for the keys.

"Here, let me help." Billy Ray deftly pulled two bags from her arms. "You have your hands full."

She hadn't noticed him coming toward her, and jumped at his voice. "Oh, thank you. Thought I had it under control." She retrieved the key and clicked the unlock button. "Obviously, I didn't."

Jack growled low and menacing.

"Down, Jack," ordered Sam. "He's a friend."

Billy moved away from the dog, holding the bags until Sam transferred them to the front passenger seat. "Not very friendly, is he?"

"I'm afraid not."

When Jack growled again, Billy looked at Sam. "He won't bite me, will he?"

"No. Unless he thinks I'm in danger, then yeah, he will. Could be it's just a guy thing."

"A guy thing?"

"You know, like flexing your muscles or showing off." She

put the last bag away and faced him. "He does that anytime a strange man comes around." She reached down and stroked the mutt's head. "He's really a big ole softy, aren't you, sweetie?"

Jack sat on his haunches, eyes still on Billy.

"Yeah, well, of all the words I'd use to describe him, softy wouldn't be one of them."

Sam went to the back of the truck and lowered the tailgate. "Once he knows you better, he'll be fine." She motioned for Jack to jump in, but he remained on the ground beside her. "Get in, Jack." She snapped her fingers. "Now."

The dog gave Bill one final *I'm watching you* look, and jumped in.

She closed the gate, and returned to the driver's side door. "Thanks again. I would have dropped the whole mess if you hadn't come along."

"My pleasure. Say, how's the house-hunting going? Did you check into the complex where I live?"

"Actually, I'm staying at Eva's for a while."

"Ahh, I see."

A strange note crept into his voice, putting her on edge. She considered telling him it was her business, but something under the wiper blade caught her eye. "What's that?" She moved around him, and plucked the single pink rose from its resting place.

She glanced at Billy.

"Don't look at me. I didn't do it."

She sniffed the fragrant bloom. *Coop. It had to be him.* "I love roses. Thanks again for your help, Billy Ray. I appreciate it." She got behind the wheel.

"Anytime, Sam. And I prefer Bill, please." He rested both hands on the bottom of the window, a smirk revealing a dimple in his right cheek, which, combined with his windblown hair, presented a rather rakish look. "You change your mind about a new place, let me know." He let his gaze drop to her chest, then back up. "I'll be glad to help you look."

A spark of desire flashed through his dark eyes so quickly she almost missed it. Almost.

"If Coop doesn't object, of course."

He turned and strolled down the sidewalk to the drug store.

Once back at The Grove, she placed the single bud in a vase and carried it upstairs with her purchases, idly wondering why she did not see Eva.

On impulse, she tapped on the door to her room, but got no response. Concerned, she made her way downstairs, and stopped to answer when the house phone rang. "Pecan Grove B&B."

"Sam? This is Anson McElroy. I hope I didn't catch you at a bad time."

"No, this is fine. What can I do for you?"

There was a slight pause before he answered, and she could almost see the leer on his face.

"Well, since you asked, how about dinner tonight? My way of apologizing for not being there when you came by to sign those papers."

How many ways can I say hell no?

"I'm sorry, Mr. McElroy, but I have plans. With Coop." Not exactly the truth, but she was kinda living here with him, so they could have plans. Maybe. If she were lucky.

"Perhaps another time, then."

"I appreciate your help, Mr. McElroy." The evasive answer and formal address were meant to reinforce her lack of interest and define their relationship as attorney-client.

"Well, if there is anything else I can do for you, don't hesitate to call."

"I will."

She hung up and headed for Eva's office. The older woman sat at the desk, hands resting in her lap.

"Eva? Are you all right?"

She looked at Sam, face pinched. "Feel strange. Dizzy."

Time slowed to a crawl as they waited for news on Eva. Coop paced the small waiting area like a caged tiger, and Sam's heart ached for him. He was so upset, he even asked her to call Jason for him, reasoning she could better answer his questions.

"What's taking so long?"

The worry lacing Coop's voice, matched her own.

"It takes time to get the necessary tests run," she soothed, "and they need to ensure she is stabilized."

"How bad do you think it was?"

"She was awake and able to answer questions, Coop, so that's a good sign. We'll know more soon, I'm sure."

Jason exited the elevator and rushed down the hall. "How is she? Is she okay?"

"We're taking no news as good news right now," offered Sam. "They are still evaluating her."

She stood between father and son as they gazed at the doors leading to the area where Eva was being treated, as though by sheer force of will they could help her.

Jason's strong fingers wrapped around her hand and squeezed. "Thank you for being there for her. And my dad."

When the double doors swung open and a man in green surgical scrubs moved toward them, Coop slid his arm around her waist.

"Benton family?"

"That's us," said Coop. "How is she? Can we see her?"

"I'm Dr. Franklin. She's had a mild stroke, but is stable for now. We're sending her up to ICU overnight to monitor, but I don't anticipate any major issues."

"Will she be okay?" Coop's voice quivered with emotion.

"All indications are there is no permanent damage. Getting her here pronto was the best thing to happen." He glanced at his watch. "She'll be situated in another half hour. Visiting hours are over, but I'll let them know you can go in. But only for a few minutes."

"Thank you, Dr. Franklin," said Coop. "How long will she have to stay?"

"We'll re-evaluate in the morning. As I said, I don't foresee any major issues. She will likely have to make some lifestyle changes, though."

"We'll make sure she does what she's supposed to," said Coop with conviction.

The doctor gave them directions to the ICU floor and left.

The large waiting area contained six oversized chairs along one wall and a coffee table in the middle. The other side held a small table with a coffee pot, Styrofoam cups and assorted condiments. They sat down as a nurse came out.

"Benton family?"

They all stood and Coop said, "Here."

"I need the next of kin to complete some paperwork."

"I'm her son," said Coop." What do you need?"

Sam's mouth tightened, but she managed to swallow hard

and hide her surprise as Coop left with the nurse.

Jason dropped into the nearest chair and stared after his father.

The ashen-faced woman in the bed looked nothing like the bright, vivacious woman Coop knew so well. Tubes and wires dangled around her like octopus arms, while machines beeped and whirred as they monitored the ebb and flow of her life-force.

He swallowed the lump in his throat as he smoothed a curl from her forehead. The icy coolness of the skin under his fingers shocked him.

Her eyes fluttered open. "Coop?"

"Hey, Beautiful. About time you woke up."

An angelic smile formed as her eyes drifted shut. "Sorry I scared you."

Scared doesn't begin to describe how I felt when Sam called.

"If you wanted a vacation, all you had to do was say so and we would have packed you off to Hot Springs."

"Jason?"

"I'm here." Jason eased closer and touched her free hand. "I'm here...Miss Eva."

Coop didn't miss his son's confused expression. He'd deal with that later.

Sam stood beside Coop, one hand resting on Eva's knee. "I'm so glad you are doing better."

"Thank you for being there, Sam." She nodded toward Coop. "Make him go home. He needs rest."

"I couldn't leave until I saw for myself you were okay." His voice quivered as he pulled her frail hand to his lips and kissed it. "There's so much we need to talk about." He glanced at Sam and beamed. "Sam is going to hang around a while. Jason is getting married." Emotions in turmoil, he swallowed hard. "There is so much good in our lives right now. So much to look forward to. You have to get well so you can enjoy it with us."

A nurse peeked into the room. "I'm sorry, Mr. Delaney, but y'all need to leave. Your –"

Coop stopped her. "We're going, thank you." He looked at Eva. "Sweet dreams, Beautiful. I'll be back in the morning, hopefully to take you home."

After a quick kiss on Eva's forehead, Coop pulled the nurse outside, leaving Jason and Sam to say their goodbyes.

"Look," he whispered, "this situation is complicated. I have to ask you not say anything about my relationship to Ms. Benton."

The nurse's face scrunched up in a frown. "I thought she was your mother?"

He blew out a breath. "She is. But…it's complicated." He paused. "She doesn't know that I know."

CHAPTER THIRTY-TWO

"I've always known I was adopted," said Coop softly. "I found out some of the circumstances when I was sixteen."

Sam and Jason sat at the kitchen table with Coop as he talked. Neither commented, letting him say what he needed to at his own pace.

"Eva gave my mother a letter for me if I ever asked for details. It told me the why, but not the names of my biological parents. I didn't find out until two weeks after my adoptive parents died." He took a deep a breath and let it out slowly. "My mother left me a letter. Said she'd leave it up to me whether or not I revealed what it said."

Sam wanted to reach out and touch him but didn't for fear she'd break the shell around him.

"My father was Jackson Cooper. They met when she was eighteen." He tore a corner off the paper napkin on the table. "He was twenty-three; home on leave from the Army. She said it was love at first sight. At the time, I didn't believe in the possibility." Love-filled eyes met hers. "Now, I know it is."

He drew in a deep breath. "They wanted to marry before he left again, but her father refused. Said she was too young, he was too old, just met, etcetera. She was heartbroken, but content to wait until enough time passed, and her father would agree."

"What happened?" asked Jason.

"Me." His jaw tightened. "Jackson was thrilled when she told him, and arranged for a weekend pass. They planned to elope." He shredded the paper napkin as he talked. "Drunk driver took him out before he got there. Eva was devastated." His voice lowered, pain radiating in every word. "Her father was a minister. He and her mother were pretty fanatical. When they found out, they disowned her. Just like that. Moved away and never spoke to her again."

"Bastards." Jason's single comment said it all.

"Yeah." His hand shook slightly as he paused for a sip of coffee. "My folks were neighbors, and took her in. They were a little older than Eva, and couldn't have children…so they made a deal. Moved to Dallas until I was born, then came back here. Eva moved back a little later."

"I can't imagine how difficult that must have been for her," Sam said softly. "For both of them."

"In her letter, mother said she always wanted me to know about Eva, and why she chose that route." He paused and took a deep breath. "She didn't want to do anything to come between me and my adoptive parents so, she settled for being the family friend."

He shook his head. "When I first found the letter, I was mad as hell. Felt like I'd been lied to by everyone I loved my whole life. Nothing was real."

"What did you do?" Jason's quiet question drew Coop's attention.

"I was a first class asshole. To Eva. My friends. The whole damn world. Joined the Army, and left everything behind.

Married your mother, did my stint in the Army and we ended up in Dallas." His voice dropped as he tore another piece off the shredded napkin. "I came home a time or two but things were strained, and I never stayed long." He lowered his head. "My biggest regret is I never told her—and you—what I knew, and that I understand why she made her choice."

This time, Sam didn't resist the urge to place a comforting hand on his arm. She squeezed gently as the muscles flexed with each clench of his fist.

"After Judy left, I finally got my head out of my ass." He drew in a deep breath, let it out through pursed lips. "Long story short, I read the letters again. This time, it all made sense. I came home, determined to tell her all of it, and make things right again."

"Why didn't you?" Jason's voice held no censure, only concern.

"Wanted the right moment to tell her. You were so young…I thought I was doing the right thing by waiting. Before I knew it, you were grown." He looked at Jason, and Sam felt the pain emanating from his gaze. "I'm so sorry, Son. I should have told you both years ago." He lowered his head. "I did the very thing to you that was done to me."

Sam swallowed the sob in her throat as Jason reached across the table and took his father's hand.

"I've always felt close to her, Dad. Maybe because I was so young when we moved here, or maybe because she always treated us like family." He gave a light shrug. "As far as I'm concerned, she's always been my grandmother." His eyes, so like Coop's, conveyed a soft, inner glow as he met his father's gaze. "It's just official now."

He rose and gripped Coop's shoulder. "We're lucky, Dad."

He looked at Sam. "We're both very lucky. I'll see y'all in the morning."

Once they were alone, Sam lightly squeezed his arm. "Are you okay?"

"Kind of ironic, don't you think?"

"What is?"

"A drunk took my family away from me. And a drunk gave my mother back." He covered her hand with his. "This has been a bitch of a day. Can we go to bed now?"

She started to argue because of Jason, but one look at his stricken face, and the protest died. "Okay."

Breakfast the next morning was a happier occasion, with both Coop and Jason giving Sam a hard time about her first attempt at making biscuits.

"But you can bake like nobody's business," said Coop after one particularly teasing remark.

"Too late to butter me up, mister," said Sam as she plucked one off the plate for herself. "They'll have snowmen in hell before I bake you another chocolate cake now."

"I happen to like your biscuits, Sam," offered Jason, "they really soak up the gravy."

She snorted. "So, you're saying they're dry?"

He sputtered and even his ears turned red as everyone laughed.

"You know we're just teasing, right?" said Coop. "You did good."

"I will admit they are not quite as flaky as Eva's, but they are tasty, if I do say so myself." She looked at them in turn.

"Since no one else will."

Before the men could worm out of the hole they dug, she asked Coop, "What did the nurse say when you called this morning?"

"They are going to move her to a regular room for one more day. If nothing changes, she can go home tomorrow afternoon."

"Great news," said Jason. "After breakfast, I'm going to sit with her for a while." Expression serious, he looked at his dad. "I won't say anything, Dad. I just want her to know I love her, too."

Sam watched as Coop swallowed hard and nodded.

"I'll be by later this morning," said Coop. "I have to check on some things at the office first." He fished a slice of bacon from the plate in the center. "How long can you stay? Do you need to get back to school?"

"Since she seems to be doing all right, I'll probably head back this evening. Couple of tests coming up I need to study for."

The phone rang and Sam got up to answer. "Hello. Sure. Hang on." She handed the cordless phone to Coop. "For you. The office."

"Delaney. Okay. Be there in fifteen." He ended the call, and stood, giving Sam a quick peck on the cheek. "Duty calls." He turned to Jason. "Thanks for coming, Son. I know Eva appreciates it, too."

"I'm going to check on Big Mama this morning," said Sam. "Then I have a couple of errands in town. I'll be in to see her later this afternoon."

Before Coop could say anything, she held up her hand. "Yes, Jack will be with me. I'll call when I leave, and keep you posted on wherever I am."

He smiled and kissed her again. On the lips. In front of Jason. "Good girl."

After they left, Sam sat alone at the table nursing a cup of coffee when a sudden chill drifted through the room bringing with it the faint aroma of gardenias. She stiffened, waiting for…whatever happened next. The air grew cooler around her head and shoulders as though being embraced by it. Instead of being comforted, Sam experienced a deep sense of foreboding. "What is it, Granny?" she whispered. "What are you trying to tell me?"

Danger.

CHAPTER THIRTY-THREE

"Sheriff?"

"Yeah, Jimmy. Come in." Coop leaned his elbows on the desk.

The deputy sank into a chair and he crossed one leg over the other. "Any good news today?"

Coop shook his head. "Just talked with my contact at the FBI. He's double checking to see if anything similar to our case is out there. I know we didn't find anything, but a new set of eyes won't hurt. How about you?"

"I got the cell phone data from Joyce's carrier. A couple of calls to her roommate the night she disappeared saying she might be home early. Nothing out of the ordinary." He pulled another sheet of paper from the folder in his hand. "I got a cell number for Peggy's phone from her mom. Still waiting for data to come back on it."

"What about the last bartender? The one who was out sick?"

"I'm headed over to Teddy's after lunch. He's due back this afternoon." He hesitated, face pinched. "What about Billy Ray?"

Coop sat back in his chair and detailed his interview with the jailer and follow up with Ruby.

Jimmy's brow furrowed as he sat up straighter. "Do you think he went back there on Sunday?"

"I don't know what to think anymore. He's hiding something. I wish I knew what." Coop tapped a pencil against the desk top. "See what you can find out this afternoon and we'll go from there."

"I saw Anson at the Dairy Barn last night. Avoided me like the plague."

"He's another one with something to hide." The tapping grew louder and more insistent. "I'm missing something. I can feel it." Resigned to another long day, Coop blew out a long breath. "Okay, we'll touch base again when you get back from Teddy's."

JD rose and stopped at the door. "How's Miss Eva?"

"Good. They're keeping her till tomorrow. All indications are the stroke didn't do any permanent damage."

"That's great."

"Yeah. We can sure use some good news right now."

Jimmy nodded. "Anything new from forensics?"

"Nothing."

"Damn."

"Yeah. We're due for a break. Keep me posted."

"Will do."

After he left, Coop pulled the file of crime scene photos and took them to the small conference room. He spread some out on the table, others he taped to the whiteboard on the wall. He studied them until his vision blurred and a headache started. Unable to get a handle on what bugged him, he headed for the hospital.

Jason's hearty laugh greeted him as he entered Eva's room. "I was a city kid. I didn't know skunks did that." He looked up when Coop entered. "We're talking about the time I got sprayed by a skunk when we first came here. Remember?"

"How could I forget?" Coop took the chair on the opposite side of Eva's bed. "The smell hung around for days."

Jason wagged a finger at the woman who raised him, shoulders shaking with laughter. "You wouldn't let me in the house. I had to bathe in some gosh-awful concoction on the porch."

Amusement sparkled in her pale blue eyes. "You did put up a fuss over that. But not as much as when I had to burn your clothes."

Jason put a hand over his heart, and his voice softened. "My favorite Troy Aikman jersey. Killed by a skunk with an attitude."

Coop joined in the laughter as other stories followed, each solidifying the atmosphere of family, and a life well-lived and loved. With sudden clarity, he knew the time arrived to tell Eva the truth.

But not until she was home again.

"Sorry to break up the party, folks." The nurse pushed some kind of computer on a cart into the room. "My patient needs to rest."

"Okay," said Coop, "We're going." He turned Eva. "Sam will be by later this afternoon to visit and I'll be back tomorrow to take you home."

"Thank you both for coming." She looked from father to son. "I appreciate it more than I can say."

Coop leaned over and kissed her forehead, voice choked with emotion. "Get well, Beautiful. The place isn't the same without you." He swallowed hard and continued. "I love you, Eva. Always will."

Tears glistened in her eyes. "I love you, too."

Jason stood and took her hand in his. "Laurie wants a Christmas wedding. That doesn't leave us much time to get it all worked out."

She blinked away the tears as joy bubbled in her voice. "Christmas?"

His cheeks turned a bright pink as he nodded. "Seems all she wants Santa to bring her is, well, me." He paused. "And all I want…is for you to get well." He brought her hand to lips and kissed the back of it. "I love you."

"Oh, Jason," she whispered, "I love you, too."

Father and son left the room in silence, each lost in their own thoughts.

The late September air forecast the arrival of fall as they exited the hospital.

"Are we going to tell her this weekend?" asked Jason when they stopped beside his truck. "Or would you rather handle it alone?"

Coop didn't have to think about it. "I want you to be there, Son. This is about all of us."

"Works for me. I'll be home Friday evening."

Coop watched him drive way, fatherly pride making his heart swell. As he turned toward his Bronco, the balmy air suddenly cooled and carried a light floral scent to his nose. Not a rose, but similar. He stopped in his tracks when he recognized it. Gardenias.

Help her.

Stop him.

"Just what I need," he muttered as he started the Bronco. "Two ghosts with cryptic messages."

CHAPTER THIRTY-FOUR

Thursday morning

Sam glanced at the clock, dismayed to see the time. She told Big Mama to expect her before noon and it was a quarter till. Determined to have the house in order for Eva's homecoming, the morning zipped by. Big Mama's displeasure at her late arrival loomed ahead.

"Can't be helped." On her way out the door, she grabbed her purse off the table and a sweater from the hook by the door.

"Jack? Come on boy. Time to go." Surprised he didn't come running, she looked around the empty yard. Frowning, she unlocked the truck, and threw her stuff in the front seat. "Jack? Come here boy."

Something caught her eye on the hood. Another pink rose. *How romantic. But why didn't he just give it to me before he left?*

She quickly dialed Coop's number. Disappointment rained down when his voice mail picked up. A message would have to do. "With all that's happened the last twenty-four hours, I forgot to thank you for the rose yesterday. And the one today. I didn't realize you were the romantic type. Not sure why you didn't just give it to me in person so I could thank you properly, but still, the gesture is really sweet. See you at home later." Soon as the phone hit the seat, she remembered her promise to call when she left. That call went to voicemail as well.

She tossed the phone in the front seat, and went to find Jack. An unfamiliar car barreling down the drive made her pause.

The driver exited and hurried toward her. "Coop sent me. Hurry. It's Eva."

Without a second thought, she got in the car with him.

Coop kept his expression neutral as he listened to JD's report.

The deputy cleared his throat again as he crossed and uncrossed his legs. "The bartender saw both Billy and Anson talking with her when he came back from the john." Mouth tight, he rubbed one hand over his knee. "At one point, he thought she might be pitting them against each other, and kept an eye on them in case of trouble."

"What time was this?"

"Around eleven-thirty. I checked with Teddy. He said it was about eleven-fifteen when Rick asked to go home claiming he was sick, and he left a little before midnight."

"Did he see her leave? Was she alone?"

He shook his head. "They were gone after his last trip to the john right before he left. Claimed he was so sick by then, he wasn't paying attention to anything." Jimmy snorted. "He puked on someone's shoes on the way out the door. Maybe Puckett's, but he didn't look up. Just saw the fancy shoes, and thought it was him."

Coop clutched the pencil in his fingers so tight it snapped under the pressure. "But he's sure it was Bill and Anson she talked to?"

"Yeah. Both are regulars, especially on Ladies Night." He blew out a long breath. "Said neither of them usually leaves alone, though Anson seems to be more particular than Bill."

Coop looked at the clock on the wall. "Did he work today?"

"Day off." The deputy broke eye contact for a moment, his expression guarded. "What next, Sheriff?"

Body tense as a bow string, Coop heard the whooshing sound of blood rushing through his body with each rapid beat of his heart. *Sometimes this job sucks.*

"I'm going to talk to Alice again. See if maybe he went by her place. Meet me back here in half an hour."

"She's not here. Took off for a wedding shower or something."

"Shit. I forgot." Thoughts racing, he picked up half of the broken pencil and spun it on his desk.

"Do you really think he could have done it?" Jimmy's fingers tapped out a silent staccato on his knee.

"If you had asked me last week I would have said hell no." He shook his head sadly, trying to reconcile the facts laid out before him to the man he knew all his life, a man he called his best friend. He pushed back from the desk but didn't stand. "Everything we have right now is circumstantial. A halfway decent lawyer, and reasonable doubt is a given. We need something solid before we act."

Jimmy nodded agreement as the sharp ring of his cell phone reverberated in the closed office. "Cannon. You're sure? Great. Thanks." He ended the call and looked at Coop. "Only calls that night on Peggy's phone were to the ex-boyfriend. Seems they were talking about getting back together. Told him she would be home earlier than planned."

"Okay. We just keep looking for whatever it is we've missed."

Coop scrubbed his face with both hands. What a shitty day. His murder investigation pointed to his best friend and a respected attorney, his mother could have died not knowing how much he loved her, and to top it all off, he deprived his son of knowing Eva was his grandmother. No father-of-the-year awards for him.

The old clock on the wall ticked away another second. Two-thirty. *No way in hell will I make five o'clock.*

He grabbed his phone off the desk, about to stuff it in his pocket. "Crap. I didn't turn it on when I left the hospital."

He powered it up and headed out the door. A quick stop at the hospital to see his mother—it sounded strange to refer to Eva that way after all these years, but it also sounded right—then home.

Once behind the wheel, he checked the phone - two missed calls from Sam. The phone rang before he could dial her back. Caller ID showed Doc Harper's office. Sam beat him to the punch.

"Hey, Baby. Was just about to call you."

"Coop? This is Jan Howard."

Aw crap. "What can I do for you, Jan?"

"Sam was supposed to see Big Mama this morning but never showed, and she isn't answering her cell." The phone hissed as she blew out a long breath. "I'm just worried you know."

The hair on the back of his neck tingled, a personal warning flag he never ignored. "I'm almost home. I'll find out what's going on. Thanks for letting me know." He cut her off and dialed Sam's number, frowning when it went to voice mail.

As he turned down the lane toward the house, he saw her truck in the driveway, and relaxed. She was home.

He got out of the Bronco and saw Jack stagger around the corner of the house, head down, tongue hanging out the side of his mouth as he panted hard.

"What the hell?" He dropped to his knees in front of the dog. "Hey, there, Jack…what's wrong?"

His doggie breath emitted a strange odor as he attempted to lick Coop's face and whined.

"Did you eat something you shouldn't have?" He looked around the yard. "Where's Sam?"

Jack gagged and whined again, looking down the lane behind Coop's truck.

"Hang on, big guy." He lifted the huge dog and laid him in the back the truck. "Let me find Sam."

Coop dashed into the house. "Sam? Where are you?" When he didn't find her, he returned to the truck. Her purse, keys and phone lay in the front seat. His heart lurched at the sight of a single pink rose beside the phone.

Chilled air swirled around him.

Look hard.

Cop senses exploded to life as he stomped to the back of the truck where Jack lay, alive but out cold. Whoever took Sam made sure the dog would not interfere.

His hands shook as he listened to her messages. The first

reminded him of her plans for the day. The second made his blood run cold. Pink roses. He hadn't left her pink roses.

Thoughts of pale, pink petals on the back of Joyce Ayers made his blood run cold. Was it the same person? Instinct said yes.

He checked the time on the last message. Just after noon. Almost three hours ago. Oh, God. Three hours at the hands of a killer.

Help her.

"Dammit, Peggy," muttered Coop, "you're not making sense." His frustration mounted as he paced and ranted. "What the hell kind of ghost are you, anyway? If you're supposed to help me, then dammit help me, and stop this cryptic bullshit. Where's Sam!"

Silence.

He sat on the tailgate, and took a calming breath. *Focus. No time to waste.*

He called JD and told him to stop whatever he was doing and get to the house ASAP. Next, a call to the vet to request an emergency visit, then a call to Eva to say something came up and he would see her tomorrow.

Those things handled, Coop struggled to slow his racing heart.

Three hours. So much can happen in three hours.

CHAPTER THIRTY-FIVE

"He had enough Ketamine in his system to drop a small pony."

The vet's statement confirmed what Coop suspected. Someone wanted Jack out of the picture. "Will he be all right?"

"I think so. We're giving him something to counter it. I'll know more when he starts coming around. Will have to keep him here a couple of days for observation."

"Thanks, Dr. Adkins. Let me know when I can bring him home."

"Will do."

"Puckett took an extra hour for lunch today." JD's voice took on a note of censure. "Supposedly to visit a client. He's back in the office now." Face devoid of expression, he looked at Coop. "Bill's not home. Went by Alice's place just in case, but she hasn't seen him. Anson had a meeting in Texarkana today, and he won't be back until later this afternoon."

"Did you check with Ruby? See if she talked to Bill?"

"Yeah. Hasn't seen him." He paused. "Jack gonna be all right?"

"Looks like it."

Jimmy shook his head. "How did he drug him?"

"Had to be his food or water. My guess is the water. Make sure you get a sample of it." Coop's fists clenched as he surveyed the activity. One deputy processed Sam's truck, while another walked the yard. "The house was locked when I got here, so whatever happened, happened out here." He looked down at the gravel drive. "Not likely to get anything useful."

"You'll find her, Coop."

JD's firm conviction failed to remove the sense of impending doom enveloping him like a shawl.

Jimmy glanced down, then back up. "We got nothing off the truck so far. Lots of prints from the back door, but probably gonna be y'alls. No signs of a struggle, though, just her stuff in the front seat."

"So, if she left with someone, it was willingly. Someone she knew?"

"Unless he forced her with a weapon."

Coop couldn't bear the thought, but knew it was a logical assumption. "Okay, let's –" The sudden ring of his phone stopped the conversation. "Delaney."

"Sheriff Delaney? This is Miriam Arnold."

"Mrs. Arnold, I -"

Miriam cut him off. "My husband went out to make some deliveries this morning and isn't back yet. Doesn't answer his cell phone, either."

Coop closed his eyes and silently prayed for patience. "There's lots of areas in the county with poor reception."

"I know that," she snapped, "he had three deliveries to make. I've already called two and he finished with them by 11:30. Your house was the last one, and no one answers the damn phone."

Coop kept his voice neutral even as his heart rate

accelerated. "What time would he have made a delivery to the house?"

"He left the Pruitt's at 11:30 so probably around noon."

Coop jerked upright. Maybe Arnold saw something. "What time did you last talk with him, Mrs. Arnold?"

A voice called to her in the background.

"Never mind. He just walked in. Where the hell have you been?"

The line went dead before Coop got an answer. He stuffed the phone in his pocket, and headed toward the Bronco. "Frank Arnold was supposedly here around noon. He just got back to the store. Maybe he saw something."

JD followed behind him as Coop got in and started the engine.

"Uh, Sheriff? You want me to talk to him?"

Coop knew the unspoken reason for the question. He was too close to the case. Too damn bad. "No. Stay here until they finish. And I want to talk to Anson and Billy Ray as soon as they show up."

"Roger that."

Twenty minutes later, Coop sat at his desk as Frank Arnold fidgeted in front of him. Miriam stood rigid as a poplar behind him, arms folded across her ample bosom, one toe tapping the floor.

"Thanks for coming in on such short notice, Frank." Coop kept his voice calm though his chest ached with anxiety. "I'm hoping you can help me figure something out."

Frank rolled his shoulders as sweat popped out on his brow. Long fingers flexed as they curled and uncurled at his side. "L-like what?"

"You were at my house today."

Frank's eyes widened as he glanced at Coop, then focused on something over his shoulder. "I h-had a delivery f-for S-Sam."

"What time did you arrive?"

The grocer stuffed his hands in his pockets, then jerked them out again. "A-about n-noon, I think."

"What did you deliver? I didn't see anything when I got there."

"I-I don't know. I didn't look at it."

"He's lying."

Arnold's head jerked around at Miriam's sharp accusation.

"What the hell did you do, Frank?"

"N-nothing, dear." His nervous glance swung back to Coop as he licked his lips. "I haven't done an-anything."

Coop studied the fidgety man in front of him. Something was off. Way off. Uneasy eyes darted all around the room, never quite meeting Coop's. Perspiration coated the man's upper lip, and his hands trembled at his side.

Miriam's fierce glare from behind was surely a factor, but did not account for this level of discomfort.

With slow precision, Coop rose from his chair. "Where is she, Frank?"

CHAPTER THIRTY-SIX

"Frank Arnold took her?" JD's incredulous voice echoed inside Coop's Bronco. "You've got to be kidding me."

"Left her tied up at the old Franklin place west of town." Coop's voice shook as he spoke to his deputy on the phone. "I'm texting you the directions."

"Why'd he do it?"

"I'll explain later. Get your ass on the road and meet me there."

He tossed the phone in the front seat without waiting for a reply and backed out of his parking spot. Siren blaring, the tires squealed as he raced out of town.

Frank Arnold. Never in a million years would he have guessed that. His reasoning made no sense, and Coop didn't waste time dwelling on it. He had to get to Sam.

Twelve miles from town, he saw JD make the turn down the lane leading to their destination.

The house showed signs of recent repair, but was still little more than a shack. The front door was slightly ajar and Coop nodded at JD.

Guns drawn, they moved to either side of the entry. At a nod from the deputy, Coop kicked the door with his foot, and they rushed in, gun hands sweeping side to side.

A lone chair rested on its side in the center of the room. An empty water bottle, discarded fast food and snack wrappers littered the dusty floor.

JD checked the room to the right. "Clear."

Coop moved to the kitchen straight ahead. "Clear."

Side by side, they inched down the narrow hall, checking each room as they went.

Nothing.

Coop frowned and forced tense shoulder muscles to relax. Sam was gone. But where? Did she escape? Did someone else take her? *What the hell is going on?*

They returned to the front room.

"He claimed he left her here, tied to a chair." Fear gnawed through his gut. This couldn't be happening. "Where the hell is she?"

JD aimed the flashlight downward over the grimy surface. "Some of the dust is smeared. Can't really make out footprints." The narrow beam traced back toward the door. "No drag marks." He looked at Coop. "Are you sure this is where he brought her?"

"Yeah. He freaked when I said he could be arrested for kidnapping and started blubbering the location."

"And you're sure he acted alone?"

"That's what he said." Coop scanned the barren room, thoughts disjointed as he sought to understand what he saw, and, more importantly, what he didn't see.

"I've known Frank all my life," said JD. "I just can't see him as our killer."

Coop slapped his hat against his thigh. "He's not."

JD's widened eyes were his only reaction.

"Frank is bat shit crazy. But he's not our killer." Lips pinched, he scanned the empty room again. "Claims they connected over a root beer float."

"What the hell?"

Frustration mounting, Coop stomped to the door and gripped the sides as he looked out, straining to remain calm. He wanted to hit something. Hard. "Fool claimed they were soulmates."

"Soulmates?"

"That's what he thinks."

"How did he get her to leave with him?"

"Said I sent him because Eva took a turn for the worse. Gambled she wouldn't hesitate." Hands on his hips, he turned back to the deputy. "He gave her some bottled water dosed with Ketamine. Same shit he gave Jack, and drove her here. Claimed it wasn't much, just enough to knock her out till he got here so they could make plans."

"What kind of plans?"

"To leave together."

"Really?"

Coop nodded.

"Why?"

"Got tired of Miriam's nagging. Bought this place a few months ago and planned to leave as soon as he had it fixed up. Somewhere along the way, Sam was nice to him. He fixated on it until he convinced himself they were destined to be together."

Coop pressed himself back into cop mode. "Let's assume for the moment that Frank told the truth and acted alone. Which means we have an unknown player in the game." He closed his eyes and concentrated as he told JD about the roses.

"Frank didn't send them. I didn't send them. Have to be from the killer."

"No shit?"

"I think he somehow saw all or part of what happened. Followed them here. As soon as he could, he grabbed Sam."

"For real?" The deputy stroked his chin, eyes narrowed as he glanced around the room. "You think our guy was here?"

"It's the only thing that makes sense at the moment." He turned for the door. "If that's the case, he must have followed Frank without him knowing it. Let's take a look around outside."

Ten minutes later, Coop called from the across the yard near a big live oak tree. "Over here!" When the deputy joined him, he pointed to the ground. "Someone stood in this spot for a while. The ground is still moist from the rain but the damn roots obscure most of the print." He squatted down and surveyed the signs. "Not a sneaker. A boot, maybe."

"Hell, Coop, half the men in the county wear boots." JD's voice showed his own frustration with the situation. "Even us."

Coop ignored the comment as he visually traced the steps leading to the tree and beyond, toward the house, till they ended in the overgrown yard. He walked the area with care, avoiding getting near the prints. "Only one track I saw might be useful. Grass is too deep to get a good print. Tracks are deeper coming back."

"He carried her out."

"Probably." Coop stared at the dense forest. "Call it in. In the back of my unit should be some plaster to make prints. It'll be dark soon and I want this place gone over with a fine-toothed comb. I'm going to follow the tracks a ways. Maybe we'll get lucky."

"Uh, maybe I should go with you for back up."

Coop shook his head. "He's got an hour and half on us at least, and is long gone by now. I just want to see where the tracks lead. I'll be back in fifteen minutes."

In due time, he returned and held up a scrap of blue cloth gripped with a gloved hand. "Found this on a blackberry vine near where I think he parked. A little blood on it, probably from a scratch." His voice shook as he continued. "Sam had on a blue shirt this morning."

Face pinched, JD nodded. "Crime scene guys are on their way."

Coop moved to his car and placed the scrap in an evidence bag as a soft breeze carried a floral scent to his nostrils. Gardenias. There were no gardenia bushes in the yard.

He remembered what Sam said about the fragrance meaning her grandmother was near. Was she here? Could she help him?

"I can't lose her, Miss Ethel," he whispered, "help me… please."

He has her.

"I know that. Tell me something I don't know."

You know him.

CHAPTER THIRTY-SEVEN

Coop stared at the computer screen without seeing its content. Exhausted, stressed to the max, his mind could only focus on one thing: finding Sam before the unthinkable happened.

The day was one fiasco after another, and he could barely function at the moment. He'd stopped by the hospital on the way back to the office to tell Eva before she heard it through the grapevine. Though understandably upset, she assured Coop he would bring Sam home soon. A call to Jason produced the same results.

He scrubbed his face with both hands, then reached for his coffee. The stale brew was strong but tepid, and he emptied the contents in one long gulp. His stomach protested right away. He fumbled in his desk for antacid tablets and popped two in his mouth. Not the food he needed but would have to do for now.

There was no doubt in his mind Sam was in the hands of a killer responsible for the deaths of two women. And he had nothing to go on beyond some half-ass footprints that could belong to half the men in the county. No leads. No suspects. Nothing.

His conversation with Arnold when they returned from

the shack yielded nothing new. He worked alone, didn't see or hear anyone else. When Coop told him his ridiculous stunt apparently spurred the killer into action, the man became so distraught a deputy had to practically carry him back to his cell.

Instinct told Coop the killer was pushed into acting before he was ready, and he clung to the hope this meant he had time to save her.

Of the three men initially questioned, only Puckett appeared to be in the clear. His long lunch today was nothing more than a mid-morning tryst with one of Teddy's waitresses. Once again, he was more concerned his wife not know of his actions than being considered as a murder suspect.

He had yet to talk with Anson or Bill. The lawyer apparently texting his secretary he would stay in Texarkana for dinner and probably not return tonight. A deputy watched his house and another watched his office. Coop would know the minute he returned.

Billy Ray had yet to appear.

The steady ticking of the clock on the wall drew his attention. Eight o'clock. Anger and desperation warred inside him as the air around him chilled.

She's alive.

He stared at the sleeping woman and sighed. So beautiful, so passionate. She would have been the perfect partner for him. Until Arnold messed everything up and forced his hand.

In hindsight, he might have been too impulsive in taking her. Maybe he should leave her somewhere for them to find.

Cut his losses. Do better the next time. No. He'd come too far to stop now. Besides, he was rather enjoying the game.

Desire surged as he ran long fingers through the ebony curls lying against her cheek, tracing the red mark above the rough rag tied over her mouth. It hurt him to do that, but, for now, it could not be helped.

When he watched Arnold drive out of town with Sam, his anger was immediate and intense. His careful plans to win her ruined. Arnold would pay dearly for that as well. Soon. For now, though, he must wait. However, he did appreciate the grocer's foresight in getting rid of the bothersome dog. He'd wondered how that could be accomplished when the time came, but Arnold took care of it for him. True, it interfered with his meticulous plans, but he would adjust.

A moment of unease rippled over him as he considered how close the grocer came to discovering him this morning. He barely managed to leave the rose and scurry out of sight, then watched from the shadows as Frank dumped something in the dog's water bowl. It was funny to watch how Arnold paled when Jack came around the house and growled at him. He had backed away slowly, then vanished from view.

The huge mutt watched Arnold leave, then scanned the yard, ears pricked forward.

The man held his breath when those watchful eyes skimmed past his hiding place, only to return. He had expected the dog to be inside as before. Cold hands gripped the deadly knife as he waited and silently cursed his foolishness. The second rose should come later, but for reasons he could not explain, he felt compelled to do it now. And it nearly cost him everything.

Jack scanned the yard once more, then trotted over to the

water bowl.

The man snickered at the noisy lapping sound. *Drink up, you worthless piece of shit. Drink up.* While the dog drank, the man slipped away into the pre-dawn darkness.

When Sam stirred, he stepped behind the sofa where she lay. It wasn't time to reveal himself yet.

Considering how deep she slept, he assumed Arnold had heavily drugged her, and she would be out for a while yet. She hadn't even stirred when he put her in the trunk. He really hated to leave her there as long as he did, but things change and plans must be altered. Thankfully, she was still out when he got here. The next phase of his plan needed some tweaks, so he didn't mind.

Arnold was a fool and nowhere near good enough for her. And the sheriff as well. So cocky and full of himself. Thought he was better, and smarter than everyone else. But he wasn't nearly as smart as he thought he was.

The evidence slept on his couch, and rested on slabs at the morgue.

Euphoria danced inside him, making him light-headed. "I am the master," he whispered. "I cannot be caught." Chest puffed out, back straight, he checked his reflection in the mirror behind him. "What a shame no one knows."

Muted light glistened off cold, dead eyes as he snipped a lock of Sam's hair.

CHAPTER THIRTY-EIGHT

A welcoming light glowed through the kitchen window as Coop pulled up to the house and saw Jason's truck parked in his usual spot. The heavy weight centered on his chest lifted.

I won't have to face this night alone.

Jay dumped scrambled eggs onto a plate as Coop walked in the kitchen.

"Just in time." His son nodded toward the coffee pot on the counter. "Hot and fresh."

"Thanks, Son." Coop filled his mug and sank into a chair at the table, worry and exhaustion sapping the last reserves of energy.

"I figured you probably didn't take time to eat," said Jason as he put a plate of bacon and eggs on the table.

Coop's hand trembled as he gulped coffee, then white knuckled a forkful of eggs. "I didn't." The gooey intrusion made his stomach roll, as images of what Sam might be enduring tormented him. By sheer force of will, he kept eating.

Jason rolled and unrolled a kitchen towel, his gaze locked on Coop. "Jack gonna be okay?"

A nod sufficed for an answer.

"What can you tell me, Dad?"

It took a long swallow of coffee for the last bite of eggs to go down. Fear constricted his chest to the point that getting enough air bordered on impossible. The constant, terrifying what-ifs wouldn't stop. Even a just-the-facts rundown threatened to unhinge him.

Never had he ever felt so helpless and afraid.

Jason remained silent until the end. "Okay, so some douchebag snatched her from Frank's place. Which means he had to have seen him leave with her, right?"

Coop sat back in his chair. "In theory, yes. But we found nothing out of the ordinary here. The shoe prints at the farmhouse were lousy at best and could belong to half the men in the county."

"What about here?"

Dark brows pinched together, and he exhaled long and slow. "Too much grass and gravel. Not to mention the in and out traffic." His voice trailed off. He had nothing.

Nervous energy made him fidget in the chair, then push back from the table. "I can't sit here doing nothing. I'm going back to the office. Look over everything again. I'm missing something. I can feel it."

"Is Eva still being released tomorrow?"

"Yeah. No idea what time."

"You focus on Sam. Laurie will help me get Eva home." He paused, then squeezed Coop's arm. "Sam's a tough lady, Dad. And I know you'll find her." Jason's grip tightened. "I know you will."

Coop wanted very much to share his son's optimism. Unfortunately, time wasn't a friend in these situations. As worst-case-scenarios played through his mind, his throat tightened. *Please let me find her before it's too late.*

The cop side, rational and systematic, competed with the personal side. His heart refused to give up hope, so he'd go through everything again. And again, till he found the thread needed to unravel the mystery of who had Sam…before time ran out.

The loud peal of his cell phone broke the somber moment. "Delaney. Now? No. Don't do anything. I'm on my way."

"What's happened? Is it Sam?"

Jason's worried voice broke through the buzz in Coop's ears.

"No, I'm afraid not. Someone I need to talk to just got home. I've gotta run. Don't wait up."

Coop sat in the car for a several minutes, taking deep breaths, forcing his cramped shoulders to relax before he knocked on Anson's door.

"Well, Sheriff Delaney. What a pleasant surprise."

The pinched expression on the lawyer's face said otherwise.

"May I come in?"

"Why?"

"It's chilly out here."

The silent standoff continued for several long moments before Anson stepped aside.

Coop eyed the twelve-foot ceilings in the foyer, the antique chandelier, and the polished hardwood floors. "Nice place. Never seen the insides before."

"I must remember to add you to my party list." He moved to his left. "We can talk in the parlor."

They entered a tidy room that could have graced the pages of any antique catalog. The furnishings, even to his untrained eye, were antiques and expensive. The thought of sitting on any of the delicate pieces filled him with dread.

He brought his gaze back to Anson. "I didn't realize lawyering paid this good."

Thin lips pressed into a tight line and heightened color on his cheeks indicated the jibe hit home.

Anson strode to a table against the wall and poured a drink from a crystal decanter. "It belonged to my grandfather." He gulped down the amber liquid, scowled and poured another. "I inherited it. As you well know."

"Oh, yeah. I guess I forgot that part, what with two murders and all to deal with."

Coop could almost hear the other man count to ten as he closed his eyes and took a deep breath. *Good. Rattled men were more apt to let something slip.*

"We've already had this conversation, Delaney—"

"Where were you all day?"

He sipped his drink. "Minding my own business. You should try it sometime."

"Murder and kidnapping make it my business. Where were you?"

Anson's cheeks took on a rosy glow, which Coop surmised had nothing to do with the alcohol he'd consumed.

"We can talk here, or we can go to my office. Your choice."

The lawyer's chest puffed out, and his eyes flashed fire. "I'm not some dimwitted country bumpkin," he snapped. "I know my rights. Unless you have probable cause you're wasting my time. And you know it."

Body tense, begging for a fight, Coop moved forward, his voice low and ominous. "Don't make me ask again."

The lawyer's jaw clenched twice and the stare down ended. "I had a deposition at eight this morning. In Texarkana. It lasted till almost noon."

Coop disguised his disappointment with derision. "Now, was that so hard?"

Thankful looks couldn't kill, he probed further. "And then?"

Anson's shoulders drew back as he swirled his drink. "Extended lunch with a friend."

"This friend got a name?"

"...Yes." The word came out strained, as though it took all his energy to say it.

Coop snickered. "Does her husband know?"

One dark vein in Anson's forehead pulsed as he silently sipped his drink.

Coop pulled the small notebook from his pocket and passed it over. "Names and contact information."

He hesitated, then reached for the pad as his brows snapped together, and his hawk-like eyes speared Coop. "What kidnapping?"

Coop watched him carefully. "Sam's missing."

The shocked expression on Anson's face said it all.

The lawyer didn't do it.

Painful throbbing pierced her skull as Sam cautiously opened her eyes. A dusty rag was tied around her mouth, and she lay on a grimy sofa, a single light suspended from the ceiling for light. Her hands were bound behind her back and a plastic zip tie secured her ankles. Pain radiated from her wrists upward when she tried to move. She swallowed a groan. Bewildered, her drug-clouded mind tried to piece together what happened.

Where am I? How the hell did I get here?

The last clear memory was Frank Arnold coming by the house. Eva. Something was wrong with Eva. No. He lied. Bile rose in her throat and her heart pounded. The gag across her mouth added to her state of near panic. *What if I throw up? I'll choke!*

She swallowed hard and sucked in a deep breath. *Stay calm. Think.*

Groggy and disorientated, she groaned and worked her jaw, trying to dislodge the gag without success. Pain raced up her arms and shoulders as she strained to free her hands. Heart racing, her breath burst in and out of constricted lungs. She bit back a frustrated cry as dizziness swamped her. *No! No!*

A soft whimper escaped and tears stung her eyes as the darkness descended once more.

Help me, Coop.

CHAPTER THIRTY-NINE

Friday morning

Coop stomped into the foyer of the courthouse, preoccupied by a night of troubling dreams, and too little sleep. Peggy's voice only bothered him once with a single comment: *basement*.

Sam was being held in a basement? Few homes in Texas had them, and he knew of none locally. But he knew someone who would know.

Alice looked up as he approached her desk. "Morning, Coop."

Her overly cheerful greeting grated on already frayed nerves. "I want to see JD as soon as he comes in."

"I just heard about Sam." Her excited voice edged up a notch. "What's going on?"

Coop ignored the question as he paced down the hall to his office. Alice hated not knowing things. Stood to reason it was just a matter of time before she picked up something to gossip about. He turned back to her desk, ignoring the hopeful look on her face. "If you so much as breathe one word to anyone about this investigation, you're fired. Understand?"

She stiffened and glared at him. "You can't fire me. My daddy's the mayor."

He took a step closer, voice clipped and firm. "And if one more person comes back to my office unannounced, you're fired." He straightened. "It's all in the code of conduct you signed when you were hired. Infractions can, and will, result in termination."

He left her muttering under her breath. It sounded a lot like *we'll see about that*, but Coop didn't care. He'd put up with her for four months. Enough was enough. Mayor or no mayor.

Ten minutes later, the intercom buzzed. "What is it, Alice?"

Her smug reply made his teeth ache.

"The mayor on line one."

The short and sweet conversation ended with the disconcerted mayor promising to have a talk with his daughter.

Ridiculous. The woman was twenty-five years old. Her father should have talked with her long before now.

Coop barely caught his breath when his cell rang. "Delaney."

"Sheriff? This is Rawlings."

Coop sat up straighter. Rawlings was the deputy assigned to watch Billy's house. "What's up?"

"Billy came home a few minutes ago. What do you want me to do?"

"Nothing for the time being. Let me know if he goes anywhere."

"Roger that."

Revitalized by the prospect of getting answers, Coop started to dial JD's number only to stop when the intercom buzzed. With monumental effort, he maintained a civil attitude. "Yes, Alice?"

"The vet on two. Said it's urgent."

"Tha –" He shook his head at the click signifying she hung up, and punched the button for the call. "Is Jack okay, Dr. Adkins?"

The harried veterinarian raised his voice over the uproar in the background. "You have got to come get this dog."

"Is he all right?"

"He's mad as hell. Barks and snaps at anyone who goes near him. If I have to keep him any longer, I'll have to sedate him again. Right now, I can't get close enough to put the muzzle back on."

Shit.

"I'm on my way."

Alice wasn't at her desk, so he scribbled on a sticky note, and left it on the computer screen.

As he approached his vehicle, he saw an envelope under the wiper blade. Forehead creased, he scanned the adjacent area but saw nothing out of the ordinary. He carefully extracted the unsealed packet, lifted the flap, and peeked inside.

"Sonofabitch!" He spun around to check the area again, but saw no one. No traffic in sight in either direction in front of the courthouse. The only people around were two shopkeepers on the opposite side of the square sweeping the sidewalk.

He inspected the contents again. A lock of hair. Sam's hair. He was sure of it. But why? A taunt? The killer's way of saying *you can't catch me?*

Lips pressed in a tight line, he turned toward the courthouse, then stopped. Whoever left it was long gone. The security cameras only covered the entrances. He placed the packet on the hood and donned latex gloves from behind the seat. After carefully securing it in an evidence bag, he stowed it in the glove box. He'd get it to the lab today. The only thing he expected to find out was the hair belonged to Sam. The killer had left no trace up to this point, so he didn't expect a change now.

When he entered the clinic a few minutes later, he heard Jack's unmistakable howl coming from the back. "I'm here to pick up Jack," he told the young man at the counter.

"Thank God," he mumbled. "I hope you can quiet him down."

He followed the kid down the hall and out to the kennel area in the back.

"When he started coming around last night we put him out here so he'd have room to roam around. As soon as he woke up, he started this."

Jack jumped against the fence as though trying to break out, all the while barking and howling as if he wanted to tear someone up. The moment he saw Coop, he ran to the gate, tail wagging so hard he shook.

"Easy big guy, easy," he crooned as he squatted down at the fence. "We'll get you out of here, just calm down."

The young man handed Coop the muzzle and leash, then stepped to the side of the gate. "I'm only going to open this enough for you to go in. You have to move quick, so he doesn't get out."

A few minutes later, a docile Jack led the way to Coop's vehicle. As soon as the door opened, he jumped up in the front seat, looking around as though searching for someone, then nosed the glove box.

"She's not here, boy." He removed the muzzle the vet insisted on and rubbed the mutt's head. "But don't worry, she'll be home soon."

Jack nudged Coop's chin with his nose and whined.

"I know, I know. I'm sorry I had to leave you there, but I had to make sure you were gonna be okay."

Another whine and a sloppy lick to the face suggested Coop was forgiven.

"Come on. Let's get you home."

Thoughts scattered, he concentrated on the task at hand. Get Jack home, then back to the office.

Instinct said the lock was a taunt, but why?

You know him.

The ghost's pronouncement bounced around his head, as worry twisted his gut. *Could Billy really be responsible for this?* He tamped down personal feelings, as he let the cop side take control.

Everything he knew about his friend was at odds with the evidence. He would do what he must to find Sam and bring a killer to justice. Regardless of who it was.

A few minutes later, Coop arrived home. Jason hadn't left for the hospital yet, so he took over getting the dog situated inside.

Back on the road, he took a deep breath and pulled out his cell phone.

JD answered on the third ring. "Morning, Coop."

"Where are you?" His supply of patience being non-existent at this point, his voice came out gruff.

"Headed in. Something wrong?"

"No. We'll talk when you get here."

Fifteen minutes later, JD sat in the chair across from Coop's desk.

"You don't think Anson's our guy?"

Coop rubbed his unshaven jaw. "No. Verified the deposition lasted till noon. He spent the afternoon with a judge's wife, then had dinner with them."

JD's right knee bobbed up and down. "Ballsy ain't he?" His knee bobbed faster. "Could he have gotten someone else to do it?"

"Not his style." Coop shook his head. "He's not our guy."

"What now?"

Before he could reply, the ringtone assigned to Jason interrupted. "Let me take this. Jason's at the hospital with Eva. Everything all right, Son?"

"Yes sir. They took her back for more tests. Something about some labs that didn't look right."

"I'll be there as soon as I can get loose."

"She's fine, Dad. Dr. Franklin just wants to double check her labs. They will most likely release her today. I just wanted to let you know it will probably be later this afternoon before she's released."

"Oh. Okay. But call me as soon as you know something."

"I will."

Head tilted to one side, JD inquired, "Everything all right?"

"Yeah. More tests." He scrubbed his chin and got back on track. "Billy's home. He works tonight so he may be in bed. Call him in now. I want you to interview him ASAP."

The look of surprise on the deputy's face morphed into one of pleasure as he leaned forward. "You want me to talk to him?"

"I think someone other than me needs to." Coop rapped a pencil on the corner of his desk. "Get it on tape, but use the conference room."

JD sat up straight, his knee no longer bouncing on the floor, dark eyes unblinking as he stared hard at Coop. "Will you sit in?"

Coop shook his head. "He might respond better if you do it alone." He dropped the pencil and sat back. "If you need me, just call. Otherwise, I'll look at the tape afterwards."

Jimmy jumped to his feet. "Yes sir. I'll get right on it."

Coop stared at the deputy's back as he hurried out the door. He was the most senior person on staff and eager to learn. Plus, he did believe having someone else question Billy would be more beneficial.

He will kill her.

CHAPTER FORTY

"Had trouble with tape. I got nothing useful," groused JD as he sat down. "Should have let you do it."

Coop waved off the comment. "I've only looked at a few minutes of it so far, but you did fine. Used the right amount of pressure and didn't get flustered when Bill got pissed at being questioned again."

"Lawyered up when asked where he's been. Said the last time he saw Sam was outside of Arnolds on Thursday. Ruby saw them talking by her truck. That's all I got."

Coop sat back in his chair and crossed his arms. "I ran into him in the hall before he left. Said he's taking some time off. I had to call Johnson in to take his place."

Eyes bright, JD leaned forward. "You think he might lead us to Sam?"

"He's not stupid. He knows we'll be watching. We still don't have anything to hold him on. Until we do, we watch and wait."

"But it's gotta be him, right?" JD's left knee bounced up and down. "I mean why else would he lawyer up? Can't we get some kind of search warrant now?"

Shoulders drooping, Coop looked away.

"I know he's your best friend and all, but surely you can see he's hiding something."

"My hands are tied. I'm having him watched until something breaks." Coop swallowed hard. "Nothing else to do at this point."

A heavy silence lingered.

"Um, I'm gonna grab some lunch," offered JD, "Maybe take a turn by his place, make sure he went home."

"Rawlings is still watching him." Coop pushed up from his desk. "I need to check on something."

"Anything I can help with?"

"Naw. It's probably nothing. Just something I want to check on." Coop chewed his lower lip. "You know any houses around with basements?"

"Basements?"

"Yeah."

"Why?"

Coop's phone rang, and he reached to answer it. "I'll tell you later."

The deputy frowned and hurried out.

A few minutes later, Coop grabbed a cup of coffee and sat down to review the tape. Crime scene photos were still up on the screen. He'd looked at them countless times, unable to shake the thought he'd missed something. A breath of cool air flipped open the folder on his desk with Sam's photos in it.

Look again.

Out of habit, he picked up the top photo and compared it to the ones on the screen.

And then he saw it. Something he had looked at time and again and never picked up on before. A piece of paper near the bush where Joyce was found. It wasn't there in the photo Sam took.

He placed a call to the lab to verify what he saw. Heart sinking, he reviewed the interview tape. As JD said, nothing earth shattering in it. Billy left in a huff and JD went to the camera, apparently to turn off the tape, then followed him out. The screen vibrated, then came back on. The breath lodged in his throat at what he saw next. Back rigid, a flush of adrenalin tingling through his body, he stared at the face of a cold-blooded killer.

A light pressure on his back, as though someone touched him, made Coop spin around. Nothing. He was alone. A stifling heaviness filled the air eddying around him.

His basement.

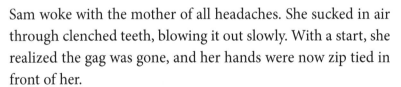

Sam woke with the mother of all headaches. She sucked in air through clenched teeth, blowing it out slowly. With a start, she realized the gag was gone, and her hands were now zip tied in front of her.

She jerked into a sitting position and immediately regretted it. Excruciating pain exploded behind her eyes, and she didn't bother to stifle the whimper rising in her throat. A wave of nausea followed, and she lowered her head between her knees. Every beat of her heart pounded against her temples, and she prayed for it to end.

Several long moments passed as she remained doubled over. Slowly, she straightened and looked around.

The room was large and filled with an assortment of furniture pieces, cardboard boxes and junk. One dirt-crusted window up high on her right allowed minimal light in. The soft white glow of the single bulb dangling from the ceiling diffused the area with shadows.

Basement? I'm in a basement.

The bindings on her hands and feet made turning around for a better view difficult. A small table on her left held a bottle of water and a convenience store sandwich. *Was it there before or did he bring it when he re-did my bindings?* She scooted closer to the table and reached for the water, grimacing in pain as the bindings dug into chafed flesh.

After carefully inspecting the cap to ensure it hadn't been tampered with, she managed to get the top off and took a small sip. A quick swish of the tepid liquid helped alleviate her powder dry mouth, and soothe chapped lips. The moment the liquid hit her stomach, it growled with hunger. She counted to ten and the water stayed put, though the hunger pains increased. Another ten count and a quick inspection of the sandwich showed it didn't appear to be tinkered with. Praying it was not a mistake, she devoured half of it three bites.

Church bells. She sat up straighter. *I'm close enough to hear the chimes from the Methodist Church.* The short musical selection preceded peals marking the hour. One in the afternoon. *How long have I been here? Since yesterday?*

Twenty-four hours. Coop would be out of his mind with worry.

Every movement sent her headache into the stratosphere. She rested her head on the back of the shabby couch and breathed deeply. *I'm in town. If I can get free, I should be able to get help. There must be something here I can cut these ties with.*

The squeak of a door opening somewhere behind her, followed by heavy steps on wooden stairs, filled her with dread. Too late.

He was back.

The hardest thing Coop ever had to do was remain calm and not rush the process. The fact Sam's life hung in the balance was the only way he managed.

One call to old Mrs. Dawson in the county clerk's office, and he knew exactly how many houses in Bakersville had basements. Two.

His prime suspect owned one of them.

He inched through the darkened house toward the kitchen, stopping when cold air surrounded him.

It's him.

"I know, Peg. I'll get him." The basement door should be on the opposite side of the small pantry area ahead.

The icy air rushed past him, pushing the basement door wider.

Weapon in hand, he edged through.

"Hello, Sunshine."

Unable to speak, Sam blinked several times as the deputy rounded the corner of the couch, a pistol pointed at her chest.

JD sauntered closer, hooked the leg of a chair with his toe and drug it forward. He turned it around and straddled it, gun hand draped over the back, a malevolent smile marring an otherwise handsome face. His unnerving silence made him all the more sinister.

She looked down at her hands. "Why? I don't understand."

He tipped his hat back with the gun barrel, bright white teeth gleaming in the muted light. "Well, I must say, this wasn't at all what I had planned, but then, I'm nothing if not flexible."

He's wearing latex gloves.

Sam never feared much of anything in her life, but she feared this man with the dead eyes. Each breath was a struggle; her head pounded, and dizziness threatened to overcome her. Try as she might, she couldn't keep the tremble from her voice. "I thought you were my friend."

"Oh, this has nothing to do with being friends."

"Y-you're n-not making any sense."

Good humor vanished and his dark eyes narrowed. "You saying I'm crazy?"

"N-no…I'm j-just trying t-to understand why. Th-that's all."

His wordless glare frightened her, prompting the need to fight back. "Coop won't rest until you pay."

One shoulder lifted in a dismissive gesture. "Guys like him are no match for guys like me."

She studied him, trying to decide if he were serious. He was.

"If he was as smart as he thinks he is, we wouldn't be having this conversation."

When she merely stared, he continued. "I got away with murder. Twice. Right under his nose." He scratched his cheek with the gun barrel. "I admit that wasn't the plan, but like I said, I'm nothing if not flexible."

"Wh-what was the plan?" If she kept him talking, maybe help would come. Maybe. *Please, God. Help me.*

"I guess it won't hurt to tell you." He sat up straight and chuckled. "I'm dying for someone to know anyway."

Fear crawled up her spine like a spider.

"Well, the first one wasn't really planned, and must admit,

I panicked a little. But days went by, then weeks and suddenly, I realized how easy it would be to get away with it. Super Sheriff didn't have a clue." He laughed again. "All those people walk that trail every day, and no one found her. I thought I'd have to find her myself." He shook his head side-to-side. "Thanks to you, the second one was discovered right away." He took a breath. "Super Sheriff thought I was careless." He crossed his arms over the back of the chair. "But I'm smart. Even left him a clue, and he never found it. Oh well, I can move on with my plan."

"Wh-what plan?"

Eyes glowing brightly, he thrust out his chest. "How cool would it be to place the blame on someone else? I have the know-how, the guts to do it, so why not?"

"Was Arnold part of the plan?"

His expression went from pleased to thunderous in the blink of an eye. "That hen-pecked idiot nearly ruined everything. I'll deal with him later." He pinned her with those dark, volcanic eyes. "I did have some serious hopes for us, though. But, that's no longer an option." He waved his gun around in a circle, dark brows drawn together in an angry frown. "I hate it when people screw with my plans. All that work shot to hell. And I really hate having to kill you, Sunshine. I truly do."

I have to keep him talking. I know Coop will find me. "You said you wanted to blame someone else. Who were you going to blame?"

The sadistic smile returned. "Super Sheriff's best friend."

"Billy Ray?"

His lips curled in disgust. "Thinks he's God's gift to women. I already got Coop doubting his innocence. Just need a little push." He tilted his head to one side. "Have you missed your gold hair clip?" He snickered. "I found it in the van after you changed. Slipped it under Billy's chair after our interview today. When I get back to the office this afternoon, I'll make sure Coop sees me find it, and I'll have a search warrant before the sun goes down. Guess what we're gonna find when we search his car?" He sat up a little straighter, voice eager as a child describing his favorite toy. "I put some of their clothes in his trunk, and I planted some of your hair in his back seat for good measure. Boom! It's over. Pretty Boy goes down with bang, and I look like a genius because I solved two murders all by myself."

He shook his head as though to banish an unpleasant thought. "I nearly had heart failure yesterday when Coop said get to his place. Hell, I'd just come from Arnold's hideaway. With you in my trunk!" He rose and pranced around the room. "Talk about a natural high. Man, watching him sweat and worry about his poor little Sam. All the while you were sleeping if off in the trunk of my cruiser." He laughed out loud then, an eerie, off-key sound. "See what I mean? I am the master!"

"Why did you kill those women?"

A muscle flicked in his jaw, and his face became a stony mask. "They shouldn't have pointed at me. I hate it when someone points a finger at me."

Sam tried not to react. *He killed them because they pointed at him?*

"We were having such a good time, too. I treated them right, gave 'em roses and everything. Then they had to go and get all uppity on me; point that damn finger like they was better than me." He made a tsk-tsk sound. "Not a good idea."

A sudden blast of cold air made dust float across the floor. Anger, fierce and deep, consumed Sam, and she tried to stand.

"You killed me for that?" A woman's voice, raspy and deep echoed in the room.

Where did that angry voice come from? Sam looked around but saw only the deputy.

A thick, vaporous fog wrapped around JD's legs.

"What the hell?" His hat flew off his head as the mist swirled around him.

The air grew colder still, and Sam shook with the ferocity of the anger swamping her.

"Your time has come," the eerie voice shouted.

Stunned, Sam watched the scene unfold.

Gaze fixed on the mist surrounding him, JD stumbled against a bookcase. "Get away from me!" He righted himself as the haze slowly rose to chest level. "Get away!" The mist completely engulfed the frantic deputy as he spun in circles, slapping at the fog with his gun.

"Drop your weapon!"

Coop's shouted warning went unheeded as the deputy circled twice, his weapon swiping at the circling mist pressed against his body. "Get away from me!"

"Drop the gun, JD. It's over. Drop it."

Sam rolled to the floor when the first shot rang out. Two more followed in quick succession.

The ensuing silence was deafening.

CHAPTER FORTY-ONE

Coop dropped into a chair in the kitchen, fatigue weighing him down. The longest week of his life was finally over. Sam and Eva were both safe and a killer was dead.

Sam moved to his side, placing a cup of coffee and slice of chocolate cake in front of him. "You okay?"

He pulled her onto his lap. "Yeah." He held her close and tried to control the trembles that erupted each time he recalled how close he came to losing her.

After several moments, she rose, and pulled a chair closer to him. "How did you know it was him?"

Coop sat back in the chair, hands resting in his lap. "The crime scene photos. My gut said I missed something so I kept going over them. I just happened to have them pulled up and one of those you took was on my desk. It was an area near the bush that I shot, too. Only in mine, a piece of paper was in plain sight. It wasn't on yours." He sighed. "I called the lab and had them look for it. Turns out it was an old teacher parking pass for Peggy Wallace. The only person besides you and I who was near there was JD." He shook his head. "I can't believe I didn't catch it before now." He paused to gather his thoughts. "I ran through the tape he did with Billy after I talked with the lab. When the interview was over, JD must have thought he turned the tape off, but it was still running." Dark brows drew together as he recalled the agony of watching someone he knew and trusted reveal his dark side. "I saw him place something under Billy's chair after he left. When I looked, I found that gold hair clip you asked me about."

"How did you know where to find me?"

He looked down, then met her steady gaze. "Peggy."

"Has she spoken to you since?"

"No."

He just said a ghost helped him find her, and she didn't even blink. Suddenly, his somber mood disappeared.

"Maybe she's found peace at last," said Sam, "and moved on."

"I hope so."

She chewed her lower lip, fingers twirling a spoon on the table. "What was the final decision?"

He intuitively knew she asked how JD died.

Neither had spoken of the strange chain of events that transpired in the basement. How could he explain the strange voice, or the fog surrounding JD that pushed him against a wall, then threw him to the floor where his gun discharged? He couldn't.

"When his gun went off, I saw you go down…I thought he hit you." He covered her hand with his. "My heart stopped. I fired on instinct, but he was already down." He swallowed hard. "He took one bullet—his own—into the heart. They're ruling it accidental because there's nothing to prove otherwise." He brought her hand to his lips and kissed it. "It's over."

"What about Billy?" asked Sam, "have you talked with him?"

"He's back at work." He sipped his coffee. "He went to see his mother in Dallas during that time. Just found out she has cancer and wanted to see him." He toyed with the cake on his plate. "Things are a little strained between us right now, but I'm hopeful we'll be back to normal soon."

Coop finished his coffee and cake, though his throat threatened to close several times. Would things ever be normal again?

"Frank came by earlier to apologize," said Sam. "Miriam was with him." She paused. "What will happen to him?"

"Up to the DA. Miriam waited two days to pay his bail." He shook his head. "Wouldn't want to be him these days."

"Rumor mill said Puckett's wife kicked him out."

"Bout time."

Jason entered carrying a covered plate which he placed on the table. "Big Mama baked these tea cakes, and said if I didn't give them to you, she'd skin me alive." He gave a very unmanly shudder. "She scares me."

Amusement flickered in Sam's eyes. "You won't find a kinder soul, Jason. She's as sweet as they come."

"Yeah, well," He looked at the counter lined with food. "Between her and all those other folks who have paraded in here bringing food this week, you won't have to cook for a while." He hesitated, then looked at his father. "So, Dad…are we ready?"

Coop pushed back from the table and reached for Sam's hand. "Yeah. We're ready."

A few minutes later, Coop perched on the edge of the wooden coffee table in front of the couch where Sam and Eva sat. "Can I get y'all anything?"

"Please stop fussing so, Coop," admonished Eva as she

glanced at Sam. "We are both doing just fine."

"Absolutely," echoed Sam.

Eva opened her mouth, but Jason held up his hand. "Yes, Dad and I are keeping a list of who brought what. We froze some and kept some out to eat now. Except for that awful spinach concoction Miriam Arnold made. I'm sorry, but I tossed it."

Coop looked back and forth between the two women who owned his heart and thanked God he hadn't lost them. He was the luckiest man alive.

"I still can't believe JD did all that," said Eva. "He seemed so nice." She looked at Coop, head shaking in disbelief. "Are you all right?"

Silence gathered as Eva's gaze found and held his. "You know, don't you?" Her voice quaked with emotion.

"Yes."

"But…"

He covered her frail hand with his and tried to keep his voice from shaking as he revealed the secret he'd kept for so long. "I always knew I was adopted." He swallowed twice before he could continue. "You told my mother to give me the letter if I ever asked for details, and she did. It told me the why, but not who you were. I didn't find out until after my parents died." He paused for a breath. "My adoptive mother left me a letter. Said she'd leave it up to me whether or not I told you what was in it." He paused to get a grip on his emotions. "I was wild and foolish, and made the worst mistake of my life. I should have said something long before now."

He glanced at his son, and back to the woman who birthed him, then silently stepped aside to let her best friend raise him, because society wouldn't sympathize or forgive. "It took me a long time to understand, but I do. I do. You've always been there for me." He looked at Jason. "For us. And we'll be here for you. Always." Vision blurred, he kissed her hand. "We love you."

Her tear-smothered voice trembled. "I was so afraid you would hate me or be embarrassed if you knew."

He drew strength from the warmth of Sam's hand on his knee. "I could never hate you. You gave me life, then saw to it I grew up in a warm and loving home. You put my welfare above everything. Even your own happiness."

"…You're the spitting image of him. Your father." Her voice cracked as tears streamed down her cheeks. "My son."

"We have a couple of weddings to plan now." Heart dancing with happiness, he looked at his mother "…Ma…I love you."

Jason moved to sit beside her on the couch, pulling her to him in a gentle hug. "So, does this mean I can call you Grammie now instead of Miss Eva?"

EPILOGUE

Sam snuggled closer to him on the big porch swing, a light blanket over her knees. "So what's this about two weddings to plan?"

"You don't want to get married?" His stomach rolled at the thought.

She pushed back to look into his eyes. "Of course I do. But a girl wants to be asked, you know, not just have the guy assume she can't wait to marry him."

He hoped his smile didn't look as smug as he felt at that moment. He tipped her chin up and brushed a kiss over those sassy lips. "I love you, Dr. Samantha Fowler. Will you do me the honor of being my wife?"

Her misty-eyed gaze, soft as a lover's caress, met his. The smoldering flame in those baby-blues was a passionate invitation hard to resist.

Love, endearing, ever-lasting, surged between them.

"Well," she whispered, "how could a girl say no to such a beautiful request?"

He bent to kiss her but stopped. "We never did have that date where you let me drive Ethel."

"Are you saying you won't marry me unless I let you drive my car?"

He pulled her closer. "I'm saying, I really, really wanna drive that car." He kissed the tip of her nose. "And make out in it."

She slid her hands up his chest. "Umm…I like how you think."

He brushed his lips over hers. "How about we go sit in there tonight and practice?"

They started to rise from the swing when a rush of cool air wafted up from the back of the porch, carrying with it the heady fragrance of gardenias.

"Thank you."

Sam froze. "Ok. Your lips aren't moving so I know you didn't just speak."

"You heard it, too?"

Her nod was barely perceptible.

Together, they looked behind the swing.

Twin pillars of mist hovered above the railings, their filmy shape oddly human-like.

"Thank you, Coop".

"Goodbye, Sammie-girl. He'll take care of you now".

The mists moved forward, wrapped around the couple as though in a tender embrace, then side-by-side, they drifted upward into the star-lit sky.

THE END

Chocolate Candy Cake

2 cups all-purpose flour
2 cups sugar
1 tsp baking soda
1 cup water
1 cup butter or margarine
¼ cup cocoa powder
½ cup buttermilk
2 eggs slightly beaten
1 tsp vanilla
Chocolate Candy Frosting (recipe below)

In large mixing bowl, combine flour, sugar and soda, mix well and set aside. Combine water, butter, and cocoa in heavy saucepan; bring to a boil, stirring constantly. Gradually add to flour mixture and mix well. Add in buttermilk, eggs and vanilla and mix well. Pour into a greased and floured 13x9x2 pan.

Bake at 350° for 30 minutes or until a tooth pick inserted in center comes out clean. While cake is warm, prick cake surface at 1" intervals with a fork; spread with frosting.

Chocolate Candy Frosting

½ butter or margarine
¼ cup plus 2 tbsp evaporated milk
¼ cup cocoa
1 16-oz box powdered sugar, sifted
1 tsp vanilla extract
½ cup chopped pecans or walnuts

Combine butter, milk and cocoa in heavy saucepan. Bring to

a boil, stirring constantly. Stir in powdered sugar, return to a boil, stirring constantly. Immediately remove from heat and add vanilla and pecans. Stir constantly for 3-5 minutes or until frosting begins to lose its gloss. Spread over warm cake and serve.

Pecan Pie Muffins
(makes 24 mini muffins)

Pre-heat oven to 350 degrees. Lightly grease mini-muffin pan (I use cooking spray- even with non-stick pans). You can use those paper cups if you like.

1 cup pecan pieces
1 cup lightly packed brown sugar
¾ cup flour
2 eggs
1 tsp vanilla
½ cup butter (1 stick) Not Margarine

Cream butter, eggs and vanilla. Add brown sugar and mix well; then add flour, mix till well blended. Add pecans and stir till blended.

Spoon evenly into muffin wells (I use a heaping teaspoon full). Bake at 350 for 15-20 minutes until muffins spring back when lightly touched.

Oven temps vary so keep an eye on them. I let them cool in the pan and they seem to release easier.

ACKNOWLEDGMENTS

There are so many folks to whom I am indebted for the completion of this book. A special thank you to Investigator Roxanne Warren, UPSO who patiently answered my multitude of law enforcement questions and helped me better understand the investigative world. Any errors in process or procedure are mine alone.

A special thank you to my critique partner and friend, Patty Wiseman, who never hesitates to tell me when I can do better. To my writers' group friends who encouraged me and supported me in this process, I appreciate you more than I can say.

And, last but by no means least, to my wonderful husband, and biggest fan. I couldn't do this without him. Love you to the moon and back.

ABOUT THE AUTHOR

Awarding winning author Dana Wayne is a sixth generation Texan and resides in the Piney Woods with her husband, a Calico cat named Katie, three children and four grandchildren.

She routinely speaks at book clubs, writers groups and other organizations and successfully coordinated multiple writing events including conferences and workshops as well as appearing on numerous writing blogs.

Her debut contemporary romance, *Secrets of The Heart*, won First Place in the 2017 Contest sponsored by Texas

Association of Authors, was a finalist for the 2017 Scéal Award for Contemporary Romance, Reviewers Top Pick and selected as a Top 10 Books to Read This Winter from Books & Benches online magazine.

Her second book, *Mail Order Groom*, released in April, 2017, has been favored with encouraging reviews as well, including 5 Stars from Readers Favorite and Book & Benches, 4.5 Stars with Crowned Heart from InD'tale Magazine, and 4 Stars from Romance Reviews Magazine. Affiliations include Romance Writers of America, Texas Association of Authors, Writers League of Texas, East Texas Writers Guild, Northeast Texas Writers Organization, and East Texas Writers Association.

www.danawayne.com

www.Facebook.com/danawayne423

www.Twitter.com/danawayne423

Preview of *Secrets of the Heart*

CHAPTER ONE

Houston, Texas present day
They died two years ago today.

Tori didn't need the calendar to remember the date. Her heart ticked away the hours one anguished beat at a time then stuttered and skipped each September fourth at 7:01 p.m.; the day her husband and seven year old son were murdered.

She sucked in a lungful of air and forced back the tears threatening to crush her resolve.

No more tears. Time to move forward.

Tori stared at the half-packed suitcase on the bed, each item new and chosen for this journey, symbolic of her mission to start fresh. She was certain her best friend since forever would understand and support her decision. Obviously not the case.

"Oh my God, Tori! Have you lost your mind?" Sasha paced in front of the closet, fingers pressed to her temples. "I am so not believing this!"

Her reaction mirrored the one from Tori's family last night. Going to Montana was one thing, keeping it secret until the night before she left was a lot to accept. Apparently.

Hands on her hips, voice rife with tension, Sassy - personifying her nickname - raved on. "I mean, really, what do you even know about this guy?" She crossed her arms, right foot tapping out a staccato. "How do you know he's not some wacko serial killer or if he even has a sick mother?"

She didn't give Tori time to take a breath much less respond.

"I can't believe you didn't tell your best friend in the whole world about this hare-brained idea weeks ago instead of the day before you leave."

"You know why." Tori held up her hand. "You're worried, Sassy, I get it. But I have to do this." She placed folded pants in the suitcase and walked back to the closet, staring at the unfamiliar items hanging there. "The past two years have been a never-ending nightmare." She wrapped her arms around herself and struggled to remain calm. "Joey died in my arms." Tori blew out a breath. "I didn't know a human could endure that much pain and live. I never thought their killers would go free, but they did and I survived that, too." Her voice dropped to a soft whisper. "I'm just existing, Sassy. I'm not living anymore."

"Rico is still out there. You know you're a loose end he wants tied up."

"I talked with Captain Lockhart last week and Rico hasn't been seen in months. Word is he took his drug plans elsewhere. Maybe even as far as Canada." She turned back to the closet and pulled a blouse from its hanger, folded it, shook it out then refolded it. "When Joey and Eddie died, a big part of me died, too." She took a breath and tried to speak without crying. "I know I can never get that back. But this job will give me a chance to...re-group, get grounded again."

"But Montana?" Sassy stood in front her. "It's colder 'n

hell there and snows like a gazillion feet a year! What if you need to go to town or get sick or hurt?"

Tori threw the blouse on the bed and faced her friend. "I can't stay here any longer!" She trembled with the effort it took to control the pain that had defined her life the last two years. Eyes blurring with unshed tears, she blinked several times, sucking air through clenched teeth. "Everywhere I go, everyone I see is a constant reminder of all I've lost. And my family, Sassy…they're smothering me."

"They love you. We all do."

She gripped her friends' shoulders. "Then please. For my sake, try to understand. I lost a big piece of myself that day and lose a little more each day I stay here."

Several seconds passed before Sassy placed her hands over Tori's and squeezed. "All right. But promise you'll call if you need anything, anything at all."

"I promise. Now, are you going to help me pack or what?"

"Fine. I'll help, but I want the whole story, start to finish. How the hell did you get hooked up with some cowboy from Montana?"

Tori released a long held breath. "It's not a big deal." She picked up the discarded blouse and refolded it. "Ted Freeman, Chief of Staff at Memorial?"

"Oh yeah, the yummy one that looks like Richard Gere."

She nodded. "He has this friend in Butte who knew about a family, the McBrides' that wanted a live-in nurse for his elderly mother. She has terminal cancer. Pretty advanced."

"They don't have nurses in Montana?"

She ignored the sarcastic comment. "He mentioned it to Ted who mentioned it to me in passing. I asked for more information, made a few calls." Tori shrugged. "And off I go."

Though not that simple, the explanation seemed to satisfy Sasha for now. True, she insisted on a background check and made a few discreet inquiries herself but not until she'd accepted the position. Tori realized significant steps had to take place if she were to have any chance at normal again. This was a significant step. A little rash maybe, but significant, so, no second guessing it now.

It was an ideal solution for her current state of mind. She would live in the McBride home and care for Mr. McBride's sister and mother, receive an acceptable salary, a private room and meals. Most important of all, she'd be free from constant reminders of her loss and well-meaning friends and family—namely her mother - now determined to fix her up with someone.

But she lacked the motivation, and, though loath to admit it, the confidence, to pursue another relationship. Eddie was her first love, and her only lover. Hell, she'd never even kissed another man—not like that - and even the thought of doing so now made her palms sweat and her heart race.

I'm a thirty-three year old coward.

"Hello in there?" Sasha tapped the side of her head. "Anybody home?"

Tori blinked. "Huh?"

"Answer me."

"I'm sorry, my mind was wandering. What did you ask?"

She heaved an exasperated sniff. "I said tell me about this McBride fella. What does he look like, is he married? And I want the good stuff, too, not whatever sugar-coated version you gave your parents."

Tori hesitated.

Sasha poked her shoulder with her index finger. "Out with

it. What are you hiding?"

"Nothing." She studied the closet's contents without seeing them. "There isn't much to tell. He runs the family ranch. His brother was the sheriff before he and his wife were killed three months ago." She took a sweater and studied it. "That's about it."

"And you never met 'im?"

"Uh-uh, just spoke with him on the phone. Got the majority of my information from his sister, Sheila. She had some sort of accident, too and needs PT."

"Okay then, what does he sound like? Old? Sexy? Gay?"

"You're incorrigible."

"Well?"

"I guess…hell, I don't know." She swapped the sweater for blouse. "It's hard to describe." *Liar. You know exactly how it sounds; a deep baritone with a huskiness to it that flows through you like fine wine, raises gooseflesh on your arms, leaving you off-balance, a strange tingling sensation racing through you.* She placed a hand at her throat and tried to breathe normally as guilt over such forbidden feelings overwhelmed her. *If just the sound of his voice on the phone has such an effect on me, what on earth will happen when I meet him?*

"Dammit! You're not listening again."

The declaration, complete with a heavy sigh, pulled Tori from those disturbing thoughts. "I'm sorry. What did you say?"

Sasha rolled her eyes and made no attempt to hide her frustration. "I said, give it to me."

"Give what?"

"I know good and well you at least got a picture of him before sashaying across the country to meet him, so gimmee."

She looked away, said nothing.

Her best friend held out her hand and snapped her fingers. "Hand it over, girl. I wanna see the man who could persuade my reasonably intelligent—"

"Reasonably intelligent?"

Sasha cocked her head to the side, one delicately arched brow raised.

"Point made."

"As I was saying, persuade my reasonably intelligent best friend to hightail it to Montana in the dead of winter." She wiggled her fingers and grinned. "I can't wait to see him."

Tori glanced at the outstretched hand and reached for her purse. She didn't bother to glance at the photo as she passed it over; didn't need to. Her mind's eye provided a vivid picture. Wind-blown ebony hair, streaks of grey at the temples. Strong, defined cheekbones anchored by heavy brows. Sky blue eyes framed by killer lashes. And his mouth. Oh God. What was it about his mouth that intrigued her so?

Full lips parted in a sexy smile that lit up his face and made her breath catch. She gave herself a mental shake and tried to focus on the task at hand. "His sister sent it. He's the one on the left. The other one is his late brother, Isaac."

"Holy-moly girlfriend! No wonder you can't wait to go. Talk about your tall, dark and handsome. He's what…six feet at least; bedroom eyes if ever I saw 'em, come hither smile… daaa-yum! I bet he's got a killer ass, too."

"Sassy!" Tori reached for the picture but her friend moved away, still studying it.

"What did you say his name is?"

"Wade McBride."

"Well, Mr. Wade McBride, you are one delicious lookin'

cowboy." She made a show of fanning herself with the picture. "And I'd be on 'at puppy like mornin' glory on a fencepost."

Her face grew warm and she shook her head. Sasha had a one track mind of late and did her best to get Tori on the same track.

"Damn. Damn. Damn!" She handed the picture back. "Sure you don't want me to come along? You're a bit out of practice you know, and he may be more than you can handle alone."

"It's nothing like that and you know it. It's a job."

"Yeah, well, it should be." She rummaged through the contents of a dresser drawer and tossed a filmy nightgown at Tori. "Better take this along. Winter or not you'll want it 'fore this is over."

"Good grief! Is sex all you think about?" She tossed the garment back to her and pulled out a pair of sweat pants.

"Hell yeah when I see a Timex man."

Tori ducked her head and sighed. "I know I will regret this, but…a Timex man?"

Sasha giggled. "Think a can of RediWhip topping, some chocolate syrup…a strategically placed cherry." She paused for effect. "And see if 'at cowboy can take a lickin' and keep on tickin.'"

Her face flamed as an image of McBride lathered in whipped topping and chocolate syrup formed. "Oh my God, Sasha! Where on earth do you come up with this stuff?" She extended her arm, palm up. "Never mind. I don't want to know."

"Trust me…one day you'll thank me."

"No. I won't. Besides, he has a lot on his plate with his sister and mother both ill and the ranch. He needs a nurse, not a lover."

"Says who?"

"Sassy, please."

"I've said it before and I'll say it again; you were too good for Eddie." She waved her hand back and forth to silence Tori's rebuke. "I know, I know, it's wrong to speak ill of the dead. He was a good cop, a decent father, but a crummy, cheating husband."

Tori sat on the edge of the bed and said nothing as her friend continued. "You've got the kindest heart of anyone I've ever known." Sassy joined her on the bed, her smile reflective. "I guess that explains why you put up with me all these years. And you have a capacity for caring I truly envy. It's why you are such an awesome nurse. Well, that and the reasonably intelligent thing."

Tori snorted. Sassy would never change. Thank God.

"I know you loved Eddie. I never understood why, but I know you did. But he's gone, Tori. You need to let him go and love again."

"I…I don't know if I can. Every time I think about moving on, of getting involved with someone, I feel guilty. Like I'm… betraying him. I know it sounds silly to you but it's how I feel."

Sasha slid an arm around her shoulders and squeezed. "I don't think it sounds silly at all. He was your husband and you loved him. But he's gone." She blew out a breath. "You're my best friend in the whole world. I want you to be happy. I want to see your eyes smile again."

"I know you do. And I appreciate that." She leaned her head on her friend's shoulder. "I'm not interested in a relationship right now." She sighed. "I don't think I even remember how to kiss anymore so a relationship is out of the question."

Sasha looked at the picture and grinned. "Wanna bet? Besides, kissing is like riding a bike, once you do it, you don't forget how." She giggled. "And if you did, I'm bettin' this cowboy is one hell of a teacher."

* * *

Tori placed the last bag on the cart by the door and called for a taxi. She stood in the middle of her living room, staring at the expensive set of matching luggage she'd splurged on, mentally checking off her preparations. Her rent was paid up for six months and the mail forwarded to her parents who would take care of any bills. Her friend had a key to the apartment and would keep an eye on things while she was gone.

She suffered no misgivings about leaving. In fact, her excitement grew as departure time approached. The need to take control of her life was of major importance right now. When she heard about the McBride's needing a nurse, it was like a rainbow following a thunderstorm proclaiming the worst was over.

Maybe it was the prospect of change itself making her tingle with anticipation or something else altogether. Wade's enticing voice notwithstanding, exactly what pulled her to Montana remained a mystery. She only knew she had to go.

The doorman rang to say the taxi arrived. Tori grabbed her purse, the cumbersome luggage cart and headed out the door. As it shut, she heard the phone ring.

She let it go to voicemail.

Made in the USA
Middletown, DE
07 July 2018